WARNING SHOTS

OTHER TITLES BY CONNIE DIAL

The Third Hell

JOSIE CORSINO MYSTERIES
Fallen Angels
Dead Wrong
Unnatural Murder
Set the Night on Fire

DETECTIVE MIKE TURNER MYSTERIES
Internal Affairs
The Broken Blue Line

A JOSIE CORSINO MYSTERY

WARNING SHOTS

CONNIE DIAL

THE PERMANENT PRESS
Sag Harbor, NY 11963

For information, address:
  The Permanent Press
  4170 Noyac Road
  Sag Harbor, NY 11963
  www.thepermanentpress.com

Library of Congress Cataloging-in-Publication Data

  Dial, Connie, author.
    Warning shots / by Connie Dial.
    Sag Harbor, NY: Permanent Press, [2018]
    ISBN: 978-1-57962-529-0
        1. Murder—Investigation—Fiction. 2. Los Angeles (Calif.)—Fiction.
    3. Mystery fiction. 4. Suspense fiction.

  PS3604.I126 W37 2018
  813'.6—dc23   2017058130

Printed in the United States of America

To Jon Dial, always

ONE

The whispering and rustling of papers stopped. Nearly everyone in the cramped space looked up at her, but Captain Josie Corsino waited until she had the accused police officer's attention before she spoke. In her experience, most cops facing termination were nervous or angry, but this one smiled as if she were about to present him with the Medal of Valor.

"This board of rights is back in session," she said, glancing at the stenographer. "Let the record reflect that the advocate, defense rep, and accused Officer Marvin Wright are all present. Captain Jorge Sanchez will read our findings as to counts one through five."

She turned to the young, dark-skinned man in uniform sitting to her right who began reading from notes. He was serious and deliberate as he described each count of misconduct and the evidence that supported a finding of "guilty." The civilian member of the board sitting on her left side nodded in agreement as each decision was explained in detail. The room was set up like a courtroom with her and the other two adjudicators sitting behind a long table on a raised platform. The slight elevation made it possible for Josie to study the faces of those who sat in the audience behind the accused and the Internal Affairs advocate. She guessed most of the spectators, including several uniformed officers, were there out of curiosity or for the entertainment value. Their expressions seemed to say they were indifferent to the outcome. There was none of the stress or worry usually exhibited by friends or supporters.

When Sanchez finished, Josie read her rationale for the penalty that board members had unanimously agreed was appropriate. She explained how the counts demonstrated a pattern of negligence and disrespect for the rules and policies of the Los Angeles Police Department and concluded by looking directly at the accused and saying, "Therefore, Officer Wright, this board is recommending to the chief of police that you be removed from your position as a Los Angeles police officer." Josie paused, expecting some reaction, but there was nothing. He stared silently at the ceiling. She continued, "That concludes your board of rights, and we are off the record." Wright leaned over and whispered something to his representative sitting beside him and they both laughed.

After five years as the commanding officer of the LAPD's Hollywood division, Josie had been told by a lot of cops that she got selected for more disciplinary boards than other command officers because her reputation was well established as fair-minded, and she was perceived as someone who would not be influenced by department politics or pressure from the chief's office. She usually felt bad when the outcome was termination, but not this time. Marvin Wright was a prime candidate to be fired. During his three-year tenure on the streets of Los Angeles he had accumulated dozens of complaints from citizens, supervisors, and even his peers. He was rude, lazy, and by all accounts unable to perform even the simplest patrol tasks with any success.

As the room cleared, Howard Burke, the civilian board member, stood and put his notes into his briefcase. She noticed his hands were trembling. He was a middle-aged, fragile-looking, civil rights lawyer. Josie thought he was too liberal for her taste, but he was smart and conscientious and had gone along with her recommendation. She was certain sitting in judgment of someone as out of control as Wright had terrified him, and she could understand why any reasonable, unarmed civilian might be concerned. Wright made several irrational outbursts during the hearing. He referred to the board as a kangaroo court with no real authority and swore he would "find justice in the end."

"I can't believe they fired him once before and let him come back. That man should never have been a police officer," Burke said in a nervous whisper. "I know we did the right thing . . . but aren't you concerned he might . . . you know, retaliate?" he asked, staring at Wright's back as he left the board room surrounded by his legal team.

"Superior court made the police department reinstate him after he got fired on probation," Captain Sanchez said, sitting on the table between Burke and Josie. "Judge said we created a hostile work environment, stifled Marvin's inner gayness, and forced him to behave like a low-life scumbag."

Josie knew Howard Burke was gay and saw him move back a little and his lips tighten before he gave her a weak smile, nodded at Sanchez, and made a hasty departure.

"Very nice, Jorge," Josie said sarcastically, shaking her head.

"What?" Sanchez asked, shrugging. "It's the truth. Jerk had ten minutes on the job and the judge took his word over a training officer with twenty years' experience."

"Not the point; you need to be more sensitive around Burke. You know he'll testify if Wright brings another lawsuit to get his job back. Burke can't have any misgivings about our attitude toward gays."

"I've never said or done anything to discriminate against anyone," Sanchez said, seeming unconcerned.

Josie sighed, annoyed she had to explain. "In your position, you should understand people like Burke. He's obviously scared," she said. "He had to go along with our decision because there was too much evidence, but he's going to be looking for a way to distance himself from us and stay off Wright's radar."

"I've got a big mouth," Sanchez said with a forced smile. He was handsome and knew his good looks made most people overlook his deficiencies. Josie had to admit his cockiness was partly her fault for having taken him under her wing, encouraging, protecting, and mentoring him while he was a patrol lieutenant in Hollywood. She had recognized his natural leadership abilities and worked hard to help him promote. She might've been too successful in bolstering his self-confidence which she feared had morphed into conceit and obstinacy.

She was firmly committed to his success even though his gritty street-cop attitude and stubbornness weren't always compatible with his role as a newly promoted command officer. When she was honest with herself, Josie knew she found it difficult to criticize him because she'd been accused by her boss of having similar traits.

"You need to get back to West LA or do you have time for lunch?" she asked.

"Can't, Stu wants me to cover while he's at a Rotary meeting."

Sanchez had made it clear to her on more than one occasion he didn't like his boss. Stuart Ames was an area captain like she was, but he had been in West LA division only a year and was already prepping for the commander's test. He was promoted to captain from the chief's office, knew procedures and paperwork, but had very little time as a working cop. His subordinates sensed his lack of experience and like Sanchez didn't show him much respect.

"He leaves you in charge a lot. That's a good learning experience for you."

"It's torture working for him; it's not in his DNA to make a decision."

"Then you make them," she said.

"I would if I was working for you. You'd back me up . . . but not shaky Stu. Want me to walk you to your car?"

"Why would I want that?" Josie asked, as they got into the ancient elevator in the Bradbury Building. She loved this late-nineteenth-century renaissance-revival landmark but knew Internal Affairs would be moving soon to a newer, cheaper place. Its decorative cast-iron interior, marble stairs, and atrium under a glass ceiling made all the hours she spent here tolerable.

"In case pumpkin head is lurking on Broadway, waiting for you to come out."

She lifted the corner of her jacket and pointed to the badge on her belt.

"This gives me the authority to protect myself. Smith & Wesson provides the means, so no, thank you. Besides, I don't think even Marvin would be stupid enough to confront the captain who just fired him. A review court would definitely frown on that."

"You give him too much credit. He's plenty stupid," Sanchez said as they stepped off the elevator.

He gave her a quick hug before heading toward his car parked in a lot down the street. She'd found unofficial police parking in a red zone half a block away. Parking enforcement usually left illegally parked police cars alone, but she wouldn't be surprised to see a ticket on the windshield. The world was changing. Police officers were getting killed or harassed every day for nothing more than being cops. There were frustrated wannabe cops writing parking tickets who took pleasure in citing a police car to show superiority.

She was a few years away from completing the last decade of her thirty-year career, but lately wondered if she'd make it to the finish line. "Bullshit," she said getting into the driver's seat and pulling away from the curb. She knew life without an adrenaline rush once or twice a day wasn't worth living. Thirty years might not be long enough.

She had no desire to promote again before she retired, but her boss, Deputy Chief Dempsey, was nagging her to take the commander's test. One of his underlings moving up in the organization would look good on his résumé, but if she passed and got promoted, it would also mean leaving Hollywood and any semblance of real police work. She'd get a lot more money in retirement but until then she'd have to sit at a desk and be a glorified adjutant to some deputy chief. She'd have none of the responsibilities she had now as an area captain supervising a patrol captain like Jorge, hundreds of detectives, uniformed officers, and civilians. She promised Dempsey to think about it but knew she'd retire before taking that promotion.

THE HALLWAYS of the Hollywood police station seemed nearly deserted as Josie stood by the back door outside the detectives' squad room. It was lunchtime, so she didn't expect to find any self-respecting detective still at his desk except maybe her homicide supervisor, Red Behan. Behan's afternoon nourishment rarely included food. He was days away from retirement, so she had stopped trying to control his drinking. Josie knew she'd miss the big redhead because drunk or sober he was not only the best homicide detective in the city but her cop conscience.

"Boss, you got a minute," Behan shouted from inside the squad room.

After four days away from the office handling Marvin's board of rights, she guessed there had to be a pile of projects and potential disasters waiting in her office, but figured anything Red wanted had to be more interesting. Before Josie could get across the squad room a couple of robbery detectives stopped her to brag about an arrest they'd just made that cleared a dozen beauty salon takeover robberies. She congratulated them and made a mental note to remind their supervisor to write a commendation. Most cops loved their work but if no one cared how well they did it or failed to recognize their accomplishments it was a morale crusher and that wasn't going to happen in her division.

Behan kept an old wooden chair between his desk and a six-foot-high bookcase that doubled as a sound barrier separating him from his raucous homicide detectives. The shelves were filled with manuals and reference materials. She suspected he might've stashed a pint or two of his favorite rye whiskey behind the stack of Municipal Code books but didn't know for certain because she'd never looked.

During the last few years, that chair had become her refuge, a place to go and breathe when the responsibilities and burdens in her office became suffocating.

After thirty-seven years in law enforcement, the big red-head had a way of putting things in perspective. "What the fuck's wrong with you?" were usually Behan's opening words of wisdom followed by, "Fuck 'em, you know what to do. Do it." They'd talk awhile, walk across the street to Nora's bar, have a drink, and she'd be ready to do battle again.

He was concentrating on his computer when she pulled the chair closer to see what he was doing. Josie recognized the statistical map on his screen. She had talked about the slight increase in homicides in the Hollywood area at the chief's last CompStat meeting where she and the other West Bureau captains detailed their strategies for fighting crime trends.

She never saw homicide as a preventable crime unless it was gang related. In her experience, serial or random killers were rare too because murder was such a personal or emotional act done for revenge, love, greed, or rage.

"What's up, Red?" she asked to get his attention away from the monitor.

"Don't know."

"So what did you want?"

"Not sure."

Josie stood and pushed the chair back in the corner.

"When it comes to you, give me a shout," she said.

"Look at this," he said before she could leave.

"It's the homicide pin map. I've seen it, five homicides in the last three months . . . a lot but not alarming in this magical kingdom we call Hollywood," Josie said.

"They're not gangbangers but all of them are young males. Three are Santa Monica bun boys but the other two are runaways with no real connection to the boulevard."

"Selling your butt on the street is a dangerous business. What's your point?" she asked.

"Maybe we've got a serial killer."

"I thought you had ruled that out because the MO was different."

"I did but . . . I don't know. It's just a gut feeling . . . reminds me of something or . . . damned if I know," he said, his voice trailing off.

"Middle of summer, plenty of potential victims hanging around the streets all night, easy pickings. You thinking about a task force . . . decoys?"

"I'll let you know. Won't be my problem after next week. Maybe I'll wait and let the new guy figure it out. By the way, Boss, who is the new guy?"

"Who says it's a guy?"

Behan groaned at the thought of a woman taking his job. Josie left because she wasn't going to discuss the pros and cons of the different applicants she had considered to fill his position. He had lobbied for one of his homicide detectives to be promoted, but as much as she trusted Behan's judgment, his personnel choices were suspect—friendship always trumped potential or talent. To spare him distress, she'd decided to name his replacement after he was gone.

Josie's adjutant gave her a big grin and a dozen messages when she finally got to her office. She had to smile whenever she saw him sitting behind the desk outside her door. He was a tall muscular man who seemed better suited to busting down doors than perching on a swivel chair taking notes and answering phones. Sergeant Dan McSweeney, or "Mac" as everyone called him, was a hard-charging uniformed supervisor who'd needed a break from the field. On the outside, he appeared strong and fit; she'd discovered he could be as fragile inside as the finest piece of Waterford crystal.

She needed an adjutant. He needed a safe place to mentally mend. The added benefit was he could write and whenever he made a request on her behalf to anyone in the division, his massive presence guaranteed speedy and positive results.

He had performed in the job for only a few months, but Josie liked him and trusted his work. She would be sorry to see him return to patrol but had promised that the decision to go back to the streets would be his whenever he felt ready. The job of a uniformed sergeant was difficult enough, but Josie heard from her snitches in the administration building downtown that Mac had been involved in a messy lawsuit before he was transferred to Hollywood. The experience had left him drained, disillusioned, and close to quitting police work. She believed trying to save him was worth the effort.

"Boss, Lieutenant Richards came by and wanted to know if you fired his problem child yet," Mac said as he put a copy of Josie's calendar on her desk and added, "The changes are on your computer and I highlighted the chief's meeting this afternoon."

"Did Richards go back to Wilshire?" she asked.

Kyle Richards had been the most important man in her life since her divorce the previous year. He was assigned to Wilshire patrol division as a uniformed watch commander and had the unenviable task of supervising Marvin Wright.

"Said he was going to see Lieutenant Bailey."

Josie left everything on her desk and went upstairs to the vice office hoping Richards was still there. He had plenty of time before his roll call at Wilshire and Marge Bailey always had a new funny story laced with her arsenal of expletives. Josie wanted to warn him about some of the bizarre rants Wright had made concerning him during the board of rights.

She always wondered why it didn't make her uneasy when her beautiful best buddy spent so much time with her handsome lover. Marge and Kyle were good friends now, but their relationship had been intimate for several months before he and Josie got together. Josie trusted them but was smart enough to know physical attraction wasn't an intellectual matter. Shit just happened and it happened to Marge a lot.

She thought it might be a peculiar flaw in her nature that as much as she loved Richards, the prospect of losing him to Marge or to anyone for that matter wouldn't be devastating. When she was candid with herself, she'd admit that assessment was probably bullshit, but her divorce from District Attorney Jake Corsino after twenty-five years of marriage had knocked her personal life out of kilter, and she was determined not to let that happen again.

Marge and Richards were sitting in Marge's office talking when she arrived. Richards got up and gave Josie a quick kiss. The department frowned on command officers dating subordinates, but they were assigned to different divisions. Technically Josie wasn't his boss.

He was over six feet, but Josie and Marge were both almost as tall as he was. Other than their size, Josie believed two women couldn't be more different. Marge was a blonde, blue-eyed beauty queen who could be wild and reckless and had a vocabulary stocked with four-letter words. Josie had been told often enough that she was pretty too, but she was thin, with dark hair and an olive complexion, rarely swore, and was deadly serious about most things. Nevertheless, after working closely for several years, a strong bond had grown between them.

"Is my psychopath gone?" Richards asked, pulling another chair from the squad room into the office for Josie.

"I recommended firing him, but it's still up to the chief. The guy said some crazy stuff and acted weird during that hearing. I thought you should know since he promised everyone would be sorry for the way he'd been treated, especially you."

"His last partner told me he thought Wright was schizophrenic or bipolar . . . talked to himself, didn't know who or where he was half the time, and thought everybody was out to get him," Richards said.

"What did shithead do when you fired his crazy ass?" Marge asked.

"Stared at the ceiling tiles with a stupid grin. I expected a meltdown, so I ended the board before his bizarre personality surfaced again."

"I have to go but I'll give my captain and guys on the watch a heads-up. Talk to you later," he said and gave her another longer kiss before leaving.

"I am fucking starving," Marge said as soon as Richards was out of sight. "Nora's?"

"Why not? I'm not getting any work done anyway. But I can't drink . . . bureau meeting this afternoon."

"Dempsey won't notice. His blood is ninety proof. Look at asshole's bloated face. He could be an AA posterchild," Marge said, putting on a light jacket to cover her holstered gun.

"One of us should be sober so the meeting won't be a total waste of time."

The lunch crowd had thinned, and the restaurant was nearly empty, but Josie preferred to eat in Nora's bar even though it was a smaller room that smelled of beer and other unidentifiable odors. There were fewer tables in there and it didn't have the nice linen found in the dining room, but paper napkins were fine. She felt comfortable at her favorite table in a corner away from the door where she'd occasionally spot one of the older detectives wandering in for a quick drink. She understood it was the nature of the beast in Behan's generation of cop and didn't interfere unless the drinking got out of hand or affected job performance. Most officers who came in for lunch were aware she might be there but kept their distance unless they had a problem that couldn't wait.

She and Marge ordered the biggest burgers on the menu with onion rings and a bottle of cabernet. Despite her good intentions, Josie decided to have a glass of wine while they waited for lunch to arrive.

"You and Kyle okay?" Marge asked, as she filled the glasses.

"Why do you ask?"

"He seems preoccupied."

"He's supervising twenty-one-year-olds with guns who can't shoot, drive too fast, and can badly piss off the public. Not to mention, at this stage of their careers they have the potential to get themselves killed."

"True, and I'm betting trying to supervise Marvin Wright didn't help either," Marge said, filling her glass again. "What's Dempsey want?"

Josie shook her head. She didn't know what the deputy chief wanted and most of the time she worried that he didn't either. Going to his bureau office was never a pleasant experience. Hollywood was a high-profile division and Dempsey never seemed comfortable with her at the helm. Her stats were as good or better than the other four divisions in his bureau, but she could sense his discomfort.

Sometimes she wondered if he just didn't like her or maybe he could tell how little she respected him.

It didn't take long for Josie's mood to improve. Wright and Dempsey seemed less problematic after two glasses of wine and forty-five minutes with the officer in charge of her vice unit. She was enjoying herself and allowed just enough time to get to the deputy chief's meeting before paying her part of the bill and leaving Marge to finish the wine and onion rings.

THE BUREAU office had that cold impersonal feel of a place where no one expected to stay very long. Josie knew Dempsey would rather be chief of detectives in a bureau where he'd supervise divisions such as Robbery-Homicide, Vice, and Narcotics. For the past year, he'd had responsibility for five high-profile area divisions with enhanced community scrutiny which meant greater potential for screw-ups. He made no secret of his ambition to fill the next assistant chief position; therefore, his often-stated goal was to get out of West Bureau and into a place where experienced detectives rarely had questionable or messy shootings or got caught on embarrassing cell phone videos.

His adjutant was an annoying clone of the deputy chief. Josie avoided interacting with him whenever possible. She did like the chief's secretary, Marion, though, who had a dry sense of humor and had no problem putting the ambitious adjutant in his place.

"Is everybody here?" Josie asked, taking the Styrofoam cup with steaming black coffee Marion offered.

"You're everybody, dear," Marion said.

"I thought it was a bureau meeting."

"No, just you and the chief."

Josie sighed too loudly. Marion laughed and said, "Chief did the same thing when he told me to schedule your meeting."

On the other side of the room, the door to Dempsey's office opened and Sergeant Scott, the chief's adjutant, stepped out. He held the door open and gestured for Josie to come in. He was pale, skinny, and several inches shorter than her. His expression was one of perpetual disdain and he rarely attempted to be cordial.

Josie slipped past him saying, "How's it going, Timmy?"

He didn't answer but feigned a smile and sat on the couch near the door. Marion told her he disliked the diminutive version of Timothy, so Josie always made a point to use it.

"Captain Corsino, glad you could make it," Dempsey said, not getting up but staring at a couple of papers on the otherwise sparkling clean surface of his glass-topped desk.

"No problem, Chief," she said, but didn't ask why they were meeting. She sat on the lone chair in front of his desk, crossed her arms, and waited.

He continued looking down at the papers for several seconds, cleared his throat, and said, "I don't like taking you away from your division but there are two items I thought we should discuss in person."

Josie waited and wondered if he'd ever make eye contact or get to the point.

"You have a field sergeant sitting in your adjutant's chair. You do realize an area captain's adjutant is a civilian position," he said, glancing at Scott sitting behind her.

"That's correct, and yes, I do."

"Field supervision should be a priority."

"I agree," she said.

"Then why is that man not in the field supervising patrol officers?"

"As his commanding officer, I decided I needed him to be out of the field for a while. The other supervisors have done a good job and there haven't been any adverse consequences. Have there?"

"Well, no, but it's a bad precedent. You need to be careful . . . other sergeants might resent it . . . the position belongs to a civilian."

"Has anyone complained?" she asked.

"No, but . . ."

"I couldn't find a qualified civilian. I'll show you the applications. It's not permanent. My division's not suffering. No one is complaining. For the time being, I want to keep him in that position."

She could've explained McSweeney's situation but chose not to for two reasons. First, she worried Dempsey might insist Mac be placed in the rubber-gun squad where stressed officers are warehoused, then stigmatized for the rest of their careers. Mac was too valuable and salvageable for that. Her second reason was she didn't want to explain something that should be her decision.

Dempsey nervously shuffled the papers on his desk. She knew he had no cause or legitimate reason to remove McSweeney as her temporary adjutant. There was little doubt in her mind that Sergeant Scott had prompted his boss's inquiry since he'd been snooping around Hollywood station for days and had commented to Mac about how inappropriate it was for a captain to have a sergeant adjutant.

"The second matter concerns your recent surge in homicides," Dempsey said, pushing the papers aside. He wasn't pleased but seemed to concede that for the moment he'd lost the adjutant skirmish.

Josie heard the door close behind her and glanced over her shoulder at the empty couch. Sergeant Scott's sudden departure confirmed her prior suspicion, and she wouldn't forget that he had attempted to interfere with how she ran her division.

"Behan is on top of that. He's planning to put some decoys on Santa Monica. He thinks we might have a serial killer."

"You didn't say anything about a serial killer at the CompStat meeting."

"I just found out this morning."

"Isn't Behan retiring? Why is he still calling the shots on your homicide table?"

"He doesn't leave until next week and I haven't made a firm decision on his replacement yet," Josie lied. She knew who was going to be her new detective supervisor, but she wasn't telling anyone, especially Dempsey, until Red was officially gone.

"Well, just be certain he stays sober and on top of this. I don't want his drinking slowing down our chances of catching a serial killer and don't drag your feet on finding a new supervisor. If you can't decide, I will."

"Yes, sir, you'll have my choice before he's gone," she said, and thought, like the day before he's gone.

Dempsey had a few more suggestions on how she could improve operations in Hollywood. Most of his ideas she already had implemented, or they were so impractical that only someone who had never run an area would believe they were helpful.

Finally he lost interest or seemed to run out of things to talk about, got up, and dismissed her with a limp handshake. In the outer office, Josie noticed the clock over Marion's desk and realized she'd been with the man less than an hour, but it felt so much longer. She chatted with Marion a few more minutes and left before Dempsey or his adjutant came up with something else to waste her time.

Once she got back to her office and dug into the pile of work stacked on her desk, she discovered that Mac had completed most of the projects. He left them for her approval or for any adjustments she might want to make. The few items she had to finish weren't difficult. One of the things she'd discovered early in her management career was that she had an aptitude for paperwork and could get it done quickly and accurately leaving more time for those parts of the job she really enjoyed—counseling her lieutenants and sergeants, attending roll calls, riding with patrol officers, tagging along on search warrants, or anything Marge's vice unit was doing. Community meetings were among her favorite activities because she'd forged a strong alliance with Hollywood's business and political leaders. The locals referred to her as their Hollywood chief of police, and Josie was certain their solid vocal support made Dempsey uncomfortable.

She had intended to sit in on a late patrol roll call and uniform inspection but by the time she looked up at the clock again, roll call was over, and the officers were lined up at the kit room for radios, shotguns, and other equipment.

Her final task for the night had been to work on Behan's exit rating report. The contents of his personnel package were spread over her desk. She'd spent hours attempting to delicately embellish his last performance rating. His lieutenant had done a fair job writing the evaluation, but to counteract all Red's personnel complaints and rehab time Josie knew she'd have to improve his image or no one outside the department would hire him. It helped that he'd always had more commendations than complaints.

When Behan retired, his LAPD pension would have to be divided among his many ex-wives, leaving him little more than pocket change. His current spouse, Vicky, was wealthy, so he really didn't need to work after he left the department, but both Josie and Vicky were encouraging him to find employment, something that didn't involve the stress of dead bodies but kept him occupied and out of the local bar.

Mac and the rest of her administrative staff had been gone for hours. She put Behan's package back in the file cabinet, turned off her computer, and looked at the couch on the other side of her office. It was nearly midnight, and she was tempted to shut the door, switch off the lights, and sleep there again instead of making the drive home to Pasadena or to Kyle's place in Long Beach. She realized he hadn't asked if she was coming. She checked her messages. There was nothing from Kyle, but her son, David, had called twice.

Her wardrobe door was open. The reflection in the long mirror inside the door told her it was probably best to go home. Her long black hair needed washing and the dark lines under both eyes meant it was time to get a good night's sleep in a real bed. Tomorrow she'd have a big healthy breakfast and try putting a few pounds back on her skinny frame. She shut the wardrobe knowing her resolutions were pointless; the job controlled her life.

The watch commander waved at her as she closed the office door. She waved back, thinking he was saying good night, but he held up the phone and pointed at it. For a second, Josie considered telling him to say she'd already gone home but didn't.

With his hand over the receiver, the lieutenant explained that one of his supervisors was at the scene of another homicide.

"I called Behan and he's got a team of detectives coming in, but I think you should talk to my sergeant," the lieutenant said.

She took the phone and listened while the field sergeant explained that a patrol unit had responded to a radio call of a man down and found the victim dead in his car.

"Your lieutenant could've told me that," Josie said, glancing at the watch commander who stared at her like a man anticipating a reaction.

"LT says I should explain, ma'am . . . I was in the Bradbury Building today to testify at another officer's board. I stopped by your boardroom. I think I recognize the dead guy," the officer said.

Josie's mind ricocheted through the parade of people who'd attended the board. For no logical reason, Marvin Wright's name was the one she expected to hear but dreaded the other possibilities.

"Who?" she asked.

"I don't remember his name. He was the guy in the grey suit sitting next to you."

"Howard Burke?"

"Yes, ma'am, that's him."

TWO

The Hollywood Chamber of Commerce had touted gentrification of their glitzy town for the last decade and a half, pointing to the construction of new restaurants and apartment buildings and the renovation of shopping malls as proof. But Josie understood the underbelly of her division. The prostitutes, pimps, drug dealers, junkie burglars, and other remnants of decadence weren't about to abandon their lucrative territory in the name of civic pride, and they were masters at survival.

Josie thought the lingering criminal element in her area resembled a cockroach infestation—resilient, hardy, and tolerant of a wide range of environments, avoiding light and aggregating when necessary to produce more damage. Removing them completely was difficult since the most potent and effective crime control measures were either temporary or deemed too extreme by elected officials. Although Hollywood might've looked new and clean when the refurbished neon lights were on, under the surface and in its darkest corners the nasty little buggers were thriving.

The parking lot behind the High-Top Bar on Santa Monica Boulevard was blocked off with yellow police tape, and uniformed officers stopped traffic from entering the side streets. Crowds had gathered on the sidewalk out front, but officers kept them away from the location. One A.M. was the middle of the day in Hollywood and patrons from the clubs and bars would be on the streets until dawn, interacting with those denizens of the underbelly.

Josie parked on the side street where one of the detectives met and escorted her to the lot where Burke's body had been discovered. Extra uniformed officers were needed to secure the area and she noticed a few patrol cars with Wilshire area's number "zero-seven" painted on the trunk. Kyle was still on duty in that adjoining division and had sent some of his patrol officers to help. It was one of the things she loved about him. He was a cop's cop.

A new black Tesla with paper plates was parked alone in the middle of the lot surrounded by more yellow tape. Homicide detectives and Scientific Investigation Division personnel were hovering around the car. Josie spotted Behan talking to a detective near one of the three massive lights illuminating the area.

Behan looked up, then finished his conversation before walking over to her. "Morning, Boss, how'd you get here so fast?" he asked. "Bunking in the office again?"

"Have we got a positive ID yet?" she asked, standing as close as she could to him, trying not to be too obvious. Lately, when he got called in, her first objective was to detect the odor of alcohol. There wasn't any. His speech wasn't slurred, and his gait was steady. She could concentrate on the death investigation and not have to worry about the slim possibility of Dempsey or his adjutant showing up.

"I was told you might be able to do that," Behan said, taking a Starbuck's coffee that had just arrived via uniformed officer and giving it to her.

"If it's Burke I can," she said, taking a sip before walking toward the car.

The driver's door was open, and the late Howard Burke was sprawled over the console and leather bucket seats. His swollen face was turned toward the open door, and Josie could identify him even with the large hole over his left ear and pieces of skull and brain splattered over the bloody interior of what had been an expensive vehicle.

She carefully leaned into the car and could see a briefcase open on the floor of the passenger side with papers pulled out. Josie started to straighten up and move away from the sickening metallic smell of drying blood when she noticed his shirt was pulled out in front and his belt unfastened. It was difficult to be certain because of the way his left leg was turned but she thought his pants zipper might be pulled down.

"It's him," she said, standing back a few feet from the car. "What's with his pants?"

"Good question . . . don't know. Looks like they were going up or coming down but don't know why or if it was his idea," Behan said.

"He's gay, in Hollywood, parked off Santa Monica Boulevard at one A.M., Red. Does that expand the possibilities?"

"It does. He's a bit older and better off than our other homicide victims, but we're in the kill zone. Their bodies were found within blocks of here."

"There is another possibility," Josie said. She'd been thinking about Marvin Wright since hearing about Burke. She explained to Behan about the board of rights and how Wright had threatened everyone including the dead lawyer.

"We've recovered the casing, but no slug yet. It's a .45. Easy enough to compare with Wright's gun."

"I'll run it by Dempsey, but I think we've got to take the precaution of letting anyone who had dealings with Wright know they might be in danger," she said.

Her first call was to Kyle. He assured her he wasn't about to be ambushed by the likes of Marvin Wright and his officers would be prepared if the man showed up at Wilshire.

"Watch your back too," he said. "You've got to be at the top of his hit list if he's responsible for this. Maybe you should stay at my place for a while."

"I'm okay . . . little wasted, probably go home. Besides, that would put two of his targets, you and me, in one place."

"Two guns are better than one."

"True, but I'll be careful; you too, lover. I'll see you tomorrow," she said, but really did want to be with him. She tried to convince herself she was an independent woman who could get along without him if he quit on her like Jake did, but Kyle had a way of making her forget how much that had hurt.

The next notification was Deputy Chief Dempsey. He grumbled about being disturbed until she explained the victim was a prominent civil rights attorney and explained his connection to Marvin Wright. Josie had called his city cell phone and figured the source of his bad temper might've been that he was not in Mrs. Dempsey's bed. She heard a sleepy female voice with a heavy Mexican accent in the background and knew from having met her that Mrs. Dempsey, née O'Reilly, was born in Boston to Irish American parents.

"Put it all in your morning report and keep Tim Scott updated," Dempsey said curtly and hung up.

Josie held up her disconnected cell phone, looked at the screen, and said, "Yes, sir, you're welcome," and whispered, "Pompous knucklehead." No one was close enough to hear but she saw Behan standing a few yards from the car staring at her. She never badmouthed the deputy chief in front of him, but the big redhead had guessed a long time ago Dempsey was her primary source of irritation.

"Chief have any words of wisdom?" Behan asked, coming closer.

She didn't answer, gave him a strained half-smile, turned, and walked toward her car. When Behan shouted, "Captain Corsino," she stopped, went back to where he was waiting, and said, "I'm going home to take a shower and get some sleep. Don't release the victim's name to the media until I say it's okay. If you can start the morning report, I'll finish it when I get in . . . thanks Red, nite."

He nodded and didn't say anything. When two cops worked together as long as they had, there wasn't much that needed to be said. She was exhausted and would get away for a few hours. It had been a long day and Burke's murder guaranteed longer hours and more aggravation when the sun came up.

Josie knew that investigating a crime, even murder, was easier than running her station. Most police officers were dedicated warriors, but their lives were never simple, ranging from the heights of glory to the depths of destruction. Her objective was to keep them in the game, save them from themselves and those internal and external forces that threatened or interfered with their ability to do their job. Some days she felt like the best goalie in the NHL; today, not so much.

After more than two decades, the drive to Pasadena was programmed into her brain, and Josie was pulling into the garage without remembering much about the trip. The lights were on as she came through the side door and stepped into the kitchen. Her first thought was she'd forgotten to turn them off that morning when she'd left earlier than usual but knew that wasn't the reason as soon as she saw her son's jacket thrown over the kitchen chair.

David still had his key to the house, but he and Kizzie lived just a few blocks away. There was no reason for him to be there in the middle of the night unless he'd finally taken Josie's motherly advice and abandoned his tiny, older girlfriend. She knew that was unlikely but kept hoping. The den downstairs and the one upstairs with the wet bar containing his favorite whiskey were dark and empty.

The door to David's room was closed. She had given him most of her furniture, including his bedroom suite, so if he was in there, he was sleeping on the floor. Curiosity was one of her weaknesses or strengths depending on the situation, but she was too tired to wake him and talk now. Instead she went to her room, took a long hot shower, set the alarm clock for seven, and crawled into bed.

It had only been a few hours but when the loud buzzing woke her, Josie felt rested and revived. The dark shadows were gone from under her eyes and her hair was shiny and clean. She found a pair of her skinny jeans and a light top to cover the gun and badge on her belt.

"I look human again," she said to her image in the dresser mirror.

David was awake and in the kitchen cooking breakfast when she came downstairs.

"Morning, Mom," he said, kissing her on the cheek. "What's up?"

"No happy to see you, how are you, son, or how's the restaurant doing?" he asked, attempting to sound unconcerned.

"What's wrong?" she asked, again. Josie knew her son wouldn't be there unless something had happened between him and Kizzie. He was almost thirty years old, tall and lanky like her, an excellent chef with his own up-and-coming restaurant, but she recognized that look. It was the same expression he had when he was a child, or a teenager, and things weren't going the way he wanted.

"I made breakfast. Sit down and we'll talk," he said, putting two plates with eggs benedict on the table.

She poured the orange juice and sat across from him. There wasn't any need to ask again. He'd tell her everything in his own way. The breakfast was delicious and she devoured it before he'd started. Finally, after picking at the eggs for several minutes, he sat back and sighed.

"I think it's over with Kizzie and me."

Josie managed to stay in her chair and held back on the fist pump. Instead, in her best consoling voice, she said, "Sorry."

"I know you've never liked her, but I can't believe she'd leave me."

"She left you," Josie said, genuinely surprised. She'd always seen Kizzie as a woman who had attached herself to a young talented meal ticket, allowing her to continue making her swap-meet jewelry and never need to get a real job.

"She's going back to San Francisco . . . says she always hated LA but came here for me."

"So she's not gone yet," Josie said, trying not to sound too disappointed.

"Today. I couldn't stay in the apartment last night. It was too much . . . I told her I can't leave LA now . . . the restaurant is just starting. It's everything I've ever wanted . . . not fair," he said, his voice trailing off to a whisper.

"What's in San Francisco? Why does she have to go so suddenly?"

"It's not sudden. She's wanted to go back for a while."

"Why?" Josie asked again. She had a feeling there was more to this story than she was getting from her son.

"She says Los Angeles is a soulless city . . . and . . . nothing."

"And what?"

"It's stupid. Dad is living in the bay area now and she thinks he's a better influence on me than you."

"What do you think?" Josie asked, trying not to say what she was thinking about his five-foot middle-aged hippie runaway.

"I want to keep my restaurant and be a great chef. I'm too old to worry about what you or Dad want for me."

"Fair enough," she said, picking up the dishes and putting them in the sink. "I've got to run. Clean up the kitchen and go to work. If Kizzie really cares about you, she won't stay away."

He was slouching in his chair, looking as if his world had crashed in on him. She touched the back of his short thinning hair, kissed the top of his head, and left. In a lot of ways, he was still her little boy, but all six foot four inches of him had to learn how to deal with one of life's most difficult lessons—love is priceless, but not everybody appreciates its value. After nearly twenty-five years of marriage,

Jake Corsino had sent her that message loud and clear in an envelope full of divorce papers.

CHANGE OF watch had just occurred so black-and-whites were lined up by the back door of Hollywood station when Josie arrived. Her parking spot was closer to the front of the station, but she always used the rear door. The lobby and front desk were usually a landmine for any area captain and dealing with community leaders, citizens, and even the better class of criminals who might recognize her wasn't something she liked doing first thing in the morning.

It was a surprise to see Mac pacing outside the back door when she turned the corner of the brick police building. He seemed agitated and immediately ground his cigarette into the asphalt when he saw her.

"Boss, I wanted to catch you before you got inside," he said, moving between her and the door. "Chief Dempsey wants his morning report ASAP and you got a visitor . . . Ed Charles, the new police commissioner."

"Really," she said, gently pushing him until he stepped away from the door. "What does Mr. Charles want?"

"Wouldn't say, but he's dead set on waiting until you got here. Didn't think you'd want to deal with him cold turkey."

She did appreciate the heads-up from her adjutant and thanked him before asking if Behan had left the morning report for her to finish. When they got to his desk, Mac handed her the pages her homicide supervisor had completed.

The captain's office had much more space than Josie needed but she appreciated not only the couch that doubled as a bed, but the round table on the other side of the room that gave her a place to work and talk to visitors without the huge pretentious walnut desk her predecessor had left creating a sea of polished wood between them.

The police commissioner was sitting on a corner of the couch with his legs stretched out, his feet resting on the coffee table directly in front of him, and watching a local news station on her television mounted on the back wall. Charles was the newest member of the police commission, those five civilians who by authority of the city charter set policy and oversee the department. They were appointed by the mayor, and the chief of police answered directly to them. In her dealings with the commissioners, the only one Josie trusted was a female Hispanic real estate developer. It was probably a coincidence that she was the only non-attorney on the commission.

When Charles was selected, Josie had read his résumé in the *LA Times*. He was a black civil rights attorney who had graduated from Southwestern Law School in Los Angeles and briefly worked in the state's attorney general's office before he went into private practice and got wealthy by suing the City of Los Angeles in police misconduct cases. Josie had heard he was buddies with the mayor, and that at his first board meeting, Charles had berated the chief of police on everything from the city's growing homeless problem to LA police officers' "out-of-control" use of force on black citizens.

As soon as Josie entered her office, Charles immediately slid his long legs off the table and stood. She was surprised how big he was, taller than she was and agile like a young college athlete.

"Captain Corsino," he said, shaking hands with a firm grip. "I'm Edward Charles. I apologize for dropping in on you without an appointment, but we need to talk."

"No problem," Josie said and pointed to a chair at the table. "Have a seat and I'll grab us some coffee."

"I don't drink coffee."

"Okay, I'll get you water, but I need coffee," she said. Before she could move, Mac came in with a bottle of water and a mug of coffee. There were times she didn't mind her sergeant overhearing what was going on in her office. All the best adjutants were by nature protective and nosy, but this wasn't one of those occasions. She would keep the contents of their conversation between her and the commissioner . . . this time. "Close the door on your way out, Mac," she said and saw him smirk as he turned to leave.

She sat beside Charles, not across the table, and he fidgeted a little as if he were uncomfortable with her proximity. Having been a captain for so many years, Josie had learned that most power players in Los Angeles weren't at their best in intimate face-to-face situations. They seemed to prefer pontificating from the safe distance created by a dais or from behind a microphone in the council chamber or in the police commission hearing room. Although it was difficult to look someone in the eye and lie, there were a few city officials who had perfected the skill. Charles was a neophyte in the political world, and he appeared uneasy.

Josie sat back, crossed her legs, never breaking eye contact with the commissioner.

"I know this is unusual, Captain, but I wanted an opportunity to speak with you about the Howard Burke investigation," he said, glancing down at the table.

"It probably would've been more appropriate to go through the bureau and Chief Dempsey, but I'll tell you what I can," she said.

"Howard Burke was my friend. We went to the same law school and worked on civil rights cases together," he said, his voice getting stronger. "Your reputation is that you are independent and not afraid to do what's right."

She waited, not responding. Flattery never meant anything to her, and she'd found most often it was used as a diversion. Her first thought was, what does he want?

"I want to be in the loop on this investigation," he said as if on cue. "I'll commit any resources the commission has to assist you."

"Mr. Charles . . ."

"Ed, please."

"This is a murder investigation. All the commissioners including you will be kept informed through department channels, and I'd expect your resources to be available. I'm not certain what you're asking for, but my detectives will handle this investigation the same way they'd handle any homicide."

"I want personal daily updates."

"Why?" she asked, and saw his jaw tighten. He didn't like being challenged.

"Because I'm your boss and I'm asking."

"Why aren't you going through the chief's office?" she asked and could see his friendly demeanor eroding quickly.

"I don't want the sanitized department version. I want the truth."

"What makes you think the chief of police won't tell you the truth? As much as he can tell you without jeopardizing my investigation."

His fists were clenched on his lap, and she could see the skin over his knuckles tighten. As he stood slowly, his eyes told her he wasn't pleased, but a tight unconvincing smile was painted on his face. She put her coffee mug on the table and got up. They were a few feet apart and Josie waited, anticipating the threat that usually came from a person who wanted something and had the power to damage careers.

"I had hoped we could work together," he said, breaking eye contact and looking away. Josie almost smiled. She was imitating Kyle's icy stare. He was better at it, but not by much.

"We can," she said. "But not the way you're suggesting . . . unless my boss authorizes it."

"Thank you for your time, Captain Corsino," he said, shook her hand again, and departed, leaving her office door open.

A few seconds later, Mac stood in the doorway. "Everything okay, ma'am?" he asked.

"I don't think so," she said honestly.

THREE

The morning report was nearly ready a few minutes after Charles made his hasty departure. There wasn't much left for her to complete. Behan had done an excellent job of detailing the Burke investigation and Mac had incorporated the watch commander's log with every significant incident occurring during the night and early morning hours.

"I think we should add a line about Commissioner Charles being here," Mac said, when she'd finished the editing.

"Why?" she asked, not wanting to prompt unnecessary questions from Dempsey.

"Sergeant Scott's been creeping around again this morning. My guess is he's already told the chief."

Josie took a deep breath, exhaled, and tossed her pen on the table. "Okay, do that, sign it for me, and have someone deliver the final version to Dempsey. Have you seen Red this morning?"

"He's in detectives," Mac said, and she caught just a hint of . . . what? His expression froze, as if he'd swallowed something sour but didn't want her to know.

"What's wrong?" she asked, detecting the early signs of discord and not about to let it fester.

"Nothing, ma'am."

"What did Behan do?"

"Nothing, everything's great," he said, took the report, and returned to his desk.

Josie wasn't buying it and went to the detective squad room where most of her investigators were either in court or filing cases, but Behan was at his desk with his back to the room, talking on the phone.

She touched his shoulder as she squeezed between the desk and bookcase to reach her chair. Behan didn't look up. He was listening intently to whoever was on the other end and judging by his irritated expression, Josie guessed he didn't like what he was hearing. She sat quietly until he grunted and hung up.

"Bad news?" she asked.

"Got a warrant to search for Wright's gun, but we can't find him or the weapon."

"Search his house?"

"Apartment . . . no gun, no Marvin . . . no clothes or other personal belongings."

"He's got a cell phone, have Kyle or his captain call and order him to go to Wilshire," she said. "Technically he's still a cop."

Behan seemed to relax and nodded.

"Okay, good," he said. "I'll set it up for later, after the post on Burke. Did you need something?"

"Thanks for doing the morning report. What's up with Mac?"

"How should I know."

"What did you say to him?" she asked.

"What did he tell you?"

"Nothing or I wouldn't have to ask, Red."

"The guy's a basket case, should be in therapy not walking around with a loaded gun."

"He's doing a good job. What's your problem? Do you know something I don't?" she asked. She trusted and liked Mac, but Behan wasn't one to bad mouth another cop unless he had a good reason.

"I know a potential breakdown when I see one. Put him in the field and you'll see what I mean."

"He is going back, but not yet."

"You're the boss."

"He's been my adjutant for months. Why all the concern now?"

Behan got up, put on his jacket, and said, "The guy's got issues. The lid is on around you but . . . what I'm saying is keep your eyes open, Corsino."

He left her sitting near his desk and she waited until he disappeared around the corner before she got up and went back to her office. The warning was clear, but she knew Behan wouldn't bring it up again. Whatever he thought he knew or had seen wouldn't be the reason she acted, if she did. He expected her to figure it out and do her job. Josie trusted the big redhead but not nearly as much as her own instincts and they were telling her there was no reason to lose confidence in Mac.

The morning didn't have a smooth start and finding her adjutant away from his desk and Deputy Chief Dempsey sitting behind hers told Josie it might not be getting better. Judging from his guilty expression, her boss had been snooping through her papers. She didn't mind because there was nothing to hide and if there had been she wouldn't be stupid enough to leave it out where he could see it.

"Can I help you find something, sir?" she asked, sitting at the table and smiling.

He cleared his throat and said, "I was looking for the Burke press release."

"A copy's attached to your morning report."

"I understand you had a visit from Commissioner Charles this morning. What did he want?"

"Burke was his friend. He wanted to know what happened."

"What did you tell him?"

"Not much, don't know much yet . . . why?" she asked. Dempsey looked worried. During his tenure in West Bureau he hadn't been subtle in letting her know that her decision-making made him nervous. He'd made it clear he viewed her leadership style as a potential obstacle to his career advancement.

Dempsey got up and paced in front of her.

"Charles called the chief of police . . . must've been right after he left here. He wanted Burke's investigation taken out of Hollywood . . . transferred downtown."

That got her attention. She could feel angry thoughts starting to fill her head but made herself calm down. The chief was a good man, but his second term depended on his ability to placate the police commission and mayor.

"What did the chief say?" she asked. Her voice was tight and controlled, the stillness before her verbal storm.

He stopped and sat on the corner of her desk. "Never mind what he said. Just be glad it was Ed Charles who made the request. The chief hates his guts for the way he humiliated him at that commission meeting. The old man didn't refuse to make the change, said he'd consider it, which means it'll happen when hell freezes over."

"So Burke is still my investigation."

"Charles can't interfere with the day-to-day management of the department. The case is yours unless the
police commission can put enough pressure on the chief to
make him take it away. My advice is don't drag your feet
on this one."

She didn't need his last bit of wisdom knowing too well
the chief's decision wouldn't survive if his contract renewal
was in danger. The investigation belonged in Hollywood
with Behan, but on a staff level, good police work always
took a back seat to career demands.

It was obvious Dempsey wasn't pleased with Charles
either. There was a pecking order in the police department and the commissioner had committed a cardinal sin
by going directly to Josie and bypassing West Bureau. She
was grateful now that Dempsey knew about the visit. His
inflated ego would keep him from supporting Charles's
request. Nevertheless she had to wonder why the commissioner was so intent in getting access to Burke's investigation that he would go to the chief of police to try to take
it away from her and give it to Robbery-Homicide division
downtown. He might expect more access in RHD since
they tended to be more politically accommodating, but that
didn't explain his intense personal interest. Was it because
Burke was his friend, she wondered, or was he attempting
to influence the outcome?

When Behan got back from the Burke autopsy, his
first stop was her office and she filled him in on what
had occurred with Charles and Dempsey. He didn't seem
surprised.

"High-profile victim, with lots of important friends, you
know they can't keep out of the way," he said and looked
up when Mac leaned into the room.

"Ma'am there's been a shooting in West LA. Captain Ames is on line one," Mac said. "It involves Captain Sanchez."

Stuart Ames, the area captain for West LA, told her Sanchez had been leaving the station parking lot in a black-and-white when someone put a round through the front window of his police car. He accelerated and hit a block wall across the street.

"Jorge's okay," Ames said. "Shook up, got cuts from the windshield glass and a few bumps when he crashed, nothing life-threatening. Paramedics patched him up . . . he refused to go to emergency. Sanchez figured considering the Burke killing I should give you a heads-up."

She hung up and told Behan what had happened. "This is looking more and more like Wright," she said and immediately thought about calling Kyle. "We should let Wilshire know what happened."

"Probably not necessary," Behan said.

"Two members of my board of rights have been attacked, one's dead. I think it's necessary to warn them they might have a rogue cop out for revenge."

"Lieutenant Richards contacted Wright on his cell phone this morning. The guy agreed to come to Wilshire station in about an hour. I think Kyle will be ready for him," Behan said. "That's one of the things I came to tell you. The other was about the post, but I want to get to Wilshire. You coming? I can fill you in on the way."

She wanted to see Sanchez to make certain he was okay, but that would have to wait. Having an opportunity to confront Wright was too important. Mac was waiting just outside her office when they left. He stared at Behan as he passed but didn't say anything. Behan ignored the adjutant, but Josie noticed the redhead's ruddy complexion got a shade brighter. There wasn't time to deal with them now, but their behavior was pissing her off and she was determined to fix whatever was going on between them before this day was over.

"The head shot killed Burke, no surprise there," Behan said as he drove out of the parking lot.

"Any signs of sexual activity," she asked, thinking about Burke's disheveled clothes.

"Nothing recent, but we recovered a syringe in the parking lot not too far from his Tesla the night he was killed, and the coroner found a couple of suspicious puncture wounds near his groin area."

"Drugs?"

"Won't know until toxicology comes back but it's looking that way. We'll have the syringe tested too and look for prints."

WILSHIRE STATION was a fifteen-minute drive from Hollywood. During the short time it took to get there she was trying to absorb what Behan had told her about Burke's autopsy while reconciling what had happened to Jorge Sanchez with Wright's willingness to meet with them. If he killed Burke and attacked Sanchez, why would Marvin Wright walk into Wilshire station where he could be arrested on the spot? Either he was very cunning, very stupid, or had nothing to do with any of it.

FOUR

The Wilshire area captain wanted Lieutenant Richards, who was sitting in for the patrol captain, to conduct the interview with Officer Wright. Kyle had told Josie on other occasions the area commander preferred not to deal directly with his uniformed officers, something she found odd. She had a patrol captain too but insisted in matters of discipline she be included. Everything that happened in her division was her business.

They used the patrol captain's office, a cramped space where Richards had managed to fit an additional three chairs around the desk. He left enough space so Josie and Behan wouldn't have to sit too close to the unpredictable cop.

Wright arrived about fifteen minutes late with an entourage that included his private attorney, union representative, union lawyer, and two bodyguards who looked like tattooed NFL linebackers in tight T-shirts and Levi's. Richards ordered everybody except Wright, his private attorney, and the union rep out of the room. The others began protesting but Wright told them to leave and wait outside the door. There was room for one more chair and the attorney

took it. The union rep either had to sit on the edge of a
small bookcase or stand.

Wright was a big man, but Josie hadn't seen him this
close during the board of rights. When he unbuttoned his
coat to sit, she noticed how his belly bulged out over the
top of his tight pants. His face was flabby and his eyes
bloodshot. He looked tired and out of shape. She tried to
imagine him in the tight-fitting blue uniform. It wasn't a
pretty picture.

"I'm taping this meeting," the union rep said, taking a
small recorder out of his briefcase.

"That's fine, so am I," Richards said, before giving the
officer his Miranda and administrative rights warning.

Wright seemed unconcerned, even cocky, nodding at
Josie and Behan when Kyle introduced them for the record.
He waited until Kyle had finished, then smiled and winked
at Josie.

"Officer Wright I have a search warrant for your vehicles,
work locker, and residence to seize your service weapon
and any other guns you might possess," Richards said.

"You already searched my place," Wright said with a
smirk. He giggled as if he'd just heard something funny.
His lawyer took a copy of the warrant, but didn't bother to
look at it.

"We both know you don't live there," Richards said,
ignoring the weird outburst.

"I temporarily lost my employment, so I had to move
for financial considerations."

"Where are you staying?"

"Don't need no search warrant. I'll give you my damn
gun."

"Is that the only gun you own?" Behan asked.

"That's it."

"Where is it?" Richards asked.

Wright pulled a gold chain out of his pants pocket and held it up. A key with a Mercedes-Benz emblem dangled from the end of the chain. He said, "In the trunk of my ride. You know I ain't got a badge or police ID to be carrying a loaded weapon on my person."

"I'll get it," Behan said, snatching the chain out of his hand.

"It's the silver one parked near the back door. Feel free to search around while you're in there," Wright said, snorting a laugh and pretending to shoot at the ceiling with his finger.

They waited in silence until Behan came back with a Colt .45 semiautomatic pistol in a black holster and four empty magazines. He immediately asked Wright where he was on the night of Burke's murder.

"Where I've been staying, at my mama's house, watching a Blu-ray DVD."

"Anybody beside your mother see you there?" Behan asked.

"My cousin Fred and his lady Jackie."

Richards handed Wright a pen and tablet and said, "Give us their full names and addresses so they can be interviewed to corroborate your alibi, and give us your current address."

Josie expected the attorney to intervene, but he didn't.

"Don't need no corroborating. You tell me why I'm gonna waste that skinny-assed lawyer when we all know some judge's gonna give me my job back with lots more money for my trouble," he said, grinning, and began slowly printing names with addresses and phone numbers. The letters were big, uneven, almost childlike.

"Where were you this morning?" Josie asked. She could understand his smugness. The first time the department fired him, the court not only reinstated Wright but gave him back wages and considerable punitive damages.

"With him," Wright said, pointing over his shoulder at the union rep perched on the bookcase.

"He's been downtown in our league office with his attorney all morning . . . we drove here together," the rep said, and the lawyer nodded in agreement.

"What about the steroid twins in the hallway? Were they with you all morning?" Josie asked.

Wright chuckled and said, "Yes, ma'am, the brothers do travel with me."

Josie turned to the union rep and asked, "Is that true? Did you see them?"

The union rep shrugged and said, "Saw them come in . . . not my job to watch them all morning."

"Give us their names and addresses too. Why do you need bodyguards?" she asked.

"There's a conspiracy against me . . . I got protection." His voice grew louder. He looked angry and pounded the arm of his chair once with his fist.

"Conspiracy?"

"People telling lies, trying to hurt me . . . accusing me of all kinds of terrible stuff I didn't do."

"Where's your ammo?" Behan asked, holding up one of the empty magazines.

"Shot it up. Didn't get a new box yet," Wright said.

For the first time, Josie saw some uncertainty in his expression, that look away and down told her he might be lying about the ammunition, but she didn't know why. It was probably the same ammo all cops carried. The department gave it to them to reload their service weapons after monthly qualifications.

The interview continued for almost another hour, but none of the questions seemed to unnerve Wright who appeared for the most part to be enjoying it, even bouncing on the chair once or twice before answering. The lawyer never spoke, smiled a few times as if the interview were amusing but of little consequence. The union rep didn't participate either but kept looking at his watch and squirming as if he couldn't get comfortable either with Wright's behavior or being relegated to the corner of a bookcase.

"I think we're done here," Behan said abruptly after one of Wright's outbursts.

Josie could tell from the tone of her detective's voice he might've been contemplating wiping the snide expression off Wright's face with a "C" clamp or some other inappropriate choke hold. She stood quickly, blocking temptation.

"Until the chief officially fires you, I'm ordering you to call Lieutenant Richards every day," Josie said, standing a few feet from Wright. "If you don't, it will be insubordination . . . another firing offense." She was looking at the lawyer for the last part of her warning.

Wright stopped grinning and lumbered out of the office where he pushed past his bodyguards, went out the door, and disappeared into the lobby.

"Crazy prick needs to be taught some manners," Behan said when he was alone with Josie and Richards.

"But not by you," Josie said. "San Quentin's not the best retirement spot."

"Something tells me his gun isn't going to be a match," Richards said. "Can we get a warrant for his mother's place?"

"Probably not," Behan said. "The exigency disappeared when he walked in here and gave us his service weapon. The original warrant was weak. The rationale probably won't fly now. His lawyer knows we've got nothing."

"Be nice to know what kind of ammo he was using," Richards said.

Behan opened his hand and held out a single round of .45-caliber Ranger SXT and said, "When dumb-shit took out the magazine, he didn't clear the round in the chamber. We'll see if it matches the round that killed Burke."

"What's your gut feeling about this guy?" she asked Behan.

"He's a certifiable nut job. He's capable of killing Burke, and he's got motive, but we have nothing that puts him anywhere near our homicide or the hit on Sanchez this morning."

While Behan went to Wilshire records to run the names Wright had given them, Josie and Richards waited in the patrol captain's office. It was the first occasion they'd had any time alone for days. He closed the door and kissed her, a long passionate kiss as if he hadn't seen her for much longer.

"Your place or mine tonight?" he asked.

"Is your daughter back?"

"Nope, still in London with my mother."

"Yours," she said and told him about her son's visit and Kizzie's departure. "He should have gone back to his apartment, but I'd rather be certain we'll be alone."

Josie liked Richards's daughter but as the girl got older she seemed to grow more distant. Beth had just graduated from high school and was smart and pretty, but Kyle's wealthy mother had a strong influence on her. Both his mother and daughter had in subtle and not so subtle ways let Josie know they would have preferred him to find someone more like his first wife, a delicate artistic woman. The job of a police captain might have given Josie a few rough edges, but she wasn't about to soften or change her personality to get their approval. It had taken years to get her own son to accept the idea that a strong independent mother who packed a gun could love him just as much as one who devoted her life to making his easier. She was determined not to go through that adolescent drama again, not even for Kyle's sake.

They agreed to meet at Richards's house in Long Beach and he promised to have dinner and a good bottle of pinot noir waiting when she got there. Josie's ex-husband had been a great cook and she was convinced David had inherited his culinary talent. Although Kyle wasn't as skilled in the kitchen, he enjoyed cooking and made their time together special regardless of how the meal turned out. Maybe it was because they were both cops, but the bond between them was more than love, sex, or friendship. It was difficult for her to understand but despite her firm desire and repeated resolution to keep an emotional distance and protect herself from being hurt again, Kyle Richards had become an essential part of her life.

FIVE

Although Behan was eager to get back to his desk, Josie insisted they make a stop at West LA station to check on Sanchez. She knew Red was irritated and guessed it wasn't just Wright's bizarre behavior that was bothering him. The lack of evidence in Burke's murder and for that matter in all their recent Hollywood homicides had to be frustrating. He was an old-school detective who relied as much on his instincts as the physical evidence, but the scarcity of clues in these cases was unusual. Other than the fact they were all homosexuals, the victims seemed to have been chosen at random.

A serial killer was a possibility but that meant today's shooting in West LA probably had nothing to do with Burke's killing. Josie wasn't ready to eliminate Marvin Wright as a suspect. She was old-school too and her instincts were telling her the lawyer's death and the attack on Sanchez were somehow connected.

They located Sanchez in his office at the back of the station. The mini blinds were closed and the door was shut, so Josie knocked. He opened the door and smiled when he saw it was her and Behan.

"You don't look too bad," Josie lied. His handsome face had a couple of bruises and the area around his left eye was black, with a deep red border, and the eye was swollen shut. His dark skin minimized the visible bruising. The damage looked like what she'd seen in traffic accidents from airbag deployment and considering everything, she was relieved he wasn't more seriously injured.

"Thanks, Boss, but I know I look like Quasimodo's twin," he said, his left arm hanging limp at his side as he imitated the fictional character's humpback walk.

"It's actually an improvement," Behan said, sitting in the leather chair behind his desk.

Sanchez had been a drinking buddy of Behan's when Jorge was a uniformed watch commander in Hollywood. Several nights a week, the homicide supervisor and a couple of his senior detectives would work overtime until Sanchez finished his shift and then they'd go to Nora's or one of the other cop bars in Hollywood. Behan always said how much he liked the younger man because he was one of the few patrol lieutenants who listened and learned what was needed to make an arrest result in a successful prosecution.

"Maybe it would help your ugly mug if you crashed into a wall a couple of times," Sanchez said with a painful smile.

"You should go to the emergency room and get that eye looked at," Josie said, gently touching his cheek.

"Paramedics cleaned and disinfected around it. Doesn't hurt too much anymore."

"Did you see who fired the shots?" Behan asked.

"No, I guess they came from across the street, but I didn't see anything . . . tried to get out of the driveway . . . I panicked like a rookie and crashed."

"Ames told me they hit the windshield on the passenger side, more than one round, maybe two or three . . . you were lucky," she said.

"We'll compare the slugs and see if they match the Burke killing, but Wright's got a solid alibi for this morning," Behan said, pushing himself out of the chair.

"How's that?" Sanchez asked.

Josie told him about Wright's interview at Wilshire, and the people who were with him in the police union office at the time of the West LA shooting.

"But it has to be him. It's the only thing that makes sense. Somebody's got to be helping him," Sanchez said, becoming agitated.

"Maybe," Behan mumbled, opening the door. "We need to get back, Boss," he said, glancing at his watch.

Sanchez escorted them as far as the back door. It looked as if every bone in his body hurt as he tried to keep up with their slow pace and she could feel his muscles tighten as she gave him a careful hug before leaving.

THEY DIDN'T talk much on the drive back to Hollywood station. Josie was angry thinking about her protégé's painful condition. She was determined whoever had targeted him had to be caught quickly to prevent a second attempt.

While at work, Josie always anticipated a heightened risk of danger, but given the events of the last two days, that awareness took on a whole new meaning. She figured it was reasonable to assume there was a target on her back too.

Behan must have been thinking the same thing.

"Are you living with Kyle yet?" he asked as he parked near the back door of Hollywood station.

"None of your business."

"You shouldn't be alone. Maybe you should get Metro to watch your house."

"Thanks, Red, but I'm good. We don't know for sure this has anything to do with Marvin Wright," she said, but they both knew that's exactly what she believed.

He didn't respond but got out of the car and walked ahead of her. When they were inside the station he went directly into the detective squad room and she turned the other way down the hallway toward her office.

Behan had to know from years of working with her that arguing was pointless. She'd always listen to him, but in the end, made her own decisions. There was one thing Josie did know for certain—she wasn't Sanchez or Burke and wouldn't get caught by surprise. If somebody was coming after her they'd better be damn good, a lot better than what she'd seen so far.

The admin office was nearly deserted except for Mac and the secretary. Her adjutant never left until she did, or she told him to go home. It was one of the things she liked about him, but it was a concern too. He didn't seem to have a personal life outside the station, no wife, girlfriend, or activity that wasn't directly related to Hollywood.

"Anything critical," she asked as Mac dropped a stack of papers on the desk.

"We can do it in the morning," he said. "All routine."

"Good, sit down. I want to talk to you."

He didn't hesitate and sat at the table. She leaned against her desk a few feet from him.

"What's going on between you and Red?" she asked and before he could answer said, "And don't say nothing or I swear I'll bury you behind a desk for the rest of your career."

Mac sighed and said, "I know you're trying to help, ma'am, but I can handle this one."

"Hollywood is my station. I want to know what 'this one' is, then I'll tell you who's going to handle it."

"Don't yell at him, it's me," Behan said. He was standing in the doorway, looking sheepish.

"Get in here and close the door," she said.

He did and sat at the table across from Mac.

"Well?" she asked when Behan hesitated.

"He's worried about me," Mac said before Behan could speak.

"That's not what it looks like to me," she said.

"Let me explain," Behan said, raising his voice. Josie sat between them, clasped her hands on the table, and stared at him. "I had a partner in patrol . . . years ago, before your time, Corsino. He got lung cancer. It messed up his head. He went on the roof of the station and blew his brains out. I've seen that same panic in your eyes," Behan said, turning to the other man. "You need to get away from this shit before it kills you. You're done. I've been doing this a long time and I know the signs."

"Like I told you before, you're wrong, Red. I'm not like your partner. I'm not going to kill myself. In a couple of weeks, when the new deployment starts, I'm going back to patrol," Mac said, looking at Josie. "If that's okay with you, Boss."

Josie didn't answer right away but watched for Behan's reaction. There wasn't any.

"Red, it's his life," she said, after a few seconds.

"I'll back off if . . . never mind, you're right, it's your life. If I made a mistake, I apologize but . . ." He didn't finish, got up, and patted Mac on the shoulder. It was friendly, a partner's encouraging gesture, and he left without saying more.

It's over, Josie thought as Mac stood and followed Behan out of her office, his stoic expression unaltered. Behan had relented and given him the benefit of the doubt, supported him, but judging from her adjutant's demeanor, it was difficult to know if he was pleased or unhappy. Detached was the word that leapt into her head and then came the second thoughts, something she rarely had.

There wasn't much time to dwell on his behavior. Marge Bailey squeezed past him on her way into the room and Mac did manage a smile and some whispered conversation with her.

"What's up with him?" Marge asked, dropping onto the chair Mac had just vacated.

"Nothing," Josie said, not certain she could explain. "What are you up to?"

"My guys just made an arrest on Santa Monica . . . wait 'til you see him . . . swears a John picked him up a few days ago, tried to strangle him, two blocks from where Burke got killed."

"Did you tell Behan?"

"Can't find Red, but you gotta see this one, Boss. My description can't do this shithead justice."

Josie told her to bring the arrestee down to detectives and put him in one of the interview rooms and she'd locate Behan. It wasn't difficult. He was at his desk when she got to the squad room. She was talking with him when Marge arrived with a tall pale young man who had shoulder-length thick white hair, pinkish-blue eyes, and was dressed all in black with a long black silk cape. Josie immediately recognized his albinism. His choice of clothes was a lot more distracting.

"What the fuck," Behan mumbled.

Marge put the man in the interview room closest to the homicide table and shut the door.

"Prince of Darkness," Marge said, grinning, as she stood beside Josie. "That's what shithead calls himself."

"What am I supposed to do with him?" Behan asked.

"He can kind of describe the turd that tried to choke him, and he knew a couple of your homicide victims, including Burke," Marge said. "Actually, he's pretty bright for a street whore."

Behan's homicide team was in the field. He decided that he and Marge should interview the "Prince." Josie was ready to leave for Kyle's house in Long Beach but couldn't make herself go without hearing what the strange man had to say. She could watch on video from the adjoining room for a few minutes to determine if his information was worth delaying her glass of pinot.

As Marge opened the door to the interview room, Josie walked past and got a whiff of lilacs. It smelled like a cheap perfume or powder. She went next door to the closet-sized room and turned on the monitor. The Miranda warning was repeated by Behan even though Marge had given him his rights after the prostitution arrest. The man waived his rights again and said he was eager to talk to them. Josie was surprised by his clear articulate speech. He wasn't the usual type of young man found selling his body on the streets.

"What's your real name?" Behan asked.

"Prince of Darkness, I've changed it legally," he said, then responding to Behan's scowl added quickly, "Anthony Charles."

"Any relation to . . ." Behan started to ask.

"Eddie Charles, your police commissioner, is my big brother. But we're estranged," he said, squinting. "Can we lower those lights a touch?"

Josie pulled a chair from across the room and put it in front of the monitor. The quality of the video wasn't as sharp with lights turned down, but she wasn't going anywhere.

"Does he know you're peddling your ass on the boulevard?" Marge asked.

"Hardly, we've had no contact for years. I'm twenty-five; I left home when I was seventeen while he was distinguishing himself at Southwestern. Family never really searched for me," he said, matter-of-factly. There was no self-pity in his voice.

"You're a smart guy, why do this?" Behan asked, indicating his outfit.

Anthony swallowed a laugh and shook his head before reciting in iambic rhyme, "My fate hath been defined by evil gods. My visage doth condemn me in men's eyes." He waited a few seconds, but Behan and Marge just stared at him, so he added, "I'm fucked up. Nobody really wants to look at me."

"What does that have to do with whoring on the boulevard?" Marge asked.

"I live in the night's shadows where pigmentation is irrelevant, and I can find love . . . well, sex if adequate cash is offered."

"Okay, we all agree you're completely fucked up. What happened when you were attacked?" Marge asked.

For the first time, Anthony genuinely laughed before saying, "I really do like you, Lieutenant Bailey." He explained how he was trolling on the boulevard two blocks from the High-Top Bar a few days ago when a big man in a dark hoodie and tinted glasses approached him. There were no lights in the area where they met, and the man kept his head down making it difficult to see his face, but Anthony thought he might've been black.

"He wanted a blow job and told me to go with him behind the building."

"Did you?"

"We walked down the alley but when we got behind the building he pushed me to the ground. It scared me. I kicked at him and tried to get up. He pulled off his belt and wrapped it around my neck; his zipper was down like he was going to force me but I was passing out when a car came down the alley . . . guess it spooked him. He let loose and ran."

"Let me see your neck," Behan demanded.

Anthony's tunic top had buttons over his shoulder and up the neck. He opened them and exposed his neck and chest. Even on the video, Josie could see the ugly red welts on both sides of his neck.

"Did he leave the belt?" Behan asked.

"No, I looked for it."

"Can you describe him better or did you notice anything unusual about him that might help us find this guy?" Marge asked.

"I'm pretty sure he had darker skin . . . not much light but I saw his hands . . . taller than me, maybe six two or three, strong, but he wasn't from the street."

"Why do you say that?"

"His shoes were shined and looked expensive. Belt had something metal like a big buckle, see," he said pointing to a large vertical bruise on the right side of his neck."

"Hear anything unusual in his voice like an accent?" Marge asked.

"No, but . . . yes, there was one thing. It was as if he were trying to sound uneducated, but he slipped up and used a word . . . can't remember, oh yeah 'rambunctious' and his grammar was almost too perfectly awful."

Behan left the room and came back with a picture of Howard Burke taken by the department for his photo ID.

"Do you recognize him?" he asked, pushing the photo in front of Anthony.

"Uncle Howie, most guys on the boulevard knew him. He did pro bono work whenever we got busted, too bad what happened to him."

"Why 'uncle'?" Marge asked.

"Howie and my brother went to school together." Anthony hesitated then grinned. "How can I put this; he spent time at our house and was my . . . got me into the game so to speak."

"Pimp?" Marge asked.

"No, I'd say more like a tutor."

"Did he get shot by one of those boys he picked up?" Behan asked.

"Doubt it, he could afford a better class of bitch, besides he never did anything in his car. Always took his date home . . . wouldn't even drink water in that Tesla."

By the end of the interview, Josie wasn't put off by the man's appearance any longer. She was impressed by his thorough answers and obvious intelligence and thought it was such a waste that he seemed to believe or had been told his looks condemned him to the status of a night crawler confined to the alleys and back streets of Hollywood.

Anthony agreed to take them to the exact location where his assault had occurred and said he'd work with Marge if she'd OR him on his prostitution arrest which would allow him to go to court on his own recognizance. He said he was angry about the attack on him and the murder of Burke and vowed he was willing to do whatever it took to catch the assailant because, "Violence at the workplace is seriously affecting my business."

Josie waited until Marge escorted Anthony back to the holding cell to process him for release before she left the interview room. She found Behan sitting at his desk with one of the murder books open in front of him. He was turning pages quickly and seemed to be searching for something.

"Look here, Corsino," he said, motioning for her to come closer. "This was our first homicide victim. He was found within a block of Anthony Charles's attack."

She leaned on his chair and peered over his shoulder. He was pointing at two five-by-seven color photos with enlarged images of the victim's neck. One picture displayed the red horizontal markings usually seen in strangulation deaths, but the other showed a unique vertical bruise similar to the pattern they had just observed on Anthony's neck.

They both knew what that meant.

SIX

It was the typical warm, breezy summer night in Long Beach when Josie drove her city car up the driveway of Kyle's Spanish craftsman bungalow a few blocks from the permanent docking place of the Queen Mary. She could smell the ocean air mixed with the unmistakable aroma of sautéed garlic and onions as she got out of her vehicle and knew Kyle had kept his promise to cook dinner.

This neighborhood was quiet with bike paths, round-abouts filled with colorful flowers or blossoming trees, and lots of millennial, two-income couples and their dogs. The stay-at-home moms drove BMWs or Porsches and had the figures to wear stylish tennis dresses or yoga pants to their trendy markets. Not exactly Josie's crowd but she knew Kyle's deceased wife had fit in easily.

She had been thinking about the albino man during her drive. His assault had given them a solid reason to pursue Behan's serial killer theory. The mark left on the first homicide victim's neck was a close enough match to Anthony's.

Behan said he would work with Marge Bailey first thing the next morning on a game plan to deploy decoys along

Santa Monica Boulevard in the vicinity of the High-Top Bar. Anthony was willing to work with them, but Josie preferred using undercover police officers. They would be armed and better prepared to protect themselves.

"Hey, Corsino, you want your drink out there?"

Kyle was waiting on the porch holding a glass of red wine, grinning. She realized she'd been standing on the driveway for several minutes lost in thought about the investigation and had forgotten where she was going.

"Sorry, daydreaming," she said. "Can't seem to get work out of my head."

"How unusual," he said, kissing her as she took the glass out of his hand. They went inside, and she told him about Anthony Charles. She put her briefcase and semiauto in the bedroom, then sat near the narrow butcher-block table in the kitchen and drank while he finished cooking. They talked for a few minutes about Marvin Wright and what had happened to Jorge Sanchez, but he was more interested in convincing her to move in with him and stay away from Pasadena at least until the Burke investigation was over.

"I'm not sure your mother and daughter would be keen on that move," she said, knowing what his reaction to her words would be.

He stopped chopping carrots and stared at her for a few seconds before saying, "You're joking, right?"

"Pretty much, but we both know they're not crazy about me."

"I stopped caring what my mother thought when I was ten and Beth can't figure out her own life yet. Besides, they're living in London now. I've already converted Beth's bedroom for my gun cleaning."

"What about when she comes home?"

"She's eighteen. She can stay with my mother or find her own place," he said.

Josie put her glass on the table and watched him for a sign that he wasn't serious, but he was. Beth was his only child and the spitting image of his dead wife, but Kyle spoke as if he were ready to cut her loose. He had been a very protective father when Josie first met him, but maybe like her with David, he realized the time had come to step back and let his daughter live her own life.

"I'll stay for a while," she said. "What's for dinner? It smells great."

"Pork roast. We can drive to your place and pick up whatever you need after dinner."

"Not necessary—have you looked in your closet and dresser lately? I've got more clothes here than in Pasadena."

"I have found some strange bottles in my bathroom, smell great, reminds me of you."

"My shampoo, conditioner, soap . . . I spend a lot of time here."

He didn't respond. Her refusal to sell or rent her house and live with him permanently had become a sore spot between them. He was ready to marry again; she wasn't. Her reluctance wasn't because she didn't love him; she did, but her independence had become valuable. Josie cherished the freedom of an individual life, but Kyle kept reminding her of the words from that great American philosopher Kris Kristofferson, "Freedom's just another word for nothing left to lose."

He was right, of course, and maybe this temporary move-in would change her mind, allay her fears. She watched him working in the kitchen with that same determination and ease he did everything. Kyle was a good man, not only handsome and intelligent, but a dedicated cop and honest about his feelings, which was a refreshing change after her bumpy ride on the Jake Corsino emotional roller coaster.

"Still thinking about work?" he asked, sitting on the stool beside her.

"No, I was thinking about you, us."

"Good," he said and took the wine glass out of her hand.

He led her into the bedroom. They undressed, took a shower together, and made love on his messy bed until they were both exhausted. The french doors leading to the enclosed patio were open and the warm breeze gently caressed Josie's naked limbs as she tucked in close to Kyle's sweaty body. They stayed like that until he had to get up to rescue the roast from incineration. She rinsed off in the shower again and found a clean nightshirt in the dresser.

When she got back to the kitchen, Kyle had dinner ready. He'd opened a bottle of pinot noir and they sat at the kitchen table, ate, and drank. Josie was ravenous and couldn't remember the last time she'd eaten this much food at one time.

"We should have sex before every meal. You might actually put on a little weight," he said when she'd finished her third helping.

After Josie cleaned the kitchen and filled up the dishwasher, they took the bottle of wine outside on the patio to finish it, and stayed there snuggling on the spacious lounge until almost midnight. He'd been quiet but then she started talking about his daughter. She guessed Beth was on his mind, and he finally admitted he'd been concerned the young woman was moving away from him, not just physically but emotionally. When Beth was a child, Josie knew they were inseparable and she sensed his bold declaration about Beth's bedroom and her living with his mother was just bravado, and it was.

"It's like I told my son about Kizzie. She loves you; she's going to want you in her life," Josie said.

"My mother is rich and gives her things I can't or won't. I'm afraid getting too much too soon will destroy her ambition, her passion." He exhaled and added, "Guess I was really hoping she'd be more like her mother and not mine."

"I was hoping David would play piano with the LA Philharmonic. It doesn't work that way, love. He was blessed with extraordinary talent, but he wants to make roast duck not Dvorak. I know he loves and respects me, but I wanted more for him. It took me a long time to understand my dreams weren't his."

"You're a wise woman, Corsino," he whispered, rubbing his soft unshaven face against her cheek.

"No, just a disappointed realist."

They could have fallen asleep on the patio but decided to retreat into the bedroom. Kyle left all the french doors open so it was almost like being outside. They never worried about intruders. Her semiauto was on one nightstand, his Colt 1911 on the other, and both she and Kyle were light sleepers.

The big meal, a bottle of wine, and great sex should have guaranteed them a good night's sleep, but Josie's cell phone woke her at three thirty A.M. Years of being an on-call civil servant meant she wouldn't and couldn't ignore it. Kyle groaned as he rolled over and covered his head with a pillow.

"What?" Josie asked in a raspy voice, coughing to clear her throat. She was sitting on the edge of the bed but not quite fully awake.

"Captain, this is Jerry Saunders at Robbery-Homicide. We got a call from Pasadena PD asking us to contact you."

Now she was awake. "Is my son okay?" she asked. David immediately popped into her mind.

Kyle must have heard her ask about David. He sat up in bed, moved across the mattress to sit quietly beside her.

"No, it's not your son, ma'am. It's your house. The PD says it's been firebombed. They checked; nobody was inside."

"I didn't stay there last night. I live alone. Nobody should have been . . . are you certain they checked all the rooms on every floor?" she asked, having a sudden panic attack thinking her son might've stayed over again.

"Yes, ma'am, every room, but they need you or some-body to secure the property. There's lots of damage, no way to lock up."

"Who's there now?"

"Fire department, arson investigator."

"Call back, tell them I'm on my way and not to leave. I want to talk to them."

She hung up and looked at Kyle.

"David okay?" he asked with a puzzled expression.

Josie nodded and said calmly, "Somebody tried to burn down my house."

They dressed and drove their own vehicles to Pasadena. Kyle would leave for work from there and she didn't know how long it would take to make her home secure from trespassers. The arson investigator was still on scene sifting through the debris near the front door when they arrived. He explained that two Molotov cocktails had been tossed onto the porch and one was thrown through the front bay window. Most of the damage inside was in the downstairs front den and the porch had been destroyed. There was smoke damage on the first floor, but the other floors were less affected.

"You're lucky the next-door neighbor is an insomniac," the inspector said, after they had gone through all the downstairs rooms. "He called as soon as the flames started, and the fire station is close, or it could've been worse. I'd say given the time of night and number of devices somebody wanted you dead."

Josie watched Kyle as the inspector talked and saw his agitation growing. She knew when he was upset. The little vein near his left temple and the ones in his neck throbbed. He was very angry.

"Did the neighbor see who did this?" Kyle asked, looking around as if he wanted to hit something.

"I'll give you a copy of his statement. He saw what looked like a big man in a dark hoodie running from your house and around the corner. Not much help," the inspector said. He told Josie sometimes he could trace the accelerant and lift prints from pieces of the bottle. He didn't seem too confident about identifying the perpetrator but added, "I'm really good at what I do so you never know. You got any idea who might've done this?"

"I'll give you some background on events during the last few days and a possible suspect, but he's a long shot," Josie said. She knew Marvin was the logical culprit, but it didn't feel right because he seemed to truly believe superior court would give him his job back, plus damages, so why go after the board members? Besides, he did have an ironclad alibi for the Sanchez attack.

All that aside, she couldn't help thinking about what Jorge Sanchez had said to her after Marvin's board of rights—i.e., not to underestimate how incredibly stupid Marvin Wright could be.

SEVEN

J osie wasn't surprised that Kyle refused to leave her alone in Pasadena. She had to wait for a local carpenter to patch up the house with plywood and for the security company to replace the sensor that had melted onto what was left of the front door. A few hours after sunrise, they had nearly completed the work. She tried to convince Kyle to leave and get some sleep in the Wilshire cot room before his shift started, but her suggestion was met with a cold stare.

She was admittedly concerned because someone had tried to harm her, but she really didn't want or need a bodyguard. Her only fear now was for David's safety. She called him at his apartment and described what had happened. She ordered him to stay away from the house until further notice. He snorted and she could visualize his well-practiced cynical military salute on the other end of the line. He always accused her of being more drill sergeant than mother.

"Got it, Mom. What about you? Can you stay with Kyle? Stay here if you want. I'll sleep on the couch."

"You're missing the point, Son" she said. "I'm telling you to stay away from me until we catch whoever's doing this."

He was quiet for a few seconds, then said, "We both know that isn't gonna happen," and the line went dead.

"Stubborn, mule-headed . . ." she mumbled, gritting her teeth and looking at the phone.

"Wonder where he gets that from," Kyle mumbled. He was sitting on the hood of his car waiting to escort her to Hollywood. "You ready to head out?"

"Look, I know you're worried and you love me. I love you too, but I really don't want you following me around all day," she said, getting into her car.

"I won't. I'm just following you to Hollywood. Marge and Red can follow you around the rest of the day."

"Great," she said sarcastically.

"Marvin claimed he lived with his mother in Wilshire. Pasadena PD is going to let me tag along today when they try to contact him about the fire. I'll let you know how that turns out," he said and leaned into her driver's window to kiss her before whispering, "Don't try to lose me, Corsino. Remember, I worked surveillance."

When they got to Hollywood, she parked in the lot and watched Kyle drive past the station, continuing in the direction of Wilshire. She took a long careful look around at parked cars and pedestrians before getting out of the car. Being aware of her surroundings wasn't new but today it had taken on a whole new meaning.

Marge and Behan were waiting in her office with Mac when she arrived. They were seated around her worktable and stopped talking when she entered the room.

"I take it Lieutenant Richards has already told you what happened," she said, unlocking the wardrobe and throwing her purse and briefcase on the floor.

"Yes, ma'am," Mac answered. "Chief Dempsey called too. He wants to bring in Metro to protect you and Sanchez. He said to call him as soon as you got in."

Josie sat beside Marge and took the full mug of coffee on the table in front of her friend.

"Thanks," Josie said.

"No problem, anything else I can do for you like dragging Marvin's fucking ass in here and beating the shit out of him."

"We've got no proof it was him. Kyle's going with Pasadena PD today to talk to him at his mother's house," Josie said. "Let's wait and see what happens."

"Knowing Kyle Richards, there's a good chance Marvin won't survive that encounter intact," Behan said.

Josie didn't respond. She'd seen how angry Kyle had become at the house but was certain he wouldn't let his personal feelings interfere with doing his job. He was a professional and on more than one occasion she'd witnessed him control his temper when a lot of cops would've lost it and their advantage.

"Do you have a game plan for tonight?" Josie asked. She was tired of talking about Marvin Wright and knew if a serial killer had murdered Burke, they might have unrelated incidents.

"We have our decoy," Marge said, grinning.

"No, we don't," Behan said and turned to Mac. "You want to go out while we discuss this."

"Not really," Mac said.

"My adjutant?" Josie asked.

Marge stood and walked behind Mac's chair. "He's fucking perfect. Look at that body. Put him in a tank top and tight jeans, shitheads will be falling all over themselves . . . Besides, Mac's never been out of your office. Nobody in Hollywood knows him on the street."

"I don't like it," Behan mumbled. "He's never been trained to do this."

Mac laughed and said, "How much training does it take to act like an idiot."

"Okay, then maybe I don't think you're ready to do undercover work. Patrol's different. It's structured. Undercovers have to think on their feet. You two know; you've done it," he said, indicating Josie and Marge with a sweeping gesture.

"If you're willing, Mac, I have no problem with it, as long as Marge preps you," Josie said, avoiding Behan's glare. "But are you sure you want to parade up and down the boulevard all night with hordes of drag queens sniffing at your butt?"

"Sounds like my dream evening," Mac said, grinning at Marge, and added, "I'll get your paperwork done and ask one of the clerk typists to answer the phones when it's time for me to get ready."

A few minutes later, Mac left the office still chatting with Marge. Josie noticed her adjutant always became a little more animated around Marge. Most of the time he showed little emotion, moving passively and efficiently through the day's activities. It was obvious to Josie that her vice lieutenant had made a rare connection with the man and she wanted to encourage anything that helped him adjust and become a stable working cop again.

"You're pissed," Josie said to Behan when they were alone. He was hunched over the table staring at his empty hands.

"No, disappointed, worried. There are some things you can't fix, Corsino. Dan McSweeney is one of them."

"I'm not buying that. I'll bet you a very expensive steak dinner he's on track by the end of this summer. Between Marge and me, I know we can put this Humpty Dumpty back together again."

Behan got up slowly. He looked weary. She realized the toll this job had taken on him. He was only fifty-eight but looked and moved like an old man. His red hair had strands of grey, but that wasn't it. "Worn out" was the description that came to mind, and she worried maybe she was asking too much from him in these last few days. Next week he'd be gone, and she'd have to operate without him. Josie really didn't want to contemplate the consequences of losing her loyal and most trusted adviser.

The buzzer startled her as she watched her friend leave, and seeing the blinking light on the phone, she shouted, "Who is it, Mac?"

His answer came from just outside the door. "Chief Dempsey's on line one, Captain."

Josie grimaced and picked up the receiver, "Morning, sir," she said with as much lightness as she could muster.

He started the conversation with his usual exposition on how much he worried about his captains and how he valued their careers as much as his own. Finally he asked, "Are you all right?"

She explained that the house had been vacant; repairs would begin soon, and there was no need to worry about her safety. But he insisted that given the death of Burke, and Sanchez's attack, she should have protection.

"Does Sanchez have protection?" she asked, after reminding him about Wright's alibi for the time Sanchez was attacked and the possibility that Burke might've been the victim of a serial killer.

"No, against my advice, he refused."

Josie smiled and thought, "That's my Jorge."

"Given what you're saying now, it sounds as if Burke and Sanchez probably aren't related at all."

"Well, they might not be related to Marvin Wright, but it's too soon to know anything for certain," she said.

She updated him on the Burke homicide investigation and the decoy plan for that evening, and eventually convinced her boss that a team of Metro babysitters wasn't necessary. Josie didn't know Sanchez's reasons for refusing, but she didn't want a uniformed escort to her lover's house every night.

As soon as Josie finished her conversation with the chief, Richards called on another line to tell her Marvin wasn't at his mother's house and the elderly woman hadn't seen or talked to her son since the day before. Richards had checked with Marvin's police union rep and his lawyers, but no one seemed to know his whereabouts.

"What about cousin Fred and his girlfriend, Jackie . . . the bodyguards? Didn't he give you addresses and phone numbers for them?" she asked.

"He did, all bogus. They've moved, and the phones have been disconnected."

She was quiet, trying to come up with a logical reason for Marvin's disappearance.

"Maybe he's taken a trip, Vegas or someplace, with the steroid twins. He's such a goofball he probably wouldn't think to tell anybody," she said, thinking out loud.

"Maybe, but you need to be careful. I don't know how he did it, but I'm thinking he probably arranged that hit on Sanchez and killed Burke," Kyle said. "My instincts are telling me there's only one reason he'd be hiding and that's to finish what he started."

DURING MOST of that day, Josie didn't have a lot of time to worry about Marvin Wright or for that matter the heartbreaking condition of her house, a place she'd loved, where she'd lived for decades with a man she'd once loved and had raised their son.

She began overseeing preparations for the homicide/ vice task force as soon as Marge and Behan left her office that morning. Marge planned to use some of her vice officers to saturate the area and others would stand by in teams to make arrests if necessary. The homicide detectives would coordinate from an observation van parked on Santa Monica Boulevard in a location where the High-Top Bar and several blocks in either direction could be seen and monitored. Josie called in favors to borrow the van and electronic equipment from the narcotics division captain for two nights.

Roll call was scheduled to begin after dinner because Behan insisted everything had to be in place before dark. Josie gave one of the uniformed officers at the front desk enough cash to buy fried chicken and pizza to feed everyone in the station including the task force. It was delivered and carried up to the break room where officers and detectives could get their fill and still be on time for roll call.

She knew no cop worth his salt ever missed a free meal and they didn't disappoint her. The desk officer had put a plate with chicken and a couple of pieces of pizza on her desk, but after she ate those, Josie went upstairs to see if there were any leftovers. For a skinny woman, her appetite could be impressive.

Silly me, she thought, surveying the graveyard of empty pizza boxes and chicken bucket crumbs scattered throughout the break room.

"Thanks, Boss," one of the senior training officers said, as he walked out gnawing on a fried chicken leg. "Don't worry, ma'am, boots will clean up this mess before we leave if they want to make probation."

He hadn't lied. When she went across the hallway, the uniformed probationers were in the roll call room collecting all the dirty paper plates and napkins, filling the trash containers, and wiping the desk tops before their training officers allowed them to return to their black-and-whites. They had almost finished their clean-up duty when Behan arrived and chased them out to make room for the task force officers.

"Whole damn station looked like KFC and Shakey's had a food fight," he said.

"You get anything to eat?" Josie asked.

"You're kidding," he said, grinning. "Thanks."

Behan's roll call was quick and no nonsense. Everyone was given an assignment and before he dismissed them, Behan said he wanted to introduce their UC and pointed to the back of the room.

"Memorize that face, those clothes; that man's safety is your primary responsibility."

Josie hadn't noticed him come in, but Mac was standing, leaning against the back wall, and held up both hands when Behan introduced him. One of the female officers in the room whistled and the other women clapped. He was wearing a white, low-cut, sleeveless T-shirt, skintight Levi's, and sandals. His thick dark hair was combed straight back, and he had a gold chain with a cheap looking medallion that Josie figured was a transmitter with a built-in microphone. His daily workouts and running regimen had given him a taut, tanned body.

"OMG, I think I'm in love," one of the male vice officers squealed in a high-pitched voice and the others laughed.

Mac held up his middle finger, smirked, and didn't appear to be bothered by the teasing.

"Knock it off," Behan said. "Get your asses out there and set up. Sergeant McSweeney will be on the street in exactly one hour."

There's no denying the man is gorgeous, Josie thought, as Mac walked past her talking with one of the vice sergeants. She glanced at Marge who didn't seem amused. She looked serious and even a little worried. Josie stayed behind, waiting until the room cleared before sitting on the bench beside her friend.

"What's wrong?" Josie asked.

"I'm not comfortable putting a cop out there as a target," Marge said.

"Any cop or just Mac."

"What? Fuck no, any cop. He's fine, more than fine, but there's too many ways this can all go sideways."

"Then we'll stand down. I'll cancel it."

"Hell no, this could work."

Josie sighed and said, "Following your train of thought can sometimes be exhausting, woman. What's really going on?"

"Dan's a special guy. I don't want him to get hurt."

"You're sleeping with him, aren't you?" Josie asked, but she knew.

"What the fuck has that got to do with anything."

"Nothing," Josie said getting up. She left the roll call room thinking, "If we handle this operation right, nobody will get hurt . . . at least not on the street tonight."

EIGHT

Hollywood station looked like a ghost town by ten P.M.
Josie sat on the couch in her office with the
police radio nearby and watched Behan working at her
table. The radio was set on the task force frequency, so
they could listen to the detective in the observation van.
He was the point man and the only one who should've been
talking.

His transmissions were detailed but slightly X-rated
until Josie called his cell phone and told him to clean up
his act. She understood cop humor and the temptation to
use it when describing the human circus sashaying along
Santa Monica Boulevard, but she didn't want the impor-
tance of this operation to get sidetracked by his wit, allowing a killer those precious seconds he needed to strike
again.

Marge was in the field, but Josie had decided not to
go out until activity picked up. From what the point was
reporting, Mac seemed to be easily interacting with the
other men hustling for johns, but their clientele pool was
still slim. The bars and clubs would provide more business,
putting additional customers on the street near closing

time. The point, who was able to hear Mac's conversations, said the UC appeared to be relaxed and enjoying his
performance.

After midnight, Marge suggested Mac be told to move
away from the crowd milling around outside the High-Top
Bar and get closer to the spot where Anthony Charles had
been attacked.

"It's more isolated if he relocates a little east . . . oh,
shit," Marge blurted out.

Josie picked up her radio. "What's up, Lieutenant?" she
asked.

"Just noticed the Prince decked out in the party cape
working his corner," Marge said.

"What do you think about setting up on him and telling
our guy to back off awhile?" Josie asked. "Can the point see
that corner?"

"Yes, ma'am," the detective answered. "But there's no
street light. I'll need some help on the ground."

"What are you doing?" Behan asked, getting up and
moving closer to the couch.

"Anthony's the real thing. The killer went after him
once. He's much better bait than Mac."

"Stand by," the point detective said. There was some
tension in his voice. "We've got a guy in a dark hoodie
approaching our UC, fits the description."

"Let us hear the conversation," Josie ordered and immediately the feed from Mac's transmitter was broadcast.

"Not into small talk, is he," the detective said as they
heard the hoodie man graphically describe what he wanted
for his forty dollars. "They're walking behind the club, get
a take-down team ready. Mac, slow it down, give them a
chance to set up."

"Let's go," Josie said, grabbing the radio and getting a few steps ahead of Behan as they sprinted out of her office.

Behan's car was parked in front of the station and in a few minutes, they were close enough to see two vice officers arrest, handcuff, and push the suspect into the back seat of their unmarked vehicle and drive away. The entire episode took seconds. Mac waited a little longer before returning to the front of the bar, counting money he'd already had in his pocket but pretending it was for services rendered.

Josie got into Marge's car when Behan went back to the station to interview the arrestee.

"Asshole is very close to Anthony's description, but I don't think it's him," Marge said as she parked on a dark side street behind the bar.

"Why not? He's wearing the black hoodie, glasses, same size and build."

"No belt, grubby tennis shoes, and I detected a little east coast accent I think Anthony would've mentioned."

"Can't be that lucky, can we."

By the early morning hours, Mac had moved to several locations along the boulevard. He turned down offers from a dozen men who approached him. He was waiting for someone who either matched Anthony Charles's description or was creepy enough to warrant a trip to Hollywood station for Behan's interrogation.

"I am so fucking hungry," Marge said, yawning. "How much longer before we call this?"

Josie glanced at her watch and said, "At three, I'll wrap it up and get you fed. Let's give it just another half hour." She knew most of the killings happened between one and two but really didn't want to leave empty-handed.

"Looks like the paying customers are drying up out there, Boss . . . want to call it a night?" the point asked.

Josie knew everyone was tired; she was too. The only promising activity they'd had all night was the man in the dark hoodie who not only wasn't wearing a belt or nice shoes and had an accent, but Behan reported he had an ironclad alibi for the night Anthony was attacked. He was a guest of LAPD's central jail on an assault charge.

"Thirty minutes, we'll wrap it up," Josie said. A deluge of quick double clicks on the radio told her everyone had not only received and acknowledged the transmission, but they were eager to go home.

"Anybody got eyes on Count Dracula?" the point asked. "He went behind the brick building and hasn't come out for a while."

"Go," Josie ordered, and Marge started the car and drove toward Anthony Charles's location. "What team has him?"

"Team three, ma'am, we saw him go in the back door of that building, but he hasn't come out yet."

"Did he go in alone?"

"Yes, ma'am, and nobody's come out."

Marge parked in the lot north of the location. Josie took the police radio and jogged to the rear door of the brick office building with Marge and two vice officers. The door was closed but unlocked. She told the point to get their UC off the street and at a safe location and directed everyone else to set up on the brick building.

There were four vice officers who entered the location with Josie and Marge. One of the male officers shouted "Prince," several times, but there was no answer. The electricity had been turned off and judging by the obnoxious smell and rampant filth, Josie knew the abandoned building had been used as a crash pad. Dirty blankets were strewn on the concrete floor and covered with items of clothing, empty beer bottles, food containers, used condoms, syringes, and other drug paraphernalia. Broken pieces of wooden office chairs, desks, and bookcases were stacked near a rusted oil drum that probably had been used during the winter as a fireplace. Melted candles were stuck to the bottom of coffee cans and strategically placed around the large main area. Shutters covered all the windows, so the light wouldn't have been detected from the outside, at least not from the street.

As they cautiously finished searching every small office adjacent to the lobby, one of the vice officers called from outside a doorway close to the back entrance, "Ma'am, you better come see this."

Josie had to squeeze past two plainclothes officers who blocked the entry but seemed unable to move out of the way as they stared into the dark room. She used her flashlight to inspect what looked like a small kitchen with a sink, refrigerator, ancient microwave, and lots of empty dirty shelves. She slowly moved the light down from the counters onto the floor and instinctively took a step back as the body of Anthony Charles came into full view of 320 lumens.

He was kneeling on the floor with his back against a cupboard, his head bent forward as if he were praying, his arms limp at his sides. Josie moved closer and shined the light directly on his neck. It wasn't a belt this time, but some sort of thin cord still embedded deeply in his pale flesh, that had been used to strangle him.

"Where's his cape?" she asked, lighting the floor around the dead man. Nobody answered. He was dressed in a black tank top and tight black pants. His long white frizzy hair had been braided. It was a sloppy job, Josie thought, as if he'd done it in a hurry by himself without the benefit of a mirror. She turned off her light and backed out of the room experiencing an odd mixture of feelings . . . a little guilt, but disappointment and relief too. Relief because she believed Anthony was a lost, sensitive soul who'd been hurting. Some fiend had taken him out of his misery. The guilt and disappointment came because she was thinking what might've been her best chance to catch that fiend was dead.

THE TASK force was shut down, and Behan came from Hollywood station with a team of homicide detectives. One of those detectives had been the point man in the van. He apologized to Josie for letting her down, insisting he should have reacted sooner to the amount of time Anthony had been gone from the street.

"Anthony wasn't your responsibility; keeping Mac safe was, and you did that," Josie said. She believed he should have reacted sooner but knew telling him that wouldn't help anybody now. "I feel bad for Anthony, but he knew the risks of putting himself out there."

The detectives brought generators and bigger lights with them from the station making the inside of the building as bright as the middle of the day. Behan ordered all nonessential personnel out of his crime scene and had the watch commander deploy additional uniformed officers outside to guard the yellow police tape. The tape extended not only around the building, but secured the parking lot and a block in either direction.

It didn't take more than a few minutes for Behan to formulate a theory on how their killer escaped. There were stairs in the utility room that led to the roof. The killer could have gone up and from there climbed down a roof escape ladder on the west side of the building where no one had been watching.

It was midmorning by the time the coroner removed Anthony's body from the abandoned building. Josie and Marge watched the gurney being rolled out the back door and pushed into the waiting wagon.

"Should've listened to you, Boss," Marge said. "If we'd set up on him, he'd still be alive, and we might've caught a killer."

"This was different. Why wasn't he attacked on the street like the others? It's almost as if the killer knew we were watching."

"Or the fucker saw something that spooked him."

"But how could he know Anthony would come in here?"

"Maybe the Prince lived in this garbage dump," Marge said.

"Where's his cape? You saw it. The point saw it. So where did it go?"

"Killer took it . . . souvenir," Marge said, shrugging. "If we're done with a hundred annoying questions can we go eat now?"

"If he's a serial killer . . . usually they do take something from their victims," Behan said. He was standing behind Josie looking through a box of plastic bags containing items he and his detectives had recovered from the building. He put the box on the floor and came closer. "That's how they relive their killings. I need to check if the other victims had anything taken."

"I've got to notify Chief Dempsey before we go," Josie said, holding up her cell phone.

Marge chuckled and mimicked her, "I'm sorry, Chief, but Commissioner Charles's brother got choked to death this morning while thirty of my Hollywood officers stood around with their thumbs up their asses."

"Thanks, that helps," Josie said and dialed the number.

"You're an asshole, Bailey," Behan said.

"I know, but as much as that pompous turd worries about his career, you and I both know he's going to dump on her to take heat off himself."

"Nobody expects us to protect every bun boy on Santa Monica Boulevard."

"Casper wasn't every bun boy; he was the fucking police commissioner's albino brother."

Josie listened to their conversation while she waited for Dempsey to come on the line. Sergeant Scott had answered and put her on hold. She knew the adjutant wouldn't be in any hurry to put her through to his boss, but on this occasion, that might not be a bad thing. Marge was joking but she was right. Trying to explain how a police commissioner's brother got murdered in the middle of a Hollywood operation, while the point man was sort of watching him, wasn't going to be her finest moment.

NINE

The conversation with Chief Dempsey went a lot better than Josie had anticipated. She began by emphasizing Anthony's deviancy and finally his relationship to Edward Charles. The tactic seemed to work. Dempsey didn't assign any culpability to the task force and despite her thorough explanation of the night's events, he didn't seem to comprehend they might've assumed some duty to protect the man. The narrative satisfied her boss but didn't help ease Josie's conscience.

"I'll let you notify the commissioner and his family," Dempsey said, and then added before hanging up, "Since he seems to prefer dealing directly with you."

"That was a masterpiece," Marge said, as Josie put her phone away. "The truth is all in the way you tell it . . . what did he say?"

"Wants me to notify Anthony's family, but he didn't seem to have a problem with the way our operation went down," Josie said. She figured that might change as soon as the chief talked with his adjutant. Sergeant Scott was always looking for some way to criticize Hollywood. But then again, she still wasn't too worried because Scott, like his boss, might not recognize a possible screw-up when he saw it.

"When are you going to tell the family?" Behan asked.

"I'm not, we are."

"Okay, when are we going to tell the family?"

"As soon as we finish breakfast. Murphy's is the closest place; we'll meet you there," she said to Marge.

"I'm not hungry," Behan mumbled.

"It's not a suggestion, Red," Josie said in a way that didn't leave any doubt about him having a choice. She knew if she didn't order him to eat he'd stop at the closest bar to take the edge off a stressful night.

Behan didn't argue but his face was nearly as red as his hair when he picked up the evidence box and carried it out to the trunk of his car. She followed him and got into the passenger side, expecting silence for the few minutes it took to reach the restaurant, and he obliged. Behan was her friend and partner, but when he retired, Josie knew she wasn't going to miss riding herd over his alcohol intake.

When they arrived at Murphy's, Josie was surprised to see Richards in uniform waiting for them.

"How did you know we'd be here?" she asked, sitting next to him and feeling very happy to see him.

"Your phone's been off all night. I finally called Marge to find out why you didn't come home. She invited me to breakfast. David's been trying to reach you too."

Josie started to dial her son's number, but Richards told her he'd already talked to David and told him what had happened.

"I turned my phone off and forgot about it," Josie said. "What did David want?"

"He found a contractor; repairs have started on your house."

"I told him to stay away from there," she said.

"He doesn't listen . . . but then he is a Corsino," Richards said.

"Not funny," Josie mumbled.

"How'd Mac do last night?" Richards asked.

"Great," Marge answered. "If I didn't know better, I'd think in another life he'd made a good living hustling."

"Great," Richards said, nodding his approval.

Richards's interest in her adjutant struck Josie as odd since she and Kyle had never talked much about Mac. She wondered if Behan had expressed concerns to him about her decision to use Mac as a decoy, hoping Kyle might change her mind. Just the possibility of Red interfering was annoying.

"Why are you so interested in Mac?" Josie asked.

"I partnered with him in Metro before he got promoted and had his problems. I'm happy to see him back at work, taking chances again," Kyle said. Looking a little puzzled by her tone, he asked, "What's wrong with you?"

"Nothing . . . I'm tired . . . grumpy . . . embarrassed about Anthony getting killed while we were a block away."

By the time they finished eating, Josie was struggling to keep her eyes open. Richards insisted on driving her to Hollywood station where she could sleep for a while before she and Behan talked to Anthony's family.

"Sorry if I snapped at you about Mac," she said when they were alone in Richard's black-and-white. "I thought Red was undermining me. I should've known better."

"I've never talked to Behan about Mac."

"I'm sorry. Just forget it. I'm not thinking straight," she said.

"You do know the whole story on Dan McSweeney, right?"

"He went off on stress . . . that's all I know. His package tells me he's an exceptional cop and supervisor, lots of commendations, worked high-profile assignments . . . probably worth the effort to get him back on track."

When they got to Hollywood station, Richards parked the patrol car at the red curb in front.

"You're right," he said, turning off the engine. "Dan's a solid cop who made the mistake of getting caught up in LAPD's political correctness machine."

"What do you mean?"

"When he promoted to sergeant, he got sent to the valley from Metro, much slower pace. One of the other sergeants in his division was a female who was about to be promoted to lieutenant. She had an advanced case of risk aversion . . . never rolled on anything dangerous or complicated, always got to the hot calls or requests for a supervisor as the last car, so naturally some other supervisor already would have taken charge. It was obvious she was dodging responsibility and avoiding the tough decisions trying not to derail her promotion. One night in the field, Mac took her aside and confronted her about not doing her job. She went to the watch commander and complained he was harassing her."

"By telling her the truth?" Josie asked.

"The watch commander panicked because she was a female who was being mentored by a deputy chief and on the fast track. He wrote a personnel complaint on Mac and everyone up the chain of command accepted her version of events which painted Mac as some sort of Neanderthal woman hater.

"After his captain sustained the complaint and transferred him to another division, Mac took it to a board of rights and won. He won in court too and got the complaint taken out of his personnel package, but the damage had been done."

"Are we talking about Stephanie Mack who made the complaint? I think I remember the rumors about this one . . . from what I've heard, she wasn't much better as a watch commander."

"The settlement was sealed. Stephanie got promoted. Mac got a clean package and a nervous breakdown after more than a year of the department brass making his life miserable and everybody else whispering behind his back."

"That's why he wanted to quit."

"He's a man of principle and integrity; his reputation means everything to him," Richards said.

"And we all know once you get a tag in this LAPD it sticks like Gorilla Glue, and that's who you are regardless of the truth. All the good job offers dry up and a promising career gets derailed," she said, immediately feeling very bad for her adjutant. Josie had known too many good cops who got labels that dogged them and guaranteed mediocre or short careers.

"Have to get some sleep, love, but I'll talk to you later," she said, leaning over and giving him a quick hug before getting out of the car.

"Watch your back, Corsino," he warned as she closed the door.

An hour later, Josie woke up on her office couch. The door was closed and the lights out. She was still a little groggy but went to the locker room, took a cold shower, pinned up her long hair, dressed in a clean uniform, and strapped on her utility belt with all its paraphernalia. Her boots and leather gear were shined and as she checked herself out in the full-length mirror on the door of her wardrobe, thought, I look pretty damn sharp.

She always liked wearing her uniform, but most of the time didn't get the opportunity to change from civilian clothes once her busy day began.

"Ready?" Behan asked, from just outside her office.

"Morning, ma'am," Mac said, working on his computer as she passed his desk.

"Did you get any sleep?" she asked, but thought he looked a lot fresher and more rested than she felt.

"Same as you, but it's enough."

"Good job last night. You up to it again tonight?"

"Yes, ma'am," he said and almost smiled. "I'll take another shot at it."

Behan seemed weary and didn't talk much during the drive except to tell her they were going to the Baldwin Hills area of Los Angeles, an affluent, diverse, and mostly African American neighborhood in the southern region of the city. Wealthy athletes, celebrities, and professionals, even a former mayor, had occupied large houses with scenic views of the Hollywood Hills and San Gabriel Mountains.

The Charles home was a colonial-style mansion set back on a spacious lot within walking distance of the Kenneth Hahn State Regional Area off La Cienega Boulevard. Behan parked the city car behind a shiny, four-door, black Mercedes-Benz and a silver 911 Porsche Carrera lined up in the driveway.

"Hard to believe the Prince of Darkness came from all this," Behan said, as they walked to the front door.

A maid answered the door and led them through the foyer, under a crystal chandelier and behind sweeping stairs to a den at the back of the house. It was a small room decorated with french provincial furniture, delicate and lovely but far from welcoming. A large bay window kept the space well-lighted, but Josie felt a coldness in the room's dainty austerity. There were religious pictures of Jesus and Mary on the walls and a colorful twelve-inch mosaic glass cross had been hung over the door.

The view from the window was impressive. The back patio was uncovered but had an enormous flagstone surface with stairs leading to at least a half-acre lawn with a swimming pool on one side and tennis court on the other.

"Nice shack," Behan said, looking over Josie's shoulder as she stared out the window.

When the door creaked open, they both turned to see Mrs. Allison Charles enter the room. She introduced herself, apologized for keeping them waiting, and said something else, but Josie didn't hear it because she was surprised by the woman's appearance. Mrs. Charles was Caucasian, blue-eyed, with disheveled snow-white hair and almost translucent skin. She was dressed in riding boots and tan jodhpurs. Given the ages of Anthony and Edward, she looked frail and so much older than Josie had expected.

Josie asked her to please sit on the love seat before telling her what had happened to her younger son and expressing her condolences. She'd anticipated some sort of emotion from the woman, but Mrs. Charles calmly made the sign of the cross, pushed a loose strand of hair away from her face, then asked, "Would you care for ice cream? I've had such a craving for caramel ice cream all day."

"Is your husband home?" Behan asked immediately.

"Hardly," Mrs. Charles said, with a giggle. "Colin is at his office or in court," she said, pointing at a picture on the fireplace mantel of a tall, handsome black man in a judge's robe. His expression was severe, Josie thought. "He and Anthony haven't spoken for years . . . our child drifted."

She stopped speaking and seemed lost in her memories, but no tears, no words of sorrow or loss. Josie believed Mrs. Charles was behaving as if she'd just heard someone else's son had died.

"Would you like us to tell your husband about Anthony?" Behan asked.

"I shouldn't think so," she said, cocking her head slightly, almost childlike.

"Is there another family member here with you?" Josie asked. She had engaged enough mentally challenged people during her police life to eventually recognize the symptoms.

"I don't know. That would be nice."

Behan and Josie exchanged a long look, but before they could discuss the situation, the door opened again and a pretty, well-dressed woman in a business suit entered.

"I'm sorry, officers, the staff just told me you were here," the woman said and held out her hand to Josie. "I'm Sandra Charles, her daughter."

"Anthony's sister?" Josie asked. "He never mentioned having a sister." Sandra's brothers had African American features, but she was fair skinned and looked like her mother.

"No mystery there, we weren't close . . . Mother hasn't been well. If you don't mind I'll have her taken upstairs," she said and slowly led the older woman outside the door where she was met by a woman in a nurse's uniform who escorted Mrs. Charles away. Sandra watched for a few seconds then came back to Behan and Josie. "Now, how can I help you?"

Josie repeated the information about Anthony and watched the woman's face for some sign of grief. Not seeing any, she asked, "Did anyone in the family have contact with Anthony during the last few days, weeks?" But was thinking—or gives a shit the poor guy is dead.

Sandra sat on the love seat and gestured for them to sit on the other uncomfortable-looking furniture.

"Anthony cut ties with this family . . . preferred his chosen life . . . well you've seen him. My father disowned him years ago . . . Frankly, I wasn't sorry he left. I know that sounds harsh, but my brother was . . . difficult," she said.

"What do you mean by difficult?" Josie asked.

"He went out of his way to embarrass us . . . the way he dressed, his friends, his ideas," she said and hesitated before adding, "everything."

"What's wrong with your mother?" Behan asked bluntly.

"I'd call it mild dementia, harmless but she's simply not rational most of the time. It has aged her terribly."

"But she rides horses."

"No, not for years, but likes wearing her riding clothes," Sandra said, shrugging.

"Can you think of any reason someone would want to kill Anthony?" Behan asked.

"I've been told he lived on the streets. I imagine that lifestyle would be dangerous," she said.

"Who told you he lived on the streets?" Behan asked.

"My brother Edward, he tried to keep track of Anthony . . . from a distance . . . gave him money, other assistance from time to time."

"What sort of other assistance?"

Sandra sighed and shifted her position. She was visibly uneasy. "Edward would bail him out of jail, pay for his medical care if Anthony or one of his friends called . . . that sort of thing."

"Are you married, Miss Charles?" Josie asked, not certain why she wanted to know—idle curiosity or maybe she was searching for something conventional in this family.

"No," Sandra said with a tight smile and stood. She didn't seem to like that question. "I'm sorry but I have an appointment and I'm already late. Would you like Edward or father to contact you?"

"That's not necessary. We won't release Anthony's name until someone tells us the rest of the family has been notified. However, if we don't hear from you by tomorrow morning, we'll have to issue the press release."

"That's fine. I'll call them immediately. Edward will want to know. Father . . ." She didn't finish but walked with them to the front door, closing it as soon as Josie and Behan were on the porch.

"You need to talk to Edward Charles," Josie said as she and Behan stood on the driveway in front of the mansion. "If what she's saying is true, he should be able to tell you a lot more about Anthony's life."

"Our police commissioner is connected to two homicides. That's a little interesting; don't you think?" Behan asked.

Josie didn't answer but said, "We need to get back to Hollywood, Red."

On the way to the station, Josie couldn't stop thinking about Marvin Wright. The fired officer didn't have ties to any of their victims except Howard Burke. If he killed Burke out of revenge maybe he had a motive to firebomb her house and get someone to shoot at Jorge. But if he didn't kill the lawyer, who would have a reason to do those other things and want everyone to think Marvin was responsible.

"You coming?" Behan asked, standing in the station parking lot knocking on her car window. She hadn't noticed they'd arrived.

"Sorry, I was thinking," she said, getting out of the car.

"About?"

"The possibility we have two killers and Burke just happened to get murdered in the middle of our serial-killer zone. Sanchez getting shot at and my house getting torched don't make much sense, if Marvin didn't kill Burke."

"The fact that Marvin has disappeared doesn't look too good for him either. We'll keep an open mind about two killers and you keep your head down until we figure it out," Behan said.

"Captain Corsino!" someone shouted from behind her and Josie turned to see a grim-looking Edward Charles standing on the sidewalk near the front of Hollywood station.

"Need backup?" Behan asked.

"No, but I guess he does," she said, recognizing the tall, distinguished-looking older black man who had just gotten out of a limo parked by the curb and joined his son.

TEN

Her feet felt as if they each weighed about fifty pounds as Josie made the trek from Behan's car to the front steps of Hollywood station. It was bad enough having to talk to Edward about his brother's death, but facing their father wasn't something she wanted to do. In nearly thirty years of police work, she'd never found the right words to comfort or console the parent of a murder victim, and for some reason, it was always worse if the child had been estranged. Guilt was a potent catalyst for grief's rage.

The two men waited at the bottom of the steps until she reached them and without a word turned and led the way into the building. She invited them into her office and closed the door.

Edward introduced his father and Colin Charles shook hands with Josie. His grip was strong and he held on a few seconds longer and tighter than was comfortable for her. She asked them to sit on the couch and pulled her desk chair over closer to the coffee table.

"Can I get you something to drink . . . water, soda?" she asked.

"This is not a social visit, Captain Corsino," Judge Charles said in a deep baritone voice.

"Excuse me a moment," she said, got up, and opened the door.

"Drinks?" Mac asked from his desk.

"Water for me," she said and waited until he returned with the bottle before closing the door and sitting again. She took a sip and then offered her condolences for the loss of Anthony.

"I want to know one thing," Colin Charles said. "Was my son working for you when he was killed?"

"No," Josie said quickly. Not technically, she thought.

"I understand you arrested him shortly before he was murdered and discovered he had been attacked by your serial killer," he said.

"Who told you that?" Josie demanded.

"What difference does it make?" Edward said, before his father could answer.

"This is a murder investigation. Details are kept confidential for a good reason. I need to know who gave you that information."

"I'm a police commissioner, your boss; I have the right and responsibility to know about any investigation this department conducts," Edward responded.

"And what about your father, does he have that right? The answer is no, but he damn well knows, doesn't he."

"Captain, you do realize who you're talking to," Colin Charles bellowed and stood. His fists were clenched, and he looked angry enough to hit something. Josie had a feeling she might be his preferred target.

She stood too and faced him. He was about six inches taller than she was and at least fifty pounds heavier.

"Yes, sir, I do, and I apologize if I've offended you, but we both know I'm right."

He stood silently staring at her for a few seconds, turned to his son, and dropped onto the couch again. His hands on his knees, staring down at the floor, he said softly, "Of course you're right. I'm the one who should apologize."

"Father, you have every right . . ." Edward started to say, but Judge Charles put his hand on his son's shoulder and the younger man stopped talking.

"My son was attempting to help me cope. I needed to know what happened."

"I understand how you got the information, sir, but I need to know who gave it to the commissioner," Josie said, looking at Edward.

"Deputy Chief Dempsey's staff is a lot more accommodating than Hollywood," Edward said.

"Sergeant Scott."

Edward didn't respond but she knew it was Scott and wasn't surprised that Dempsey's ambitious adjutant would be willing to compromise a murder investigation to win the approval of a police commissioner.

"Look, I'm sorry I went around you, but you made it perfectly clear after Howard Burke's death you weren't about to tell me anything. Anthony was my brother. My family needed to know what happened to him," Edward explained.

"Anthony told me his family had disowned him."

"That's not true and even if it were, that doesn't mean I wanted my son dead," Colin Charles said and hesitated a moment before asking, "Did you put his life in jeopardy, Captain?"

"Why would you think that?" Josie asked.

Edward sighed and said, "I was told you had an operation that night at the same time and location where my brother was killed."

"We had an undercover officer on the street that night, not your brother. If you want to know who killed Anthony, help me and tell us everything you know about him and his life."

"How could we possibly know anything?" Colin Charles asked.

"I've met a few of his friends . . . they used to live in that place where he was killed," Edward said, avoiding eye contact with his father. He explained that he had given money to his younger brother on several occasions and once or twice had asked Howard Burke to represent Anthony on soliciting charges. "My brother told me his lover was someone he called Matador, but I've never met him. This Matador supposedly gave him that stupid black cape he wore all the time. I thought they had argued and split up. Truly that's all I know about this Matador." Edward agreed to meet with Behan and give him a list of names and any other information he had about his brother.

The longer they talked, Josie found Colin Charles wasn't as unpleasant as he appeared to be at first. When his anger dissipated, he revealed a natural charm and humor. She began to genuinely like and even admire the man. He had a UCLA-Harvard education, but grew up on the streets of Los Angeles and knew the realities of life and politics. It was obvious he cared deeply for his family but didn't allow his love or affection to interfere with telling humorous, bittersweet stories about them, especially his wife.

"I came home one night, and she asked if I would mind driving the limo downtown to pick up her husband and a pizza," Judge Charles said. "When I finally convinced Allie

I was her husband, she demanded to know what I'd done with the pizza."

After each story about his wife, he'd get this wistful smile, the look of a man who'd lost something precious, irreplaceable, but who had come to terms with the one thing he never wanted or thought he'd have to do—live without her.

Josie couldn't imagine how difficult it had to be for him to learn of his son's death on top of his wife's illness. When Edward went to the detective squad room to talk to Behan, Josie escorted Colin Charles through the lobby and out to his limo.

"I like and trust you, Captain Corsino," he said, as he climbed into the back seat of the limo. "I hope you won't disappoint me."

The uniformed chauffeur closed the car door and drove away, leaving Josie standing on the parkway. She liked Colin Charles but couldn't guarantee that finding his son's killer wouldn't be a disappointment. Every finely tuned cop instinct in her body was telling her Edward Charles was hiding something.

ELEVEN

By late afternoon, the nap was wearing off and Josie was thinking about going to Long Beach to sleep a few hours before the task force roll call. The prospect of driving that far in her drowsy condition wasn't appealing but sleeping in her office guaranteed constant interruptions. She would have made Mac her "Do Not Disturb" sign for a couple of hours, but he'd already gone to the officers' cot room to rest. When her secretary promised to guard the door like a bullmastiff, Josie decided the couch would do.

She had just closed the door, turned out the lights, and dropped onto the cushion, when someone knocked. My mastiff is a poodle, she thought, getting up and putting on the lights.

"Yes?" she asked, as she opened the door. Sergeant Scott was standing there with her secretary fuming behind him.

"I told him you were sleeping," the secretary said, in her best guard-dog voice.

"It's all right, Carol. What do you want, Timmy?" Josie asked, not sounding nearly as annoyed as she felt.

"Chief Dempsey wants you to cancel your task force tonight."

"Because?"

"He didn't tell me why. You'll have to talk to him."

"Is he in his office?"

"No, he's out, probably for the rest of the day," Sergeant Scott said with a noticeable smirk.

"Fine, the message has been delivered. I'll talk to the chief as soon as he's available."

"Is the task force canceled?" he asked, still standing by the open door with a concerned expression.

"Not to worry, Timmy," Josie said with a slight smile.

"What should I tell him?"

"That he and I need to talk," she said.

She turned to go back to the couch, but he kept the door from closing and stepped into the office. He moved a little closer to her and said with a slight quiver in his voice, "I'd prefer if you called me Sergeant Scott."

"Really, why is that?" Josie asked.

"I'm a supervisor. Using my first name is demeaning around the officers or staff. It gives me less respect . . . lessens my authority."

"Is that how you think a supervisor gets respect?"

"Yes, I think it matters."

"Okay, Timmy, here's a valuable lesson. Respect is earned. Officers can tell if a supervisor has been field-tested, knows his job, and has their backs. They respect a person who makes tough decisions, takes responsibility, and does what's right even if it won't help his next promotion. I call my adjutant Mac, and I'm pretty certain every officer in this division respects him and would follow Sergeant McSweeney into hell."

Sergeant Scott's cheeks were a bright shade of pink now. He sucked in his lower lip and his eyes narrowed. He was livid, but his survival instincts kept him from saying nasty things to a captain. Josie guessed he had to be aching to say something.

Finally he turned to leave but stopped in the doorway and said, "I think you might find your sergeant has an unfounded complaint early in his career that's worth looking into given Hollywood's rash of homo-strangulation homicides."

"Hold on," Josie demanded. "You don't throw out something like that and walk away. You're supposed to be a cop; act like one and tell me what you know."

He came back and stood in front of her with his arms crossed, looking like a defiant child eager to snitch on the favorite brother.

"We were probationers together in Rampart. McSweeney had a complaint that he'd harassed drag queens and nearly choked one to death."

"You said it was unfounded."

"Because none of the victims would cooperate. He was the division's 'Boy Wonder' and since it was just drag queens complaining, everybody covered for him," Sergeant Scott said, taking a deep breath, and adding, "That's all I know."

"Is that why Dempsey canceled my task force?"

"I don't know. I have to go," he said and moved quickly to get out of her office.

Josie didn't try to stop him, figuring it was probably best if he got out of her sight. She sat on the arm of the couch but didn't bother to close the door again. Her mind wasn't about to shut down now.

She took Mac's personnel folder out of her file cabinet and spread the contents on her worktable. His rap sheet showed two unfounded complaints, both labeled 'excessive use of force.' There was no trace of the harassment complaint made by the Valley female sergeant that Kyle had mentioned. Unfounded, use-of-force complaints were so commonplace, Josie wasn't surprised she didn't pay attention to them when Mac came into the division. It was ludicrous to give an ancient unfounded complaint any credibility, but she wasn't surprised Dempsey would think it was significant, especially with Timmy whispering in his ear.

She'd get a copy of the complaints from Internal Affairs and read them but was irritated Dempsey hadn't done that before canceling her task force and behaving as if her adjutant were a serial killer.

"Boss, you hungry?" Marge asked. She was holding up a paper bag, covered with grease stains, and two cans of Coke as she came into the office. "I got pieces of fried chicken here floating in about a quart of oil."

Josie quickly picked up the pages in Mac's file and put them on her desk, then helped Marge spread paper towels over the table.

"Needs wine," Josie said, biting into a crispy, greasy thigh.

"Almost forgot," Marge said, taking a small bottle of hot sauce out of her jeans back pocket and pouring some over the piece Josie was eating. "Better?"

"Perfect."

"What's up with Mac?" Marge asked.

"Nothing, why?"

"You were looking in his package."

Josie swallowed, wiped her hands on one of the towels, took a sip of Coke, and told Marge what Sergeant Scott had revealed.

"Not exactly a fucking news flash. Queens are notorious for making complaints. It's what they do," Marge said. "Look in my package. I got twenty of them."

"I guess it's the choking accusation Dempsey thinks makes it relevant."

"Nothing about Dempsey is relevant. Doesn't even have the balls to talk to you himself. Fuck him. I say we go ahead tonight like we planned."

Josie shook her head. "No, we'll cancel the task force, but that doesn't mean you and Red can't have a UC working on the street."

"Mac?"

"I need to talk to him first," Josie said and hesitated before asking, "What's your impression of Mac's mental state?" Marge started to protest but Josie interrupted and added, "Don't go all indignant and crazy on me. For the record, I think it's a good thing you're together, but I also rely on your talent for detecting bullshit. Is he okay or does he just want me to believe he is?"

Marge threw a well-chewed chicken wing into the empty bag and wiped her hands. She sat back and stared at Josie for a few seconds before saying, "Okay, Boss, I know you're trying to help, but I can't be sharing my guy's intimate thoughts . . . it's personal shit."

"I don't care about your pillow talk. I just want to know if you think he's stable enough to be put in a high-stress situation."

"He's different . . . there's a lot of crap bouncing around in his head, but he's solid as a rock with work stuff. I'm positive he won't do anything stupid or unsafe. He's taken down assholes to protect himself or his partners but he's not the sort to kill for recreation."

They talked until the chicken and hot sauce were gone and Josie almost felt comfortable about putting Mac on the street. She wanted to use him again because he'd made some good contacts the previous night and with his friendly face could ask questions without raising suspicions among that tightknit group of young men who trolled the boulevard. She was hoping one of them knew something about Anthony's Matador friend. Mac might be their best chance of getting honest answers.

Josie told Marge to brief Behan on the cancellation of the task force and have everyone meet in her office in a couple of hours.

"Tell your crew the task force is canceled, same for Behan's detectives. Pick two officers you trust to work with tonight. I'll have the watch commander assign a black-and-white. That's it. Nobody else needs to know."

"Yes, ma'am," Marge said and collected the greasy dinner debris scattered over the worktable. She stuffed everything in a trash can behind Josie's desk before leaving.

Josie knew her adjutant had returned from the cot room because she could hear him talking with Marge outside the door. They were mostly whispering but Josie could tell from her tone Marge wasn't happy about something. A few minutes later, Mac carried a stack of paperwork into her office and dropped it into the in-box.

"Nothing critical here," he said. "Lieutenant Bailey told me about the task force. Just so you know, that complaint I got as a probationer was bullshit. My training officer taunted the queen, and he made bogus allegations about both of us. If you check you'll see he made at least a dozen similar complaints against other cops."

"I want you on the street tonight," Josie said. "I will read the complaints because I have to, but I wouldn't put you out there if I had serious doubts. I don't, so put on your sexy street pants and be back here in a couple of hours."

He almost smiled and said, "Good enough, Boss."

After he left, she had a burst of energy and finished all her paperwork in an hour. There was nothing else to do and Josie was contemplating another attempt to pass out for a few minutes on the couch when Mac told her she had a visitor.

"David Jacobson to see you," he said, leaning into her office.

"David?" Josie asked, but got up and hurried to the door.

The honorable David Jacobson was a judge in the LA Superior Court and one of her oldest, dearest friends. They'd met when she worked an undercover assignment in the LAPD's intelligence division, and he liked to tell everyone she had saved his life. He was David's namesake, godfather, and one of the few people she knew who could play the piano better than her son.

"I was having lunch down the street and thought I'd stop by. We haven't talked for a while. Is this a bad time?" he asked, when she stopped hugging him.

"I've missed you," she said, sitting beside him on the couch. He was older than her, tall, with white hair like her ex-husband, but he wasn't nearly as healthy or robust looking as Jake was.

"I saw my godson last night at the restaurant. He looks great, but he mentioned you've had some trouble."

"Business as usual in the world of cops and robbers. Are you okay?" Josie asked. "You're looking a little pale." She'd also noticed a slight tremor in his hands.

"I'm fine, about to retire, as soon as my paperwork comes through."

"Wonderful, I'm happy for you."

When they had finished catching up on family news, Josie asked if he minded talking about work for a few minutes. Jacobson was the supervising judge in the Criminal Courts Building and had been there so long he knew everything about everyone.

"What can you tell me about Colin Charles?" she asked.

"Does this have something to do with his son's death?"

"Yes, I can't get a read on that family . . . especially Edward."

"They're all extremely intelligent," Jacobson said. "I'm not certain what you're looking for but I know Edward. He's the most ambitious of Colin's kids . . . not exactly someone I'd pick as a police commissioner. He's not fond of cops, just the opposite."

"The mayor's not fond of cops either. Did you know Anthony Charles?"

"Yes, he was in my class when I taught criminal law at UCLA."

"He was a lawyer?"

"He graduated but never took the bar . . . broke Colin's heart. Colin is a fine man. Anthony was brilliant, too, but troubled. I know Edward tried to help him. I'm not surprised his life ended the way it did."

"Why not surprised?"

"Anthony saw himself as a poet living among brutes and philistines. Edward did everything he could to protect him, mostly from himself, but I think he knew his brother was intentionally playing Russian roulette and eventually the game would kill him."

"Did you know Howard Burke?" Josie asked.

"Yes," he said. Wrinkling his forehead, he asked, "Were they killed by the same person?"

"Don't know," she answered truthfully. "I think there's a connection but so far Edward Charles seems to be the only link. Was there any courthouse gossip about Burke?"

Jacobson smiled and said, "What do you think, Josie? His clientele were almost exclusively young gay men and there were rumors about how he got paid."

"Somebody's killing a lot of his customers on Santa Monica Boulevard. Burke was murdered in the same neighborhood, but he doesn't fit the victim type. He was older and the only victim who was shot. His death was different, but my gut tells me it's connected somehow."

"Maybe he figured out who the killer was . . . put the pieces together, confronted whoever it was, and got killed," Jacobson said.

"You knew Burke. He wasn't the confrontational type, very timid for a lawyer," she said and sighed. "And then there's the very real possibility his death had nothing to do with our other killings." Jacobson looked puzzled, so she added, "Never mind, it's a long story."

They talked for a few more minutes until Jacobson told her he had to hurry home to Brentwood for a dinner party. She promised to get together with him and David as soon as she could manage an evening away from work.

After he left, she closed the office door and sat on the couch thinking about that time, decades ago, when she and David Jacobson had met. It seemed like another life and in many ways, it was. Working as an undercover cop in Los Angeles during the turbulent antiwar years had given her a certain freedom and a bohemian lifestyle she enjoyed. She'd met Jake Corsino during those years, fell in love, and later began a life she thought would last forever.

She got up, opened the door, and telephoned Kyle Richards. The last thing she needed was a trip down memory lane, wasting time thinking about her ex-husband and the 'not so' good old days.

TWELVE

Wilshire patrol officers were engaged in a citywide car pursuit, and Lieutenant Richards was in the middle of it when she called. Josie left a message on his cell phone and a text saying she'd get to Long Beach sometime that night. She had never been involved in a serious relationship with another cop and couldn't believe how little time they had to spend together. If she just went through the motions of being a manager it would be easier, and she'd be home for dinner every night, but she loved hands-on police work and couldn't do that. Kyle was the same, but tomorrow and the next day were his regular days off, and she intended to be with him as much as possible.

Josie couldn't remember putting her head down on the desk but sometime after texting Kyle she had fallen asleep. Mac was gently shaking her shoulder when she woke, and sitting up, she stretched and tried to recall where she was and why.

"Sorry," she said, when her head cleared, and she could focus on the wall clock. "How long have I been out?"

"About two hours," Mac said, putting a mug of hot coffee in front of her. "I'll buzz Red and Lieutenant Bailey, let them know you're awake."

Josie finished the coffee before going to the lady's locker room, changing into her jeans, and splashing cold water on her face. By the time Marge, her two vice officers, and Behan got to her office, she was feeling rested and surprisingly energized. She began by explaining why the task force had been canceled.

"Doesn't look like it's canceled to me," Behan said. "Are you planning on putting him out there without backup?" he asked, nodding at Mac, who smiled and looked down at his tight jeans and sandals but didn't say anything.

"He's got quality instead of quantity tonight," Marge said, grinning at her two officers. "Your fucking observation van and small army didn't do Anthony a hell of a lotta good."

"This isn't a task force. Mac has one mission, find out all he can about Anthony and a guy called Matador. That's it."

"And what if something goes sideways?" Behan asked.

"If the five of us and those uniformed guys I have on standby can't protect one armed officer, we're all in the wrong business," Josie said.

Behan was quiet, but Josie knew he wasn't convinced or satisfied. Marge started to say something, but Josie gave her a look that must have conveyed the intended message of "don't provoke him or you'll feel the full measure of my wrath" because she stopped and looked down at the floor.

"Where do you want me to set up?" Mac asked.

"Closer to Anthony's corner," Marge said.

"But start in front of the High-Top Bar," Behan said. He'd made it clear he didn't agree with what they were doing, but Josie knew it wasn't in his nature to be a nonparticipant. "That's where most of these guys hang out. We want information. You should be where there's the biggest crowd."

"Why's this Matador so important?" Mac asked.

"He gave Anthony that cape he always wore, and the cape was missing after the killing. Edward Charles claims his brother had an erratic relationship with this guy," Josie said. "Find out anything you can. Don't ask too many questions but get them to talk."

"Who's going to monitor the wire," Behan asked.

"You and me," Marge said. "We won't be in the van. We'll stay close enough to watch him and still be mobile. My UCs will be on the street nearby," she said, pointing at the two vice officers, and adding, "The uniforms will be parked in a black-and-white a couple of blocks away."

"Sounds safe enough," Behan mumbled.

"Where do you want to be, Boss?" Marge asked.

"In my car, but I want to monitor Mac's wire too," Josie said. Everyone got up and started to leave. She added quickly, "One more thing, if anyone spots Sergeant Scott in the area, let me know. I'll deal with him."

"Poor Timmy," Mac whispered to Marge as they left the office.

It was nearly midnight by the time everyone was set up outside the High-Top Bar on Santa Monica Boulevard. The crowd milling around the front of the business was larger and much more fluid on a Saturday night. Mac easily slipped in among them without creating attention. A few of the younger men immediately recognized Mac and when they casually welcomed him, Josie felt a little relieved.

She drove around the block, down an alley across the street, and parked behind a dumpster where it was dark and quiet. She knew Marge had chosen a spot away from the street lights in a parking lot across the street. It was on an angle from the bar where her unmarked vice car was hidden behind a row of plumbing trucks. The two vice officers weren't on Santa Monica, but Josie was confident they would be close. She listened and watched as Mac socialized and was impressed by how easily he fit in. He was friendly but immediately let it be known he wasn't in the mood to do business that night and just wanted company.

He went into the bar and came back with a couple of bottles of beer, kept one, and gave the other to a man sitting on the handrail near the entrance. They had been discussing how "fucked-up" most of the crowd was that night. The other man was wearing cut-off shorts and was bare-chested with two long gold chains around his neck. He looked to be about Mac's age, in his thirties, and made it clear he found Mac very attractive.

"After those bitches and Prince got killed, I almost quit coming here," Mac said. The man responded but he was soft-spoken and not close enough for the wire to clearly pick up his voice. All Josie could hear was Mac's half of the conversation. "Yeah, he was fucked up but who isn't. Why kill a sick wacko? Bullshit, who told you that? Is he still around? What's his name; what's dickhead look like in case he hits on me? Is he here now? No shit," Mac said and laughed.

Several men joined them, and the conversation turned to other subjects. Mac lingered a few minutes, eventually wandered away from that group, and sat on a planter closer to the corner where Anthony had worked. There were smaller gatherings at the new location, but a couple of those men sat with Mac and talked for a few minutes before getting up and moving on toward the bar. Two scruffy-looking, most likely homeless, young men sharing a joint were standing nearby and came over to him. They must've offered him a hit because he held up the beer bottle and shook his head. They sat on the planter close by and started joking boisterously about queers and queens. Josie picked up enough of what they were saying to know it was probably an attempt to bait the UC. When Mac got up and walked toward them, she grabbed her microphone and said, "Bailey, tell him to back off, walk away."

"Little late for that," Marge said, as Mac grabbed the bigger man around the throat with one hand and shoved him on his back into the planter. The second man jumped up as if he wanted to help his buddy. Mac held up his other hand and said, "Take one step toward me, bitch, and I'll break his neck and beat you until you look as bad as you smell." The second man begged for his friend's life, swore they were sorry. Mac released his hold, let him get up, and chased them away with a parting butt kick to the bigger man.

"Everything okay?" Marge broadcast.

"I'm good," Mac said.

"Damn straight," she said.

He stayed on the street until two A.M. when Josie decided to shut down the operation. Mac had covered the area from the bar to Anthony's corner and spent nearly two hours talking to several men. Josie told the vice and uniform officers to go end-of-watch; they were done for the night. She asked Marge to pick up Mac and meet behind the Wells Fargo Bank on La Brea for debriefing.

The bank parking lot was small and not visible from the street. She backed her car into the shadows and waited until Marge arrived. Marge drove close, parking so they could open their driver's windows and talk without having to get out.

"You're not fucking gonna believe this," Marge said before her window was all the way down.

"Try me," Josie said. She was tired and wanted to get to Long Beach, fall asleep next to Kyle before she passed out in the car.

Mac was sitting in the back and leaned over the seat between Marge and Behan.

"I had four different people tell me they knew the name Matador. Carl, the guy I bought the beer for, he told me he kind of saw him once in a cab when Matador picked up Anthony but he didn't get a good look. The others said they were told Matador was tall, dark, and handsome, but they barely got glimpses of him. They said he has to be rich because he buys gifts for his boy toys."

"Who are these boys? They're the ones we need to find and talk to," Josie said.

"That's the problem," Behan said, pushing Mac out of his way. "They're in the morgue. At least two of our homicide victims had dated him . . . three if you count Anthony."

"But that's not the worst part, Boss. He's got a good reason for not wanting anyone to see him," Mac said. "They swear . . ."

"They're saying our fucking killer's a cop," Marge said before he could finish.

"Why would they say that?" Josie asked.

"Because our victims bragged before they were killed that they wouldn't get arrested because Matador was a cop," Mac said.

"I'm thinking one of these geniuses did get arrested, talked to his lawyer Burke about Matador . . . and probably signed scumbag lawyer's death warrant," Marge said.

"We're still trying to figure out if any of our other victims had property taken," Behan said. "Most of them were transients so it's hard to know just what they should've had."

Josie leaned back against the headrest and closed her eyes. After a few seconds, she said, "Okay, tomorrow make that a priority, Red. Have your detectives interview everyone on Santa Monica Boulevard if necessary. Find out what gifts Matador gave our victims. If we can track even one item back to a retailer, maybe we can figure out who bought it. Start with Anthony's cape. Marge, you try to locate Matador's current lover. From what Mac was told it sounds as if he probably would latch onto a new boy."

"I'm pretty sure he's not a Hollywood copper," Mac said. "Street people pretty much know everyone who works this division and word would get around."

"They didn't know you," Marge said. "And there's lots of other so-called cops who've been in office jobs most of their careers."

"Hey," Mac said, feigning hurt feelings. "Just insult me to my face."

"You know I don't mean you, asshole," Marge said, playfully pushing him back into the rear seat.

Josie started her car and said, "I'm going to take some time off the next couple of days but call me if you dig up something important. Mac, don't put anything in the morning report about Matador. Just say you worked with vice trying to gather information—nothing significant to report, but make it clear the task force was canceled."

"Yes, ma'am."

She would tell Chief Dempsey about the possibility their killer was a police officer, but not now, and not until she was certain the rumor had some substance. Leaving Mac's or any cop's reputation to the likes of Timmy Scott wasn't going to happen.

THIRTEEN

The driveway was empty, and the small craftsman bungalow was dark when Josie arrived at Kyle's Long Beach residence. He usually left the driveway open for her city car, but she didn't see his car parked anywhere on the street.

She used her key to enter through the side door off the patio. It felt twenty degrees hotter inside the house. She opened the rear french doors and all the windows as quickly as she could. Almost immediately, the ocean breeze cooled down the interior. She poured a glass of chardonnay from an open bottle in the refrigerator, turned out the lights, undressed, and lay on top of the bed. Her .45 was on the nightstand, close enough if she needed it. She never worried about her safety in the Pasadena house, but here for some reason it was always on her mind. Familiarity had to be the difference, she guessed.

In the dark, with her head propped up on pillows, she sipped the cold wine and looked out at the small enclosed Spanish-tiled patio. It was a peaceful, secluded space where she and Kyle had made love on more than one occasion when retreating inside would have ruined the moment.

The only sounds were a chorus of crickets and stray cats wailing in a noisy standoff in the alley behind the garage. The wall fountain wouldn't start again until sunrise. Kyle had set the timer intending the gentle flow of water to be the first thing they'd hear in the morning.

She finished the wine and felt completely relaxed. Everything seemed perfect for her to drift off into a deep sleep, but her eyes refused to shut. There was the hint of an idea floating in her weary brain trying to surface among all the information she'd accumulated the last few days. Retrieving it felt like lifting a heavy box with one hand— just wasn't happening. Maybe in the morning, she thought, closing her eyes.

The deadbolt lock on the side door clicked. She sat up, instinctively putting her hand on the semiauto.

"If you're awake, don't shoot; it's me," Kyle said, from the living room.

She slipped on a nightshirt and found him in the kitchen rummaging through the refrigerator. He straightened up and gave her a kiss before returning to his search.

"How'd you know I'd be awake?" she asked.

"You weren't answering your phone earlier . . . no surprise there. I called Marge and she told me what happened. I know you, Corsino. There's no way you're sleeping."

"You work overtime because of the pursuit?"

"Nope," he said, removing the bottle of chardonnay and three eggs before closing the refrigerator door. He held up the eggs, "Hungry?" he asked. She nodded. "Pasadena PD got a lead on Marvin Wright's whereabouts in Wilshire. I went with them, but he wasn't there. They've got one of their people sitting on the location."

"Marge told you our suspect might be a cop?" Josie asked. She sat on a stool near the long butcher-block table where he was chopping onions for his omelet.

"She said that was the rumor among the street boys. Could Marvin be this Matador?"

Josie yawned, got a couple of clean wine glasses from the cupboard, poured a little of the chardonnay into each. She took a sip before saying, "No one's had a good look at him. At least that's what they told Mac. Could be anybody." She explained how they intended to track Matador through his gifts or other contacts. "Burke obviously wasn't his type, not young, not reckless, didn't need the killer's gifts."

"Marvin is the most likely suspect for the Burke homicide; isn't he? The only reason to lump him in with your other killings is the location, right?" Kyle asked, putting a plate with half the omelet in front of her. He sat across the table and started eating.

"I'm too tired to think clearly," she said and because it was on her mind, asked, "Did you know about Mac's personnel complaint when he was a probationer?"

"No, why?"

"Nothing . . . it's stupid, another Timmy Scott sabotage."

"I'd imagine Mac had a few of them."

"Why's that?"

Kyle almost smiled and said, "He came to the department from the Marine Corps. He's always been a hard charger, in the middle of everything, first one to respond when someone requests backup. If there's a fight, a shooting, he's in it or close enough to know what happened. Cops like him get complaints."

"I didn't, you didn't, and we worked that way."

"We've been blessed with good verbal skills and that innate ability to bullshit our way out of trouble. I've seen you in action, Corsino. You're the only captain I know who can hand an officer a suspension and have him thank you."

After they finished eating and filled the dishwasher, Josie went back into the bedroom and curled up on top of the bed, asleep in seconds this time. She never felt Kyle lie beside her, but sometime before daybreak she woke briefly and realized she was tucked in his arms. She slept until late morning when the room got too hot to be comfortable. It was the first good night's sleep she'd had in weeks.

There weren't any missed messages or calls on her cell phone which meant nothing critical had happened in Hollywood. Behan could be relied on to let her know when she needed to be there, and Marge had a network of spies in the station who told her everything. Mac had proven to be one of the best adjutants she'd ever had. He always seemed to be one step ahead of the bureau, so she felt comfortable spending some time with Kyle.

The banging noises coming from the kitchen meant he was still home and probably cleaning up from their late-night snack. She glanced at her watch on the nightstand. It was almost noon. A long luxurious shower before she dressed was another rare treat. Shorts, sandals, and a halter top were perfect for the lazy day she anticipated.

"You're alive," Kyle said when she came into the kitchen and he hugged her. "You look great. I was beginning to think you might sleep all day."

"With a little breeze, I might have. I'm starving. Want to walk to that little restaurant down the street."

They locked up the house and strolled the two blocks to Bonjours, a small family-owned restaurant that served breakfast all day. It had four tables on the sidewalk patio and a dozen inside. Kyle hurried to get the one empty table on the patio. He knew she liked to eat outside and watch people with their dogs walking past. Although she kept her phone on the table where she could see it, there was no hurry to either eat or get back, and their conversation didn't include anything work-related.

She stretched her long legs and realized they hadn't seen the sun for some time. Her Sicilian skin was a natural olive tone, usually a little darker. Jogging was the way she kept in shape, got some fresh air and sunshine, but lately there didn't seem to be enough time to sleep let alone exercise.

"What are you smiling at?" Kyle asked as she slid her legs back under the table.

"I was just about to make myself that promise about getting up and jogging every morning."

"What's funny about that?"

"I'm lying," she said.

"I'll get you up. We'll run together."

"You can try," she said, grinning.

"Do you mind if I ask you to marry me again?" he asked, smiling back with that Kyle Richards penetrating stare. The question came out of nowhere but wasn't unexpected. He'd made it clear on numerous occasions that her fear of commitment wasn't going to deter his love or his desire to make her his wife.

She was quiet for a few seconds, petting a golden retriever whose owners occupied the closest table. The big dog was sitting beside her with one paw resting on her lap. "No," she said, not looking at him.

"No, you don't mind or no, you still won't marry me."

"I don't mind."

"Will you?"

"Yes."

"Really?"

"No, I'm screwing with you. Yes, of course really. I love you. I want to be with you."

He nodded as if he still wasn't certain she meant what she said, slowly got up, and gave her a long kiss. "You won't be sorry," he said.

"I just hope you won't be sorry. I'm a bossy workaholic who hates housework. I can't cook, not exactly the *Better Homes and Gardens* little wife."

Josie noticed the dog's owners smiling at her. She guessed they were close enough to overhear the conversation, but their smiles faded into masks of confusion when Kyle announced, "Martha Stewart is boring. I want a beautiful sexy woman who can shoot good on a two-way range and won't run from a knife fight." The dog couple paid their bill and left. Josie had the impression they wanted to get away as quickly as they could.

She expected to feel some apprehension about promising to tie herself to another husband, but instead she experienced relief and a sense of having done something very right.

Given her father's Italian genes, Josie knew big decisions always resulted in a bigger appetite. She finished a huge ham and cheese panini sandwich, two stacks of thick-cut french fries with a vanilla shake and had to unbutton her shorts before they started walking back to the house.

As soon as they reached Kyle's front lawn, Josie remembered something her crazy Irish mother always said—usually after downing a pint of cheap whiskey. The woman would warn her children, "Don't be fooled by a touch of happiness and good fortune. It's the devil's way of teasing you before your next disappointment."

There on the front porch was proof positive that even paranoid drunks occasionally got it right.

FOURTEEN

They stopped at the curb for a few seconds before Kyle, in a subdued greeting, said, "Hi, Mom, Beth . . . what are you doing here?"

The elderly Mrs. Richards and Kyle's daughter were standing behind the wrought iron railing, waving at them. Beth opened the gate and hurried down the stairs to the sidewalk to hug her father. Josie was surprised how grown-up the girl looked. She was a beautiful young woman now as well as the spitting image of Kyle's dead wife. Suddenly Josie felt like an outsider, an intruder on the edges of this family. She stood quietly while his mother and daughter embraced him, fussed over him, asking nonstop questions. She seemed to occupy space again when he finally had an opportunity to announce their engagement.

"That's wonderful, dear," Mrs. Richards said without a hint of enthusiasm.

"Wonderful," Beth repeated, hugging her father again and giving Josie a quick peck on the cheek. "I'm so glad we came back early. Aren't you, Grandmother?"

Mrs. Richards didn't answer, but managed a forced smile before leading the way back toward the porch and into the house.

It was almost as if Kyle could read Josie's mind when he suggested that Beth continue living with her grandmother. They were sitting on the patio now, drinking iced tea, and Josie was pleased to hear him say it but felt a little uneasy too. She wanted to get along with Beth. Throwing her out of the family home probably wasn't the best way to accomplish that goal.

"That's fine," Beth said. "I'll be starting university in a few weeks. I wouldn't be home much anyway."

Josie studied her face but couldn't tell if the words were sincere or simply an effort to please her father. There was no doubt about Mrs. Richards's feelings. Her expression was remarkably clear—bitter disappointment.

They stayed there talking for more than an hour, everyone except Kyle's mother. She was sulking and sat quietly, nodding or shaking her head when asked a question, otherwise fixated on the fountain. Beth asked Josie to help her pack some things in her room, and even when they were alone the young woman was upbeat and seemed happy for her father.

"Don't mind Grandmother," Beth said, closing the bedroom door. "She adored my mom, but dad's been alone too long. Anybody can see he's happy with you."

Josie hugged her and said, "Thank you . . . as long as you're okay with it I'm fine."

"I love my father and he loves me, but I'm pretty sure he'd dump me like a smelly stray dog before he'd let you go," Beth said, smirking and raising one eyebrow. "So when do I meet my handsome, soon-to-be stepbrother that dad has told me about?"

Josie didn't answer. She changed the subject and thought, "Great, my son finally gets away from a woman old enough to be his mother, and now a teenager is drooling over him."

The visit ended shortly after Beth had collected everything she wanted to take to her grandmother's Long Beach mansion, an early twentieth-century, two-story Victorian sitting off Ocean Avenue with a million-dollar, panoramic view of the Pacific. Josie knew Kyle's father had left his mother a small fortune when he died. Beth's change of address wasn't likely to cause her any discomfort.

"What did you and Beth talk about?" Kyle asked when his mother and daughter had gone.

"You."

"That's interesting; all mom wanted to talk about was you."

"I'll bet," Josie said, but didn't pursue it. She had no need nor any desire to discuss his mother's animosity. He'd made it clear to Josie that she was his priority and that was enough.

They were alone again and had made it through an entire day without a call from Hollywood. Josie knew Behan and Marge would handle everything they could to allow her a few uninterrupted hours but had to admit she was curious about what progress had been made on tracking their serial killer.

The next morning an update arrived unexpectedly with Marge Bailey. She opened the side gate while Josie and Kyle were finishing breakfast on the patio.

"Sorry, hate to do this, Boss, but we got a shit storm that needs your attention," Marge said, dragging a chair across the patio to the table and then disappearing inside the house.

"Another homicide?" Josie asked when Marge returned with a glass of orange juice.

"No, worse. Dempsey has assigned Mac home until we ID our serial killer. Might as well put a fucking sign around his neck saying, 'I'm a suspect.'"

"What's Dempsey's reason?" Josie asked.

"I guess asshole doesn't have to explain himself because he's a deputy chief," Marge said.

"That's bullshit," Kyle said. "He can't just order something like that without a reason. The union will be all over him."

"All I know is Dempsey told the watch commander to assign him home until further notice," Marge said, drinking the juice and taking a slice of toast off Kyle's plate.

"Is Mac okay?" Josie asked.

Marge swallowed the last bite of toast and said, "Fuck no."

"I'll get dressed and meet with Dempsey. Has Mac contacted the union?" Josie asked. She got up, collected the dirty dishes, and carried everything into the kitchen.

"Yeah, but they're about as much good as tits on a bull . . . unless they've got something personal to gain from it," Marge said, trailing behind her.

Kyle followed them, told Josie to go get ready and he'd clean up the kitchen. He wasn't due to return to work until the next day, and said because she was leaving, he'd probably go to his mother's house to spend a little time with Beth.

It only took a few minutes for Josie to change her clothes. She realized she wasn't all that eager to leave. For the first time in years, she wanted to stay and be with someone more than she wanted to be at work.

She and Marge arrived at her office about the same time. Josie was irritated as she passed Mac's empty desk. Her secretary had attempted to fill in for the missing adjutant, but her stressed-out appearance told Josie the workload might be too much for the woman.

Josie gathered a stack of projects from the secretary's desk, put them on the table in her office. She could handle the paperwork. The bigger problem was getting her adjutant back.

"What are you going to say to Dempsey?" Marge asked, falling onto the couch.

"Don't know. Where's Red? I didn't see him at his desk."

"Last time I talked to him he was still trying to track down Anthony's cape."

Josie thought about calling Chief Dempsey and making an appointment but changed her mind. The best tactic would be to go to the bureau unannounced, not give Sergeant Scott an opportunity to interfere.

Her secretary knocked on the open door and came in. She was holding a single sheet of paper but seemed hesitant to speak.

"What is it, Carol?" Josie asked, expecting more bad news.

"Ma'am, they've scheduled you to give Detective Behan his shadow box at the retirement party tonight . . . also they've penciled you in to deliver a short speech. Sergeant McSweeney never had an opportunity to ask if that was okay with you. Is it okay?"

Josie groaned. She'd forgotten about Red's party. "Yes, of course, I'll do whatever they need me to do," she said. She'd already seen the shadow box. It was a wonderful gift from the Hollywood division officers. All his medals, ribbons, handcuffs, his first handgun, and other paraphernalia he'd accumulated over the years including some of his Marine Corps medals were arranged in a glass-covered mahogany box.

Red was going to hate all the attention. Josie wouldn't be surprised to find him hiding in the Police Academy's rock garden halfway through the endless speeches and presentations. Behan was something of a legend among LAPD homicide detectives. The retirement committee had easily sold enough tickets to fill the academy's newly renovated bar and banquet room.

She would be honored to speak at his party but had decided she wasn't about to let him walk away from Hollywood until he solved the Santa Monica Boulevard killings. He had planned on taking some vacation time before his official retirement date, but she'd find a way to bury her guilt, hide from Miss Vicky's wrath, and keep him working longer. There wasn't a doubt in her mind he could find the killer or killers and also help clear Mac's name and reputation. She figured after that night's gathering, he'd only be allowed a few days to continue the investigation before his wife or Dempsey dragged the big redhead away from that homicide table forever.

A QUICK call to Kyle's cell phone solved the problem of what to wear to the retirement. He agreed to bring her simple white summer dress to Hollywood an hour before the party and they would drive to the academy together.

"You need to write a speech for tonight?" Marge asked, grabbing a handful of Jelly Bellys from a jar on Josie's file cabinet. "I'll go see if my guys dug up anything on Matador's new love nest."

"No, I want you to come with me to the bureau," Josie said.

"Really . . . that's a first. You're not worried I'll offend Chief Douche Bag?"

"I'm counting on it."

"Yes, ma'am," Marge said with a sloppy salute. "Please let me choke out Timmy the weasel too."

"We'll see," Josie said with a slight smile. They both knew that wasn't going to happen . . . not in the chief's office, but she wanted Dempsey off balance and having Marge in the room was the best way to achieve that goal.

When they got to West Bureau, Sergeant Scott and the chief's secretary, Marion, were in the front office. The door to Dempsey's office was closed.

Josie went directly to the secretary's desk and asked, "Is the chief in? I need to talk with him."

Before Marion could answer, Sergeant Scott said, "I think he's busy. I'll ask if he's available."

"Go right in, Captain. He's on the phone, but he won't mind if you wait in there," Marion said, glaring at the chief's adjutant.

Sergeant Scott started to get up, but Marge stood in his way and ordered, "Sit, Timmy, we've got this one."

"You can't just . . ." he started to protest as Josie opened the door.

Marge pointed to her collar and said, "Lieutenant bars trump sergeant stripes, so, yes we can, and FYI Timmy, you're a fucking gofer not the chief." She smiled sweetly at Marion and followed Josie into the chief's office.

They sat on chairs in front of his desk and waited until Dempsey finished his call. He was in a good mood so Josie guessed he hadn't been talking to his wife.

"What can I do for you, Captain, Lieutenant Bailey?" he asked and looked over at his computer screen. "Did we have a meeting this afternoon?"

"No, I wanted to talk to you about my adjutant, Sergeant McSweeney," Josie said.

"What about him?" he asked, his smile fading.

"Why is he assigned home?"

"I thought it prudent, given his history."

"What history?" Marge asked.

"What's your interest in him, Lieutenant?" Dempsey asked.

"Sergeant McSweeney has helped uncover important information in a homicide-vice investigation. He's critical to our operation," Marge said. "But he's not doing us a hell of a lot of good sitting on his ass at home."

"I did it for his own good," Dempsey said, and looking at Josie, added, "You weren't entirely candid with me about his mental condition, Captain."

"With all due respect, sir, sending a cop home as a possible murder suspect rarely does his mental condition any good," Marge said calmly.

"I realize that," Dempsey mumbled, defensively. "I never said he was a suspect, but . . . he does have a relevant complaint and has shown some mental instability in the past . . . In my judgment it was the best thing to do."

"That complaint was unfounded. I read it. The arrestee was a chronic abuser of the system. Everyone who arrested him got a complaint," Josie said. "McSweeney is a steady, reliable cop. He's worked for me three months and . . ."

"Don't you think it's somewhat peculiar that your rash of homicides started around the same time he transferred to Hollywood."

"Fuck, no," Marge said.

Dempsey's face flushed but before he could respond, Josie said, "I'll go back and check but I'll bet there were a dozen officers on the transfer list when Mac came in. Are they all suspects?"

"Of course not," Dempsey said. He was angry but less sure of himself now. It was clear from his body language he hated being challenged, but Josie was counting on his indecisiveness and the likelihood that under pressure he wouldn't really know if he had overstepped his authority. He tapped his fingers on the clean glass-top desk for a few seconds, clasped his hands, and finally looked up and said, "If you're willing to take full responsibility for his actions, I'll agree to reinstate him . . . but I don't want that man in the field for any reason, until, one, this serial killer is caught, and two, he's had a thorough mental evaluation." Marge started to protest but Dempsey held up his right hand like a traffic cop and said, "That means find another UC, Lieutenant. If I learn he's been in the field for any reason before those two things happen, Dan McSweeney goes home and I'll make damn certain he stays there. Clear enough?"

"Yes, sir," Josie said. She didn't like the conditions but having her adjutant back at work was better than nothing. Mac was ready to return to patrol and wouldn't be pleased about the delay, but Josie hoped his situation might motivate Behan, give him the added incentive to work quickly.

FIFTEEN

The party for Behan would take place at the most popular location for traditional LAPD retirement festivities, the Police Academy in Elysian Park. Kyle was waiting in her office when Josie returned from the bureau. He sat on the couch and watched cable news while she pinned up her hair and slipped into the sleeveless dress he'd brought. He'd told her it was one of his favorite outfits because the straight lines and silky white fabric highlighted her slim figure and olive-colored skin.

"You look beautiful," he said when she'd finished and stood in front of him. "But it needs something."

"I know," Josie said smiling, and dropped a small semi-auto gun into her evening purse. "Better?" she asked.

"Not that, this," he said taking a ring out of his jacket pocket and sliding it onto her finger. It was a wide gold filigree band with a delicate circle of small diamonds in the center, a perfect fit that looked good on her long fingers.

She stared at her left hand for several seconds and hesitated before asking, "It wasn't Mary's?" The last thing she wanted, or he needed, was a constant reminder of the dead woman she was replacing.

"No," Kyle said quickly, "I gave her ring to Beth years ago. This one is much older. It was my great-grandmother's on my dad's side. He left it to me as a memento. I've never wanted to part with it until now."

"Wish we could go home," Josie said and meant it.

"Me too, but we both know that ain't happening."

"Our romantic evening will be shared with Red Behan and a bunch of cops."

"Somehow not a huge surprise," he said with a wry smile.

POLICE OFFICERS in Los Angeles enjoy a fine retirement plan that should leave them secure after they are no longer willing or able to work, but Josie knew that wasn't the case with Phillip Red Behan. He drank too much, had married too many times, and stayed too long at a rank that he loved but that would never give him much financial security after he retired. She had calculated that with his divorce-depleted pension, his marriage to the wealthy Miss Vicky would be the only thing keeping him from a life on the streets.

Most cops start thinking about their retirement as soon as they've done everything they've wanted to do, or the stress and danger have taken their toll, or the job is no longer challenging or exciting. By nature, they are inquisitive problem-solvers. When police work becomes too repetitive or too heavy a burden, physically or mentally, they retire and move on to other things. She feared Behan's future wouldn't be altered much or improved by leaving, but staying wasn't an option for him either.

The academy lounge was overflowing when Josie and Kyle arrived. She looked around and was surprised how many command officers had come and knew many of the officers and detectives were from divisions outside Hollywood. The good turnout made her happy for Red that so many of his peers had come to honor him. Even Chief Dempsey and Ed Charles had made appearances and were standing near the bar talking with Captain Ames from West LA. The chief's MO was to have a few drinks and let himself be seen for morale purposes. He'd find a way to slither away before the time-consuming festivities began. She watched Jorge Sanchez join his boss, the police commissioner, and the chief, but as soon as Kyle went to the bar to get drinks, Jorge walked over to her.

"Captain, good send-off for Red," Jorge said, giving her a hug.

"You look healed. Can hardly see the scratches and bruises anymore," she said, thinking what a shame it would've been if that good-looking face had been permanently damaged.

"Yeah, some nightmare. I heard Marvin is MIA. No news yet on that front?"

"No, Pasadena PD thinks he might be staying somewhere in Wilshire," she said, taking a glass of cabernet from Kyle.

Sanchez and Kyle shook hands, but Josie knew Kyle wasn't a fan of the young captain. He thought Josie had made a mistake in mentoring Sanchez. He couldn't explain why but said he just didn't like or trust the man.

"Isn't Pasadena after him for tossing Molotov cocktails at your house?" Sanchez asked.

"He's a suspect, but no proof yet," Josie said. "How'd you find out about my house?"

"Don't remember . . . somebody at detective bureau I think. Can't keep something like that a secret."

"Anything new on your ambush?" Kyle asked.

"No, but I know it had to be Marvin Wright or some-body he got to do his dirty work," Sanchez said.

"Maybe," Kyle said with a shrug.

"Hey, no fucking maybe. He tried to kill me and mur-dered poor Howard Burke . . . probably ought to be sus-pect number one for all Hollywood's homicides. The guy's a homicidal maniac and I'm sleeping with one eye open until he's in jail or dead," Sanchez said. He became increasingly agitated and excused himself to go back to the bar for a refill.

"Your protégé's kind of hysterical," Kyle said, taking a sip of whiskey.

Josie didn't respond right away. She was watching San-chez pace in front of the bar waiting for his drink. She was worried the shooting attack at West LA station might've had some long-lasting psychological effect when she saw him go from outrage to calm within seconds as soon as Behan approached and greeted him. They laughed and talked for several minutes until one of the other detectives announced that dinner was ready to be served.

"That's just Jorge," she said as she and Kyle walked into the dining room, but she couldn't help wondering if the young man's ordeal had left him with some emotional damage.

Marge had saved two seats for them at a table where the patrol captain and the other Hollywood lieutenants were sitting, but the place next to the vice lieutenant was empty.

"Where's Mac?" Josie asked, whispering in Marge's ear.

"He left."

"Why?"

Marge didn't answer. She seemed to be struggling with what she wanted to say before getting up and motioning for Josie to follow her outside to the rock garden patio.

"Mac was fine until that piss-ant Dempsey stumbled into the bar," Marge said. She was pacing on the narrow path near the back door.

"What happened?" Josie asked, dreading the answer. She feared nearly three months of her time and effort attempting to rebuild Mac's confidence and pride had just been flushed down the toilet.

"What do you think? He was pissed, wanted to punch the asshole's lights out. I knew he wasn't gonna hit him, but just the same I could see it was eating at him. He was accused of something he didn't do and kept saying he wasn't going through that shit again."

"Where is he now?"

"He promised he'd go to my place and wait for me. I can't bail on Red's big night, but I'll leave as soon as I can," Marge said. She tried to sound calm but Josie knew her well enough to see she was worried and maybe a little scared.

"Go now. I'll explain to Behan," Josie said, leading her in the direction of the steps. "Call me if you need anything, but make certain he comes to work tomorrow. I promise I'll get him back on track." She waited on the patio until Marge's shadowy figure hurried down the stairs and disappeared along the asphalt road to the academy parking lot, and tried not to think about how many pitfalls there'd be in keeping that promise.

A cold dinner was waiting when she got back to the table. Kyle pulled out the chair for her and cocked his head as if he were waiting for an explanation but didn't ask any questions. She leaned over and said, "I'll explain later."

THE REST of the evening went pretty much as Josie had anticipated. The chicken was overcooked, and the speeches were too long. War stories by Behan's former partners were embellished with a flair for absurdity only cops possessed. Fortunately many dubious tales fell outside the statute of limitations for criminal indictment but Josie still cringed at admissions of creative writing on crime reports, hookers delivered to a commander's promotion party, and live ducks stolen from the lake in MacArthur Park to be left overnight in a city councilman's new Mercedes-Benz.

Every organization and politician connected to Hollywood gave him a plaque or commendation with large gold seals, but his three-by-one-and-a-half-inch detective gold card, a prize among investigators, was the only item that seemed to impress him. Behan sat stoically through most of the ceremony and only blushed when Jorge got up and talked about their late-night bar-hopping jaunts during the time he was a watch commander in Hollywood. Chief Dempsey and most of the staff officers had gone but the elegant Vicky Behan in a stunning blue silk cocktail dress stared at her manicured nails with a frozen distasteful expression during the young captain's speech. His recollection of events was very funny and entertaining to a bunch of cops but her husband's drinking escapades weren't something she'd wanted to celebrate.

The last presentation was Josie's. She walked to the podium without prepared remarks but knew they weren't necessary. The big detective had been a part of her life for decades. He was her friend and that's what she talked about. She concluded her speech with a toast to him and Miss Vicky for a long, happy life together, away from the demands of a job Josie knew had taken a toll on him. Her desire for their happiness was genuine, but nonetheless she intended to do whatever it took to delay his well-deserved, idyllic future.

Behan took the shadow box from her, put it on the podium, and gave her a bear hug. Before letting go, he whispered in her ear, "Stop shoveling dirt, Boss. I'm not dead yet."

She leaned back a little and said just loud enough for him to hear, "I like you, Behan, but not enough to let you walk away without finishing what you started. Be at your desk tomorrow."

The big redhead didn't answer, but they both knew he'd be there. He hated vacations, and spending any time away from work while he was technically still a detective wouldn't have been something he'd agree to do without pressure from Miss Vicky. Josie figured she'd have to hide from his wife until the investigation was done or the City of Los Angeles declared him officially retired and banned from police work.

SIXTEEN

The next morning, Josie went directly to Hollywood's vice office hoping to talk with Marge before having to deal with Mac, but she wasn't surprised to find her adjutant already there and engaged in an intimate conversation with the vice lieutenant.

"Morning, ma'am," he said, looking a little sheepish. "I was just . . ."

"Don't worry about it," Josie said, interrupting him. "I wanted to talk to you and Marge anyway."

Marge was leaning against a file cabinet a few feet from him and looked tired, a little annoyed.

"The chief has ordered you out of the field. Are you okay working in my office awhile longer?" Josie asked and he nodded. "Good, I'm certain we'll get this investigation cleared up before next DP. You can go back to patrol then if that's what you want."

The next deployment period would start in four weeks, but Behan would be officially retired long before that. Josie believed once her best detective was gone any chance of arresting a serial killer would be slim. If they didn't have a suspect or at least identify one, she was certain Dempsey wouldn't allow Mac to return to patrol and she felt bad about making an empty promise even if it was an attempt to help him.

"Yes, ma'am," he said, without looking at her and left the office with a quick unsmiling glance at Marge.

Marge waited a few seconds maybe to let him get downstairs and then she kicked at the metal file cabinet hard enough to put another dent in the side and knock her favorite picture of former Police Chief Daryl Gates onto the floor. There wasn't any glass in the picture frame because after replacing it several times, she'd told Josie, "What's the point? I want his picture up there and I'm not gonna stop kicking the damn cabinet."

"Feel better?" Josie asked.

"No, I'm fucking pissed. Mac's convinced Dempsey wants him pensioned off and won't ever let him go back to patrol."

"That's not Dempsey's call."

"No, but he's got enough juice to make it happen," Marge said. She pulled a chair out from one of the tables and sat. She looked exhausted.

"What happened when you got home last night?"

"He stayed awake until almost dawn . . . would hardly talk and when he did, it didn't make sense. I told him you'd fight for him, get him back on the street, but he wasn't listening. I think he's convinced his career is fucked," Marge said, not looking at Josie, which meant she probably believed that too.

"Well, it's not. Dempsey isn't the final word. I'll go to Office of Operations, even the old man, if I have to. Tell Mac not to give up and not to do anything stupid. He should be back in the field in four weeks," Josie said as convincingly as she could, not knowing if it was the truth.

"He'll be okay," Marge said, and sighed before adding, "unless he keeps me awake again tonight. If he pulls that crap again, I swear I'll fucking shoot the bastard and put us both out of our misery." A raised eyebrow was the only indication she was joking . . . maybe.

Josie cleared her throat and changed the subject with rapid questions. "What progress have you made tracking down Anthony's cape or any of Matador's other gifts?" she asked. "Have you found any new boy toy yet?"

"Red's going through personal property from all the victims and interviewing anybody who knew them . . . still can't identify any item that might've been removed by the killer around the time of the murder."

"What about the cape?" Josie asked. She kept harping on the missing cape because it was unique and should be traceable.

"Judge Charles has a box of pictures Anthony left in his room. He said I could go through them. I'm hoping at least one has a clear picture of that cape with an identifying mark."

"Anthony stayed in Baldwin Hills?"

"Rarely, according to his father, but he kept stuff there," Marge said. "I'm going this afternoon. Want to come? I could use help. The judge won't let me take the pictures."

"Can't Red or one of his guys go with you?" Josie asked.

"I asked. He said no . . . his exact words were 'hell no.' He wants to finish the property searches and his homicide teams are tied up."

"What about Matador's new love interest, any progress on that front?"

"We're trying to locate a teenager who had bragged about dating him, otherwise another dead end."

JOSIE NEEDED to finish the work she was being paid to do, i.e., run Hollywood division. There were progress reports, projects, and personnel matters to handle, but she'd decided to get those done and make time to help Marge. This had become more than a murder investigation. She was certain the Hollywood killings were somehow tied to Burke, Jorge Sanchez's attack, and the firebombing of her house. Maybe Marvin Wright was responsible for some or all of those events, maybe not. Jorge's sanity and her peace of mind, not to mention Mac's prospects of returning to field work, depended on making those connections and catching the killer.

She watched Mac quietly perform his adjutant duties for most of the morning and by early afternoon he seemed to relax. Josie felt a lot more comfortable about his mental state when she noticed him chatting and joking with the secretary and the watch commander.

She had managed with his assistance to complete most of her critical paperwork and had returned a stack of phone messages by the time Marge arrived to drive them to the Charles mansion. The only call she hadn't returned was from Deputy Chief Dempsey. He'd left a message saying he needed to talk with her code-three—in police jargon, without delay. She threw it in the trash. Like any other obstacle, he was in the way and she was determined to work around him.

Fortunately his attention span was limited regarding anything other than department or city politics affecting his career. She figured he and Sergeant Scott only dabbled occasionally in police work as an afterthought or to annoy her. They would be upset she hadn't called, but the delay would give her time to use her resources without interference or arbitrary demands. She was willing to endure another lecture from Dempsey about ignoring the chain of command if it gave her time to do what had to be done.

"If Sergeant Scott calls again, tell him I had an emergency and I'll touch bases with the chief later or he can get me on my cell phone," Josie said to Mac as she left her office.

"You know cell phone reception sucks in Baldwin Hills, right?" Marge asked.

"I know."

THE NEIGHBORHOOD where the Charles mansion was located had a pleasant summer breeze making the temperature several degrees lower than the hot sticky air over Hollywood's overcrowded pink granite sidewalks.

Josie hoped the family would be as hospitable as the climate, but Colin Charles's first words on seeing her were, "What are you doing here?"

"I asked Captain Corsino to help me look through Anthony's pictures," Marge said and asked, "Problem?" Her tone challenged the older man to object but he didn't and stepped back, allowing them to enter the house.

"If my wife . . . if Allie bothers you, let the nurse know," he said and hesitated before asking, "Would you like to see Anthony before . . ." He didn't finish but led them down the hallway into what looked like a library, its shelves mostly filled with law books. He took a framed, five-by-seven picture off the top of a large cluttered desk and gave it to Josie. "This was my boy after his first year at UCLA."

It showed a tall, thin, clean-cut young man wearing sunglasses, a pullover sweater with the sleeves pushed up, and khaki pants. Unmistakably albino, but his pale arms were folded and he was smiling with the cocky attitude of someone who knew he was smarter than most and destined for greatness.

"What a shame," Josie said, thinking out loud.

Charles took the picture out of her hand and said, "After law school his life deteriorated."

"Drugs," Marge said and Josie was thinking the same.

"No."

"Then what?" Josie asked.

"Allison's legacy."

"What the hell does that mean?" Marge asked.

"It means our children will inherit not only considerable wealth from my wife's side of the family but her genetic failings as well."

"What are you saying?" Josie asked, but she had a pretty good idea what he meant.

Colin Charles didn't answer. Instead he reached under the desk, picked up a small covered storage box, and dropped it on a chair.

"You're welcome to look at these, but please don't take anything without my permission and try not to disturb my wife. I'll be in the den down the hall when you've finished."

He didn't wait for a response and took Anthony's college picture with him when he left. Josie removed the cover from the box and dumped the contents on the floor.

"We can put them back as we look at them," she said, pushing the desk chair in front of the pile of photos and sitting.

"What a pompous ass," Marge said, groaning, as she held onto the chair and squatted on the floor beside Josie.

"I'm guessing he just admitted all their kids inherited mommy's crazy gene."

"That's exactly what he said, but I'm guessing our newest police commissioner never mentioned that to the mayor before he took the job."

"Fat fucking chance, but then again he's no worse than the other losers his honor put on the commission, so who gives a damn."

Josie glanced at several photos and tossed them into the box before asking, "What if Ed Charles is already crazy enough to have killed his brother? He was almost frantic about getting inside information on Burke's investigation, and he kept tabs on Anthony, knew all the intimate details of his life."

"He's not married, doesn't seem to have a girlfriend . . . maybe it's his life too," Marge said.

"Marvin Wright has a connection to Burke, but we can't show he knew Anthony or any of the other victims. On the other hand, Ed Charles knew 'Uncle' Burke, and admitted knowing some of his brother's street friends, not to mention he gave us the name of Anthony's lover."

"That little turd Tim Scott has been feeding him any information we give the bureau which might explain why our first task force was such a bust. He's a possible suspect but we got shit for proof."

Josie grabbed another handful of photos off the floor and said, "True, but there's still something about the man that's not right."

"If you ask me, his whole family is one clown short of a Barnum & Bailey Circus," Marge said.

"Actually they're not; you just haven't met the sister," Josie said, glancing over her shoulder to be certain Colin hadn't heard her.

Marge hummed big-top music as she carefully sorted the photos, but they didn't talk anymore until they were finished. Most of the photos weren't helpful but Marge found several with Anthony and other young men standing in front of places she recognized as bars or clubs on Santa Monica Boulevard. The ones at the bottom of the pile seemed to be the most recent and most interesting.

A color photo showed what appeared to have been a costume party in the abandoned crash pad where Anthony's body had been found. One of the participants was wearing a bullfighter outfit, the traditional "suit of lights" embroidered in flamboyant gold patterns. The man was tall with an athlete's build, but he was wearing what looked like a black wig tied back in a ponytail, torero hat, and a mask over his eyes. It was difficult to see the color of his skin in the room's poor lighting.

Two pictures depicted Anthony dressed in his all-black outfit and cape. He wore a mask too but his white skin and hair were in stark contrast to his clothes. He was holding the ends of the cape with his arms extended as if he were pretending to fly and Marge noticed what appeared to be a label on the inside near the bottom of the cape.

Among hundreds of pictures, they found six that might help their investigation. Josie kept them, put the cover back on the box, and left it on the desk. She thought about leaving with those six photos, and thereby avoiding a confrontation with Colin Charles should he forbid them to be removed from his house, but decided against it. Instead she and Marge went to his study.

"I've found a few I'd like to borrow and copy," Josie said when he glanced up from the papers he'd been reading. She gave him the six pictures, and he quietly examined each one before handing them back to her.

"Keep them," he said. "This isn't a part of my son's life I care to remember."

MARGE HAD intended to bring Josie back to the station before taking the photo with the cape to SID downtown where with any luck the photo lab could enhance the label and reveal the manufacturer's name or whatever information was there. However a radio call from one of the vice sergeants changed that plan. The supervisor said a young man had just been arrested by PED, Hollywood's prostitution enforcement detail, for solicitation. He was bragging about being Matador's best friend and lover and was demanding special consideration.

"Have Behan sit in when you talk to this kid," Josie said, as she and Marge entered the back door of Hollywood station. Marge groaned but pirouetted toward the detective squad room.

"Yes, ma'am," she said. "I'll send the photo downtown with one of my sergeants."

"No," Josie said. "You or Behan should do that." She didn't know if Matador was a police officer but had a feeling the fewer people who knew what they were doing the better it would be. She didn't want to signal anything that might cause their killer to become cautious or go underground.

Marge didn't stop or turn around but gave a thumbs-up as she disappeared through the doorway of the squad room.

It was dinner time, and Josie could smell the aroma of Indian spices wafting down the stairs from the break room. Someone was warming dinner in the microwave and the grumbling noises coming from her stomach told her she needed to eat something soon. Kyle was working so she went back to her office to call him for a possible meet somewhere between Hollywood and Wilshire.

She wanted to sit in on Marge's interview but hunger and the desire to spend more time with Kyle were stronger. Her office door was closed and Mac was at his desk shaking his head when she arrived.

"Who's in there?" she asked, but he didn't have to answer. He looked upset and a little angry. "Dempsey," she said.

"Yes, ma'am and Commissioner Charles."

"Go home."

"I can wait if you need . . ."

"Go home," she repeated, interrupting him. "Thank you for everything today. I'll see you in the morning."

She waited until he locked his desk and had left the admin office before opening the door and entering her office.

The two men were sitting side by side on the couch watching a Dodgers baseball game on her television. Ed Charles stood when she entered but the deputy chief didn't budge.

"Did you get my message, Captain Corsino?" Dempsey asked, not looking away from the television screen.

"Yes, sir, did you get mine?"

He didn't answer and she knew he had probably tried to call but poor cell reception had prevented any success.

"I need to know where you are with these Hollywood homicides. The chief of police is not pleased with your lack of progress," he said, finally turning to look at her. "I'm warning you he's giving serious consideration for RHD to take this investigation and the commissioner and I are leaning toward recommending that."

Josie turned to Charles and said, "Lieutenant Bailey and I just left your father's house. He was very gracious in allowing us to look at some of your brother's pictures. Please thank him again for me."

It was obvious Ed Charles heard what she said but he seemed to be confused about how he should respond.

"I will . . . why would you want to see Anthony's pictures? What do they have to do with finding his killer?"

Josie noticed Chief Dempsey shifting his position on the couch. He didn't like being ignored and she had deftly cut him out of the conversation.

"We're trying to find an associate or someone familiar with his lifestyle who can help us."

"Were the photos helpful?" he asked, sitting beside Dempsey again.

"Not sure yet," she said with a faint smile. "But your father was very helpful in explaining your brother's mental difficulties." She met Charles's stare, detected a hint of panic, and thought he might be worrying that his father had revealed the family's genetic secret. A thin layer of perspiration had dotted his upper lip before Josie added, "But none of that really matters. Finding his killer is my one and only concern."

"Then I think we should give your detectives time to do that," he said, turning toward Dempsey and asking, "Don't you agree?"

The deputy chief looked uncertain but nodded like a bobblehead dog before saying, "If that's what you think is best . . . I can't speak for the chief, but . . . if the commission . . ." His words drifted off.

It was clear to Josie the two men had come on a mission to take the serial killer case away from Hollywood, but the sudden turnaround by Charles had baffled her boss.

She'd hoped her assurance that his family's secret wasn't her concern would ease Charles's mind and allow him to trust her. He'd been around the police department long enough to understand if detectives at RHD discovered his genetic flaw, they might not be as discreet.

There was nothing left to discuss and Dempsey seemed eager to get away, not only from Josie but from the police commissioner as well. He shook hands with Charles and was gone. Charles lingered a few seconds talking about the weather and department gossip until he said, "I don't know what my father told you, but you must realize our family history is not in any way relevant to my brother's murder."

"I mostly agree," she said. "But we both know you're still keeping something from me."

"When this investigation is done, I intend to be candid with the mayor about my . . . about everything," he said.

"Fine, but what aren't you telling me right now?"

He closed his eyes and took a deep breath, exhaled loudly. Josie could see he was frustrated and clearly suppressing anger, but he also must have finally realized how relentless and stubborn she could be and he said, "Howard Burke and I were more than classmates and friends. We were close . . . intimate. He knew this Matador person and helped arrange liaisons for him among his gay clients. That's how Anthony met him. In the days before his death, for some reason, Howard was terrified, so scared he started using drugs again."

"Why, what scared him?"

"He wouldn't tell me but I know he was afraid to go out at night. It doesn't make sense he'd be anywhere near the High-Top Bar at that hour."

"Unless he was with somebody. Were you with him that night?"

"No, I'd kept my distance . . . as soon as I found out he was on the needle again."

Josie tried to remember if there were any signs of Burke's drug use during the board of rights but had to admit she hadn't paid much attention to the high-strung lawyer.

Once Charles started talking he couldn't seem to stop. He told her about his dysfunctional family, haunted by the maternal sword of Damocles hanging over their heads. Charles insisted he and his sister hadn't displayed symptoms of the gene, although she did possess a dark moody nature. Charles promised to use his influence to keep the investigation in Hollywood, but Josie was surprised when he didn't ask for or demand anything in return.

His parting words were, "I believe you are a decent human being, Captain Corsino, who will do everything possible to find my brother's killer."

When she was alone, Josie sat at her worktable and had to admit her best suspect might've just convinced her he wasn't the killer.

SEVENTEEN

A good watch commander spends part of every night in the field observing his subordinates' decision-making abilities, monitoring patrol officers' responses to radio calls and their interaction with the community, so Josie wasn't surprised when she called Wilshire and Kyle wasn't in the office or answering his cell phone.

She got a Coke and two candy bars from the vending machines and located Marge and Behan waiting outside one of the jail's holding cells. They told her the arrestee, Andrew Romano, aka Mookie, had a lice infestation and smelled like a skid row outhouse. Behan had ordered a delousing and shower before the interview.

"This kid doesn't fit the Matador victim type," Behan said. "I think he's full of shit."

"You haven't talked to him yet," Josie said, swallowing the last bite of a Hershey's bar.

"No, but the other victims didn't smell like a mound of cat turds," Marge said. She broke off a piece of Josie's second candy bar and ate it.

The jailer appeared from behind the row of cells escorting a baby-faced man. He appeared to be barely over five feet tall and skinny with long stringy blond hair that reached below his shoulders. He looked young but his skin had the tan leathery appearance of someone who lived on the streets. As soon as he saw Marge, he smiled, revealing perfect teeth, and when he got closer they could see his big soulful blue eyes.

The high school heartthrob—with lice, Josie thought, and she could see when Mookie was cleaned up he did fit the mold of the serial killer's victims.

Behan decided to use the largest jail interview room to keep the young man and any of his surviving vermin as far away as possible. He and Marge sat at the far end of the table across from Mookie, and Josie stood near the door drinking her Coke.

"I ain't eat nothing all day. Did I miss the feeding?" Mookie whined, glancing at Josie's soda.

"They'll get you something when we're done," Behan said, pushing his chair back farther from the table.

"You ain't supposed to be keeping me. I told them cops I got me a pass."

"I didn't see any fucking pass," Marge said.

"I said 'Mad da dor,'" he said slowly, pausing for effect after every syllable. "That's all I gotta do is say his name."

"Did he tell you that?" Behan asked.

"Yeah," Mookie said, squirming and looking from Behan to Marge to Josie, not so sure of himself now.

"You're a lying piece of shit," Marge said. "If you know him, tell me what he looks like."

Not hesitating, Mookie said, "Bigger than me, looks like that movie star . . . hey, you all oughta know what he looks like. Don't he work here?"

"What movie star?"

"I dunno his name . . . you know, old dude, real famous."

"Is he white, black, Mexican?"

"I dunno could be any of 'em, I guess."

"You've never really seen him, have you?" Marge asked.

"Have too," Mookie said and chuckled at a joke only he understood. "Done lots more than seen him."

"If he likes somebody, Matador gives him a gift. What did he give you?" Josie asked.

Mookie didn't answer. He looked down at the table, shook his head, and mumbled, "I ain't telling . . . you'll take it."

"We can't," Josie lied. "It's against the law."

"Don't matter, it's mine. Jesse give it to me. You got no right," he mumbled, touching the front of his neck as if he expected something to be there. He must have remembered whatever it was had been removed and put in his property bag when he was booked. His hand slid down the front of his jumpsuit and his expression begged them, "You didn't see me try to touch what was around my neck, right?"

"Tell us Jesse's last name and we might believe you," Behan said.

"Mata! Now you gotta let me go!" he shouted and banged on the table with his fist in victory.

"Let's get you some dinner and a good night's sleep in clean sheets first," Behan said in his best fatherly voice. "Okay, buddy?"

Mookie looked confused by the kind words but nodded in agreement, got up, and went quietly with the jailer to an isolated cell. Josie had told the jailer to keep him separate from the other inmates and that no one other than Behan or Marge should talk to him. Behan put a note on Mookie's paperwork asking to be notified if he got bailed out.

As soon as the jailer returned, Behan asked to see Mookie's personal property. His clothes had been thrown in the garbage, and he'd be given a clean, donated outfit when he was released. For the moment, his only possessions were in a small sealed plastic bag containing a coin envelope with $1.50; a black, almost toothless plastic comb; and one ten-carat gold chain with a tiny red and white clown-face pendant.

Behan took the chain and pendant as evidence and left a receipt for Mookie.

"How long can we hold him?" Josie asked, when they were back in detectives.

"I'm pretty sure he's not going to make bail before his arraignment or anytime soon," Behan said. "Maybe we can drag our feet on transferring him to county, try to keep him here."

Marge was examining the chain with the pendant and said, "This looks like pretty cheap shit. Probably not traceable." She dropped them on Behan's desk and added, "And in case you hadn't thought about it, the name Jesse Mata only matches about ten thousand illegals in LA."

"But it fits with the whole matador thing," Josie said. "Mookie doesn't seem clever enough to have thought about that on his own."

"Maybe," Behan said, stretching and groaning. "I'm beat. We'll try to find a retailer for the jewelry tomorrow, but I'm done." He put the chain with the pendant in his desk drawer, locked it, and left. Marge needed to check on her officers before calling Mac. Josie was curious to hear how Mac was faring but she couldn't wait. She was tired and wanted to talk to Kyle before heading home to Long Beach.

She reached him on his cell phone, but he'd already left the station and was nearly at the house.

"I took an early out," Kyle explained. "Tomorrow morning Pasadena PD is door-knocking a place in Wilshire just off Venice Boulevard. They got a tip Marvin Wright might be staying there. I'm going with them."

"Your captain's okay with that?"

"Hope so."

Josie took a deep breath and asked, "You didn't run it by him, did you?"

"Nope, easier to beg forgiveness when it's done."

"Good luck with that one, lover."

"He's not you, Josie. My boss doesn't care as long as I don't bring any negative attention on him . . . definitely not your hands-on kind of guy."

"More the out-to-lunch sort, I'd say."

They talked a few more minutes until he got close to the house. She hung up, straightened her office, and left before the next catastrophe could hit. It was late enough that the traffic was free flowing to Long Beach and she arrived in a little more than half an hour. Given the time, Josie was surprised to see Kyle's mother's Mercedes-Benz parked in the driveway.

Josie knew her stomach was a barometer of her emotions. When she was nervous or excited, it rumbled like a San Francisco trolley car. When she was upset or angry, it ached. As soon as she spotted Mrs. Richards's car, a sharp pain stabbed at her insides. Her first thought was, "I wonder what that woman is doing to make my life miserable."

The gate leading to the patio and side door of the house was open. She found Kyle and his mother sitting in the kitchen drinking wine. He immediately got up, and welcomed Josie with a hug and a glass of cabernet.

She took a sip and sat on the stool beside his mother. "What's up?" she asked, looking over the rim of the goblet at Mrs. Richards.

"Mom's worried about Beth. My daughter wants to stay with a girlfriend near the college instead of living with her grandmother," Kyle explained. His tone said he didn't have a problem with it.

Mrs. Richards held out her glass so Kyle could fill it again but set it on the table untouched before saying, "That child should be at home with her father. She's too young to be out on her own."

Her manicured nails tapped nervously on the side of the wine bottle as she spoke. Josie stared at the enormous diamond ring on her finger and thought the woman sounded distraught but judging from her appearance she probably hadn't rushed out of her mansion in the middle of the night in a grandmotherly panic. She was smartly dressed in a black silk pantsuit with a string of pearls, high heels, and a perfectly coiffed hairstyle. This was a performance for her son's benefit and Josie wasn't about to fake interest or take it seriously.

"I'm going to bed," Josie said, finishing her wine and adding with a forced smile, "G'night."

"But don't you agree, Josie?" Mrs. Richards asked before she could get away.

"Not really. Beth is a smart, resourceful girl. She's more than capable of living away from home," Josie said on her way into the bathroom, before closing the door.

She could hear Kyle and his mother talking as she stepped into the shower, but by the time she finished, put on her nightshirt, and went back into the kitchen, he was alone.

"Are you worried about Beth?" she asked when he didn't say anything right away. She had to admit to herself she was a little annoyed and concerned his mother would continue to jump in and out of their lives attempting to draw him away from a marriage she clearly didn't like or want, and she'd forever use Beth as an excuse to intrude in their business.

"Nope," he said filling her glass again.

"Are you going to force Beth to live here with us?"

"Nope."

Josie stared at him for a few seconds before grinning and asking, "Did you kill your mother and bury her under the fire pit?"

"Not yet. I'm going to marry you and we're going to live here alone. Beth has her own life. I'll help her out any way I can, but I told my mother in my loving and endearing way to butt out of our lives."

They went to bed and she fell asleep in his arms. Her world had taken an unexpected turn. The police department had become a place of turmoil and hidden land mines, but her personal life was suddenly somewhere she was excited about and happy to be.

The next morning Kyle was up at five A.M., and his alarm woke her too. Josie figured since she was stirring she might as well get dressed and go watch Pasadena PD try to find Marvin Wright again. There was no expectation on her part that the missing cop would be at this new location. She was beginning to think either Pasadena had terrible informants, their timing was off, or someone in that police department was warning Marvin, giving him an opportunity to escape.

An hour later she was sitting in her car a half block away watching two plainclothes Pasadena detectives walk up to the front door of room number nine at the Royal Oak Motel on Venice Boulevard. The single-story motel had rows of rooms on either side of a courtyard cluttered with piles of bulging black garbage bags, old tires, broken toys, bicycles, and other debris. The outer walls of the building had been tagged with fresh gang graffiti and the rooms had several broken or boarded-up windows. Kyle's car was parked in front of hers, closer to the motel, but he had agreed to hang back unless the other agency requested assistance.

Another Pasadena officer had gone to the back of the building in case Marvin tried to climb out one of the rear windows. Josie had programed her radio for their frequency and was surprised how little these guys communicated. She had her car window open and heard one of them pound on the door, identify himself as the police, and demand they be allowed to enter. The man in back had never said he was in position. There was silence for a few seconds; the detective knocked louder and shouted "Police!" Silence again, followed by a volley of gunshots as the windows to the right of the door shattered.

The two detectives scrambled away from the door ducking under windows to find cover behind a retaining wall.

"Officer needs help shots fired," one of the detectives was shouting into his radio, but he was on Pasadena's frequency. No one in LA would hear him.

As she got out of her car, Josie switched to Wilshire's frequency and heard Kyle's calm voice repeating, "Officer needs help, shots fired at . . ." And he continued with the exact address. She and Kyle approached the motel together with weapons drawn and as they reached the sidewalk in front of the location, Josie heard several more shots as well as sirens approaching.

She switched back to Pasadena's frequency and asked, "Officer to the rear of Royal Oak Motel. It's Palmer, isn't it? What's your status?"

"Yes, ma'am, shots fired. I'm pinned in a bad spot," he shouted. His voice was nervous, excited, scared.

"You're gonna be all right, Palmer. Where's the shooter now?" she asked, looking for a safe route to get behind the building.

"I . . . I think he's in the alcove . . . might be a laundry room."

Kyle waved at her from the far end of the courtyard. He pointed to a walkway she could use to reach him without being in the line of fire. She did and when they were together, they crouched below the windows moving quickly behind the motel.

She keyed the radio again when they stopped behind a shed that had been pushed against the wall a few yards from the back window of room nine. "Where are you Palmer?" she asked as she heard sirens, shouting, and car doors slamming in the street.

"I'm on the other side of his room near a broken-down incinerator in somebody's backyard. Sorry, I think he got away."

Kyle ran toward him as uniform officers from several LAPD divisions, the sheriff's, and highway patrol swarmed into the backyard. They cleared the motel and the laundry room, but once again Marvin Wright, or whoever was in that room, had gone.

Officer Palmer wasn't wounded by gunfire. When he dove behind the incinerator he broke his ankle on the concrete blocks and couldn't move. A total of ten rounds had been fired from a .45-semiauto handgun and all the casings were recovered. Four shots were discharged from inside room nine and went through the front windows into the high wall across the courtyard; six shots were fired as the shooter climbed out the bedroom window, ran through the laundry room, and fled on Venice Boulevard either on foot or in a vehicle. It was anybody's guess where those last six shots landed. Josie suspected trees, birds, or parked cars were the likely victims of wild gunfire. The motel was surrounded by private homes, but luckily no one was injured.

A good description was provided by Officer Palmer, but he claimed to have seen two men running away and didn't know which one was firing the weapon. One was a lumbering, overweight black man who Palmer tentatively identified as Marvin Wright. The other matched the description of either of Marvin's muscular bodyguards.

"Looks like Tweedledee or Tweedledum might still be doing Marvin's bidding," Josie said. "I wonder how he manages to stay out of sight with the Hulk twins following him around."

It was early afternoon and she was drinking coffee, waiting with Kyle on the front seat of his car while Wilshire detectives and RHD finished their crime scene investigation.

"Don't know, but this shootout tells me Marvin's not only nuts but he's dangerous. I'm beginning to think Jorge Sanchez might've been right. The West LA ambush, firebombing your house, I can see now he's capable of doing those things and probably worse," Kyle said, looking worried.

"By 'probably worse,' do you mean killing Howard Burke?"

"I believe he could've done that," he said and asked, "Don't you?"

"Don't know what I believe anymore. I can't convince myself that Burke's killing wasn't somehow connected to Anthony Charles and the other murders off Santa Monica. Isn't it strange that Marvin would kill Burke in that particular parking lot?"

"Why not?"

"Marvin has no connection to Hollywood. We can't prove he knew Anthony or any of the other victims killed in that area."

"You're the connection; you fired him. He has a reason to come after you. Maybe he stumbled on Burke while planning his revenge."

"So instead of killing me he decides to burn down my house?"

"He didn't know you weren't home. That fire could've easily killed you."

Josie closed her eyes and leaned back against the headrest. Kyle was right but she'd always trusted her instincts and his scenario wasn't working for her. Marvin was a classic screw-up and not clever enough to commit the perfect crime. If he was guilty, there should've been a ton of evidence pointing at him for Burke's murder and the other crimes, but there was nothing—no fingerprints, no murder weapon, no witnesses.

Her first stop when she finally got to Hollywood station was the detective squad room, but Behan wasn't there. She was hoping Marge had taken Anthony's photo downtown to SID, but when she checked the vice office she found Behan and his wife, Vicky, sitting in the lieutenant's office talking with Marge. They all looked up as soon as she entered the room and it was too late to slip away unnoticed. Josie knew Vicky was unhappy about her husband still working in Hollywood after his retirement party, and she'd made it clear to anyone who'd listen she blamed Josie for not sending him home.

"I don't want to interrupt. I'll catch you later," Josie said, doing a perfect about-face.

"Come back, Captain. I want to talk to you," Vicky demanded.

Josie heard Behan groan and Marge snicker.

"How are you, Vicky? Sorry to delay the retirement plans, but . . ."

"Stop the bullshit, Josie. We both know you're not sorry," Vicky said. The wealthy matron who shopped on Rodeo Road, ate at the finest restaurants, drove a new Rolls-Royce, and in every way imaginable lived a life of luxury, had just thrown down the "how can you do this to me" gauntlet.

Josie needed only a second to drag another chair into Marge's office, put it directly in front of Behan's wife, and sit.

"You're right, Vicky," she said without emotion. "I really don't care about your retirement plans. I like you, but I need Red a little longer. He'll have the rest of his life to figure out how to live without doing the work he loves, but not until he catches my serial killer. I know this pisses you off and I'm sorry about that, but you'll just have to live with it." Behan's wife stared at her as if she'd just witnessed a terrible accident. Josie didn't wait for a response, picked up the chair, and put it back in the vice office before leaving.

Vicky hadn't said a word, but Josie knew from Behan's stories the woman had a temper, and she expected to feel something hard hit the back of her head as she walked out, but managed to escape unscathed. There goes my invitation to Miss Vicky's next fancy dinner party, Josie thought, as she walked through the records section toward her office. It was a joke to herself because she felt bad, not for his wife but for Behan. He needed to be away from this place for his physical and mental well-being, but she wasn't going to let that happen . . . not yet.

EIGHTEEN

There had never been much time in Josie's life for a husband and son. Police work was the kind of addiction that consumed nearly all her waking hours. She had loved Jake and certainly David but couldn't find a way to balance their needs with those of the LAPD. She did try but failed miserably, and Jake left her. David didn't. Her son seemed to have survived his nearly motherless childhood and as an adult for some mysterious reason wanted to remain a part of her life.

After she'd accepted Kyle's proposal, Josie had intended to tell David about the pending marriage but couldn't seem to find the right time. Her son called several hours after she'd retreated from Miss Vicky's tirade in the vice office, and he asked to meet her at their Pasadena house. The firebombing had done extensive damage to the family home, but he volunteered to oversee the repairs and had hired a full-time contractor, gotten help from several friends, and even did some of the work himself when he wasn't at the restaurant. It was far from finished, but he was eager to unveil what had been done. She wasn't looking forward to paying the invoices for all the work he'd arranged but figured that evening might be the perfect opportunity to tell him not only about the marriage but her intention to sell the house.

It was dinner time and if she got lucky they might even be able to have a meal together without a call from work to spoil it.

She could see some of the changes as soon as she parked in the driveway. The porch was bigger and much nicer with new posts, wood slat flooring, and new patio furniture. They hadn't talked about buying new furniture. The outside of the house and trim was in the process of being painted, a new bay window was being installed, and the landscaped yard looked much better than she remembered it. The insurance would pay for most of it, but she pictured the tally on her expenses increasing rapidly.

"Hi, Mom," David said, opening the new front door with costly etched glass windows. "Come on in."

Josie stood in the doorway and looked around the foyer and into the den—new wood floors were partly installed, different color on the walls with some of David's oil paintings in prominent places. At least the artistic improvements wouldn't leave her impoverished. The dining room was being freshly painted with more of his art work hung. The kitchen had new granite counters, a farm sink, an almost completed island, and all new stainless-steel appliances. Whose house is this, she thought, and who the hell is going to pay for all these extras?

She waited a few seconds to control her anxiety before asking, "Okay, David, it's beautiful, but what do I have to hock or borrow to afford all this when it's finished?"

"Nothing, sit down, I'll explain."

She did, and he made her a proposition. He had already paid for most of the improvements and repairs over and above her home insurance coverage and now wanted to buy the house. He would make payments to her if she agreed.

"Truth is, Mom, I've already moved in here."

"I told you to stay away. It's dangerous," she said.

"I know but the first thing I did was install an alarm system, motion lights, and security cameras. It's safe. I know you and Kyle are getting married so you don't really need this house anymore, but if you say no that's okay too. I'll move out and you can come back," he said and seemed to mean it. "I'll finish the improvements and they'll be my wedding gift."

"No," she said, shaking her head. "I . . . I want you to have it . . . no payments. How did you know I was getting married?"

"Men talk, Mom," he said, wrinkling his forehead, and she tried not to smile. "But I insist on making it a real sale with payments or I won't stay."

"Okay, fine, pay me, but make sure you keep that security system working. Where did you get the money to do all of this?"

"I've saved to buy my own place, but while I've been fixing up this one, I fell in love with it. I understand why you wanted to stay on after the divorce. Kyle asked me to be his best man, so I figured you'd probably want to sell now."

He showed her what was already done in the rest of the house and Josie was impressed with changes he'd made in such a short time and those he planned to do. She felt happy knowing he might have a family there, even if it meant tolerating someone like his tiny irritating ex-girlfriend.

"Have you heard from Kizzie?" she asked, hoping the relationship was finally over.

"No, she's moved on. Have you guys set a date yet?" he asked, changing the subject too quickly.

"Moved on to what?"

"Let it go, Mom."

"Let what go?"

They were in his piano room on the second floor. The baby grand had been moved from his apartment back where it belonged. He sat on the bench and said, "It's so exasperating when you do that. Stop asking; obviously I don't want to talk about this."

"Why not," she persisted.

"Because I think Kizzie's staying with dad in San Francisco."

"Perfect," Josie said sarcastically. "You're right; it's not worth talking about. Let's get something to eat and celebrate your new house."

"Thought I'd make dinner here. It's almost a chef's kitchen and I have a special meal planned for us."

He opened a bottle of pinot noir from a built-in wine rack in the kitchen. While he prepared the lamb, they drank and ate hors d'oeuvres she recognized from the menu at his restaurant. She sat near the island and watched him work, thinking that unlike his painting or music, cooking seemed to make him happy. It was obvious he was showing off, but his culinary skills were impressive. They talked and laughed, hunched over the plywood covering the island while eating out of pans as the food came out of the oven or off the stove, using dish towels as napkins. Her son had inherited her appetite so they finished a good portion of the lamb, roasted potatoes, broccoli, and several glasses of wine before cleaning up and afterward taking their coffee and crème brûlée into the den.

It was the first time in weeks she'd had an opportunity to relax and be around him without distractions. He was upbeat refusing to dwell in the past and excited about his future, even thanked her for making him independent enough to deal with life. She was having such a great time the phone call from Hollywood was inevitable. Call-outs had always intruded on their time together or came in the middle of good movies, excellent dinners, or a much-needed night's sleep.

The watch commander apologized and said, "Captain, this isn't in our division but Lieutenant Richards, the watch commander in Wilshire, said I should notify you."

"What happened?" Josie asked and felt the rack of lamb tumbling in her intestines. "Is he okay?"

"Yes, ma'am, the shooting was in West LA. He said the patrol captain there . . . I guess he lives in the division, shot a guy trying to break into his house. Lieutenant Richards said you'd want to know and to tell you he's on scene."

Josie gulped the rest of her coffee and asked, "Did Richards mention the suspect's name?"

"No, ma'am, sorry, didn't ask."

She got another mug of black coffee from the kitchen and finished it while she explained to David why she had to leave. He walked out with her to the city car and she watched him standing in the driveway until she drove around the corner. There was something sad, Josie thought, about leaving this house tonight knowing it wasn't hers any longer. Decades of worrying about plumbing, electric bills, mice in the attic, or how her creative, awkward little boy could possibly survive, not to mention succeed, in the world without her guidance and protection were over.

"Damn," she said, staring at herself in the rearview mirror. "I'm practically emancipated."

JORGE SANCHEZ had been leasing a one-story Spanish-style bungalow in the West LA area where practically every house on his street looked like the one next door—stucco walls, banana trees, and tile roofs. Permit parking, security signs on the lawns, and tiny overgrown yards with high walls were the norm.

Below the stop sign on every corner a placard warning "Neighborhood Watch" was prominently displayed, but serious criminals knew it was mostly a police PR gimmick. Burglars were willing to take the risk in this trendy area that attracted successful millennials who had rooms full of computers and digital devices left unattended most of the day while they worked long hours to buy better computers and more digital devices.

Black-and-whites with lights flashing were parked in front of the house and others were maneuvering to get out of the narrow street when Josie arrived. West LA detectives in their shirtsleeves were walking around the yard with flashlights even though this house was on the corner and directly under a streetlight. Jorge had installed motion lights that were staying on tonight with the constant foot traffic in and out of the house.

She located Kyle on an enclosed porch off the living room talking with Deputy Chief Dempsey and West LA's Area Captain Stuart Ames, Jorge's boss.

"Captain Corsino," Dempsey called cheerfully as soon as he noticed her. "Looks like our boy may have put a dent in Marvin Wright's reign of terror."

Before she could ask what the hell he was talking about, Kyle interjected, "One of Marvin's bodyguards came after Sanchez. Jorge shot and killed him."

Josie heard the words but it was taking a few seconds for them to sink in.

"He came here," she said.

"Why's that so hard to understand. He tried to kill Sanchez before," Captain Ames said.

"We don't know that . . . besides it was more like warning shots," she said. "If Jorge hadn't panicked and crashed, he might've gotten out of the whole thing without a scratch."

"Wright or one of his henchmen tried to barbeque you in your sleep," Dempsey said, interrupting her, his voice getting louder. "And look what he did to those poor Pasadena cops . . . and Howard Burke for Christ's sake. Would've been Jorge lying on the kitchen floor in his own damn blood if he hadn't heard glass breaking."

"Excuse me, sir," she said, walking away while touching the automatic dial on her phone for the Pasadena house. She knew David had a good security system now but she wanted to warn him to be extra cautious. He promised he would, but she called Pasadena PD, explained the circumstances, and they agreed to have a patrol car periodically check on her son's house.

"Where's Jorge?" she asked, moving back toward Kyle, who was still standing near Dempsey, but watching her.

She wanted to stay away from her boss, who seemed on the edge of a meltdown. Josie worried she might be the catalyst for his near hysteria. Dempsey liked things simple and was eager to accept the obvious as true. He always told her he really hated that she questioned everything. It was an old habit from her days as a working detective, one that had saved her from making stupid decisions on numerous occasions.

Kyle led her to a bedroom in the back of the house where Sanchez was talking with two older detectives. He looked scared, a little jumpy, and went over to her as soon as she entered the room. The detectives started to object, but he pulled rank and insisted he needed to talk to Josie. They did leave the room after Josie introduced herself and asked if she and Kyle could speak with Sanchez alone for a few minutes, assuring them it wouldn't be about the shooting.

"Shit, Josie, I didn't have a choice," Sanchez said as soon as the door closed. "He had a gun. He was going to kill me. Dumb asshole broke into my home. What's gonna happen to me?"

"Calm down, Jorge, they'll probably give you a medal. It'll be fine. You were protecting yourself. You didn't do anything wrong," she said, trying to quiet him. She knew he'd never been in a shooting and guessed his heart and head had to be pounding. Most cops only hear gunfire when they're wearing ear protectors on the shooting range. The noise in a real gunfight is deafening, especially inside a house. Adrenaline peaks; nerves are raw and senses enhanced for hours after the danger is over; then the body seems to deflate like a blow-up doll. Jorge's reaction was slightly different. He appeared excited and hyper, but she knew not everyone responded the same way.

His hands were trembling. It was a warm night and he was wearing a tank top and shorts but sweat had soaked through under his arms and down the front of his shirt. Drops of perspiration dotted his forehead, rolled down the sides of his face. Kyle had been in the military in the Middle East and had been involved in several shooting incidents throughout his LAPD career. He distracted Sanchez, talked to him, joked with him for a few seconds until the man almost seemed to revert to his cocky self again.

The two detectives from Force Investigation came back into the room, said they would finish the interview in their office, and asked Sanchez to dress and come with them.

"He's a mess," Josie said, as she and Kyle watched Sanchez leave his house with the detectives.

"Unlike you and me, Corsino, most cops, especially captains and above, have never had to use their weapon except to qualify," Kyle said. "Besides he's more hyped than scared. I kind of think he's enjoying the moment."

"What makes you say that?" Josie asked. She thought Sanchez looked a little unhinged and would never have said he was having a good time.

"Can't say, just a feeling. Some guys feed on the rush and then they might feel bad later."

One of the homicide detectives called her name from the kitchen, and she left the room but kept wondering why anyone would think that about Jorge. She understood Kyle had more experience in these situations than she did, but she'd known Jorge Sanchez for a long time and would've bet he was the sort of man who'd be sickened by having to take a life.

Josie didn't have time to give their conversation much thought. As soon as she got to the door of the kitchen, she saw the body of Marvin's bodyguard sprawled on the floor in front of the refrigerator. He was a big man, maybe six foot five or taller and more overweight than muscular. No one had told her how many times he'd been shot but it looked as if Sanchez had unloaded his semiauto and most of the rounds appeared to have found the target. A pool of blood was spreading from under the body and blood had splattered on the cupboards and appliances. He still loosely held a .45 semiauto in his hand but, according to the detective, he never got a round off before Sanchez killed him.

The same detective showed her the back door where the glass had been broken and the intruder had apparently reached in and opened the deadbolt.

"Where was Sanchez when he fired his weapon?" Kyle asked. He had been standing quietly behind her until now and had what she thought was a puzzled expression.

"Down the hallway, about where the bathroom door is."

"What are you thinking?" Josie asked. She could tell something was bothering him.

He didn't answer, turned, and walked back through the hallway until he reached the bathroom door.

"That's some good shooting," Kyle said when he returned to the kitchen.

Josie stepped into the hallway and looked at the door frame and the walls around the opening on that side. There wasn't a mark, not one errant bullet had damaged the wood or the plaster.

"I'm guessing Captain Sanchez might've actually been a little closer," the detective said, his eyes narrowing to a look of disapproval. "He's really upset and all he remembers for sure is he was standing somewhere in the hallway when he started shooting. He kicked casings all over the floor, but I marked a few spots where brass ejected and dinged the wall . . . I'd calculate he was closer."

She stayed another hour while the detectives and shooting team worked in and around Sanchez's house. Kyle had to return to Wilshire, but he'd planted a seed of doubt in her brain that kept her there watching the examination of the shooting scene and wondering if a man she trusted, her protégé, had been completely honest about what had happened. She'd been a captain long enough to know fear makes some cops do incredibly stupid things. It wasn't far-fetched to wonder if Marvin Wright's bodyguard standing in his kitchen might've panicked Jorge enough to make him shoot first and concoct a cover story later.

NINETEEN

Josie woke at six the next morning without an alarm. She got out of bed, carefully sliding out from under Kyle's arm, attempting not to disturb him. It was after midnight when she had fallen asleep and he still hadn't come home. She didn't know how long he'd been in bed but didn't want to wake him.

It would be busy today and she wanted to get to Hollywood early. Behan and his detectives had to start providing some answers or the chief of police was certain to take the investigation away before Red retired.

She took a shower, had breakfast, and checked on Kyle again before leaving. He hadn't moved and was snoring softly in a deep sleep. It was difficult not kissing him goodbye but she knew that would wake him and probably begin a chain of events that would put her back in bed and late to work. The time they spent together seemed to be shrinking, and text messages were a poor substitute for intimacy.

Behan was in her office with Marge and Mac when she arrived. They already had read preliminary reports from the West LA shooting and the background workup detectives had done on the intruder.

"Our dead guy was an ex-con, big surprise," Behan said, pushing the stack of reports toward an empty chair at the worktable. "Jerome Handy hit the weight stacks in prison, but a lot of that muscle had turned to fat. He was almost three hundred pounds of flab."

"Got a tail?" Josie asked, standing in front of the reports.

"Yep, still on parole from San Quentin for robbery, and he did time for assault with a deadly weapon, burglary, dealing heroin, stealing cars . . . your typical renaissance dipshit," Marge said.

"How about the gun?"

"They're testing it for a match with the Burke homicide and Sanchez ambush at West LA . . . for now, all we know is it's the right caliber," Behan said.

"We got the bodyguard but where's fucking Waldo?" Marge asked. "That nut job Marvin's not smart enough to stay hidden this long on his own."

"We've done background on the other bodyguard too," Behan said, ignoring Marge. "Tyler Jones has a hefty rap sheet but no hard time and nothing violent. You mind if I borrow Mac for a couple of hours to help on computer stuff. We're running a little thin."

She looked at Mac who was staring intently at his coffee mug.

"I think you should leave him out of this," Josie said, knowing computer work could lead to checking out a few things and inevitably to hooking up suspects and dragging them off to jail.

"He won't leave the building," Behan said. "I swear."

"I don't think it's a good idea," she said.

Behan got up and whispered in her ear, "He needs to do this."

Josie sighed and said, "Okay, but absolutely nothing in the field." Behan frowned and she got serious. "I mean it, Red. If we challenge Dempsey on this, he'll make certain Mac never sees the light of day. Keep him inside."

"Yes, ma'am," Behan said curtly.

"It's your future, McSweeney. Don't screw this up. Okay?" she asked, glaring at her adjutant who finally looked up at her.

"Yes, ma'am, I'll do what I can for the detectives whenever you don't need me," Mac said.

"We should let West LA and Force Investigation worry about the shooting last night, but we need to follow up on the dead guy's contacts, find that other bodyguard, and track down Marvin," Josie said. "If Jerome's gun turns out to be the murder weapon, he might not have had a reason to kill Howard Burke or Sanchez but it points directly back to Marvin."

When she finished, Behan got up and left her office with Mac following a step behind. After they'd gone, Marge sat behind the mahogany desk and watched quietly as Josie went through the stack of reports left on the table.

"What do you think?" Marge asked as Josie turned over the last page.

"Wonder how he found out where Jorge lived."

"Marvin was a cop. He's probably still got contacts in the department or a cousin or auntie in the DMV or some other government office that can get him information. He found your house without a problem."

"There's been nothing to prove my house fire or the ambush on Sanchez had anything to do with Marvin."

"Nothing but fucking common sense," Marge said, getting up and sitting at the table beside Josie. "Burke gets killed, Sanchez gets shot at, your house nearly burned down, and Marvin's bodyguard breaks into Sanchez's house with a gun . . . don't you think that might be more than a coincidence?"

"Maybe."

"Damn it, Boss, open your eyes. Marvin Wright is LAPD's resident lunatic with a fucking vendetta against your board of rights and probably Kyle Richards for sending him there."

"Maybe," Josie said. "But it doesn't feel right."

She wanted to explain but wasn't sure why she felt that way. Marvin Wright was the obvious suspect, especially after last night. If Jerome's gun turned out to be the weapon that killed Howard Burke, there would be little room for doubt.

Marge stood and paced near the table before saying, "Great, so what's your theory."

"Haven't got one. I just think Marvin's too stupid to do all those things and not leave a single clue. It's almost as if someone is trying to divert our attention."

"From what?"

"A serial killer. I can't believe it was chance that Howard Burke got shot in that particular parking lot so close to the other killings."

Marge's eyes opened wide; she inhaled, raised both arms in frustration, and dropped onto the couch, exhaling loudly.

"What's new with the cape? Was SID able to help with the label?" Josie asked. She didn't want to argue about speculation. The facts would eventually lead them where they needed to be.

"It was manufactured in a costume warehouse in Burbank near the studios, and they've got an invoice that shows half a dozen of their black capes were shipped to

Ozzie's on Hollywood Boulevard in October last year just before Halloween."

"Have you followed up with Ozzie's?"

"Yep, the manager says she sold three of them, two on credit cards and one for cash. Credit cards are both old queens who can hardly walk and the capes are still hanging in their closets.

"What about the cash sale?"

"Probably our guy. He wore dark glasses, a Dodgers baseball cap, a hoodie, and Levi's. She remembers he was tall, dark skin, maybe black, maybe Latino . . . soft spoken. She said he was wearing what looked like expensive black leather dress shoes which she thought was weird given the rest of his outfit."

"Nothing else, no car, no jewelry?" Josie asked, and Marge shook her head. She was frustrated with the lack of leads. "Did you show her Marvin's picture?"

"Couldn't say it was him. Couldn't say it wasn't, but she did tell me the next night someone broke into her store and stole a couple of costumes. One was an expensive matador jacket that wasn't for sale. It was displayed on a mannequin."

"Touch bases with the burglary table."

"Already did. The fucker was smart enough to cut the telephone line for the security system, broke the back window, and climbed in. No prints but there was fresh blood on the ledge so he might've cut himself. Don't think Marvin could get his fat ass up there but we'll do the DNA shit on him if we can get a sample."

Josie picked up the stack of reports and dropped them on Marge's lap.

"Take these back to Red. I've got captain stuff to do," she said.

"Yes ma'am," Marge said, not moving for several seconds and staring out toward the admin office.

"What?" Josie asked, sitting behind her desk and turning on the computer.

"You'll see," Marge said, sliding off the couch and grinning at her. When she was outside the door, Josie heard her say, "Morning, Chief."

Dempsey marched into the office a few seconds later. He didn't bother with small talk but sat on the corner of Josie's desk.

"I've ordered a Metro detail to be stationed at your house overnight and another one for Sanchez until Wright is caught. No argument this time. Pasadena PD's already been notified," he said, staring at her as if prepared to do battle.

"Great idea," she said. "The house has a new security system and motion lights, but I'll sleep better knowing they're watching."

She didn't intend to tell him she wasn't living there any longer. David would have the benefit of armed security and she and Kyle could keep their privacy and peace of mind in Long Beach knowing her son was safe.

The deputy chief looked confused by her immediate cooperation and seemed disappointed there wasn't an argument, but he recovered quickly and slid off the desk. The pliability of a simple mind is a thing to behold, Josie thought.

"Okay, that's settled. I've ordered Wilshire to put together a task force and I want you to cooperate with them to find Wright . . . we'll turn over whatever rock that maniac is hiding under."

"Who's heading up the task force?" she asked, seeing another headache.

"Lieutenant Richards, he's been working with Pasadena PD trying to find Wright anyway so he's got a head start . . . he's acting patrol captain . . . supposed to be a pretty sharp guy."

"Perfect," Josie said, trying not to smile. Although she and Kyle were always together at every department function, she knew Dempsey would be oblivious to the fact they were a couple. Despite the chief's frequent declarations of concern about his subordinates, he wasn't all that interested in their lives, which in this case was a benefit.

"Find this animal before he kills again," Dempsey said in his most authoritative voice.

"We can't actually prove he killed Burke."

"Well, I'm convinced he did. This isn't the time to be stubborn, Corsino. Arrest him and throw him in jail," Dempsey said, becoming agitated, again.

Knowing he didn't like his decisions challenged, she was about to elaborate on how none of the evidence pointed to Marvin Wright in the Burke murder when Behan knocked on the open office door and came in without waiting for an invitation.

"Morning, Boss, Chief," Behan said, nodding at Dempsey and handing Josie a single sheet of paper. "This is the report on the gun Jerome Handy was carrying last night. It's a match for the weapon that killed Burke and the same one used to ambush Jorge outside West LA station."

"And he's Marvin Wright's bodyguard buddy," Dempsey said, getting excited. "So, Captain, we do have proof Marvin is behind all of this." He clapped his hands once in victory. "Good work, detective."

"Not me, sir. If Captain Sanchez hadn't dumped Jerome's ass, we might've never recovered the gun."

"Right, right, well get with Wilshire, Corsino, and keep Sergeant Scott in the loop," Dempsey said as he left her office.

"What's he talking about with Wilshire?" Behan asked.

She told him about the task force and Kyle's involvement. Behan seemed pleased about the prospect of working with Richards again. They had investigated more than one case together when Kyle was a sergeant in Hollywood. Like Jorge Sanchez, Kyle Richards was one of the few people who had the type of personality that didn't irritate the grumpy detective.

"This report changes everything," Josie said, giving him back the paper.

"It's the gun that killed Burke, but Jerome's on a slab in the morgue and can't explain how or why it was in his possession. We're trying to track the history of the gun, but my guess is it's stolen, a throwaway."

"So where are we with the Matador killings?" Josie asked.

"Mookie finally admitted he stole that chain and pendant from one of our other victims. It's so cheap we haven't been able to trace it anyway. Everything he gave us on Matador was most likely gossip, but he swore Jesse Mata was the name Anthony Charles gave when he talked about his lover."

"There's got to be somebody on the street who knows or has seen this guy."

"I'm going to the High-Top Bar this afternoon. There's a waitress-bartender working there that Mookie says knows Jesse Mata," Behan said and looked at the floor before asking, "Can I take Mac?"

"Hell no," Josie answered quickly. "Boy, that didn't take long."

"Fine, can you come? Marge is tracking down a lead on the matador costume, and Mookie said the waitress likely would be more willing to talk to a woman."

Josie had work to do. She should have told him to find someone from one of the other detective tables, but they both knew she rarely turned down an opportunity to do police work and feel the adrenaline rush that only comes with the hunt.

Mookie had called the waitress from the jail phone and she was expecting Behan before the bar opened in a few hours. Her apartment was on the floor above the High-Top and she agreed to be interviewed only if he came there, where she felt safe. She told him to use the back stairs and not to park in the lot behind the bar.

There were plenty of parking spots close by, but Behan used a public parking garage half a block down the street. He wanted to be certain the police car was nowhere near her apartment. They walked in the alley behind buildings maneuvering around and over the trash and belongings of homeless men and women who were living out of sight of the uniformed footbeats or patrol cars on the boulevard. They were tucked in near the dumpsters or had attached cheap tents or tarps to the fences to make shelters. Sleeping bags and articles of clothing were draped over the fence to air out or dry. The smell of trash and makeshift toilets was magnified by unwashed human bodies.

The inhabitants of this world seemed oblivious to the presence of two outsiders and aside from a quick hard glare from one or two, they went about their business of doing whatever they did to kill time.

Josie picked up her pace until they passed the encampment. She had a touchy stomach and knew her insides could tolerate the awful smell only so long before its rumbling contents erupted onto the asphalt.

The back steps of the High-Top were steel and narrow leading up to a landing and the second-story door. There was another entry on the first level that led to the bar's storage room. Both Josie and Behan had been inside the business on numerous occasions and knew the layout but she hadn't realized there was an apartment on the second floor.

Josie waited on the landing for Behan to slowly make the steep trek up the stairs. After years of jogging and work-related abuse, his knees were in bad shape. It was painful for him to climb and she could hear the stream of expletives after the first few steps.

She gave him a few seconds to catch his breath before knocking on the metal security screen. The door was closed too and there wasn't a doorbell.

"Who's there?" a strong female voice asked from the other side of the door.

"Detective Behan," he shouted.

The wooden door opened slowly and she peeked out before removing the chain and opening it again. She unlocked the security screen and held it for them to enter. Behan introduced himself and Josie, and the woman said her name was Judy.

It was a small cluttered room with what looked like a Murphy bed, open and unmade, taking up most of the space, with a couch close beside it covered in boxes and clothes. A sink and counter were in the corner with a hot plate, microwave, and coffee maker. A large steel clothes cart overburdened by too many outfits jammed on the rod was in front of the only window. There was one other door that probably led to the bathroom.

"Mind?" Josie asked as she opened that door and saw a toilet, sink, and narrow shower.

"What are you doing?" Judy asked, moving toward the bathroom.

"Making sure we're alone," Josie said, closing the door again. "Don't like surprises."

"Look, I been thinking . . . maybe this ain't such a good idea," Judy said, nervously looking toward the window. She was a pretty woman, not in the traditional sense but she had shoulder-length brown hair in a feathered cut, clear tanned skin, big dark eyes, and a slender figure. She might've been in her early thirties but her features were hard, someone who'd seen and understood the darker side of life.

"If you can help us find this guy, you might save lives," Behan said.

"Yeah, but I ain't no hero, and I like breathing," she said, sitting on the bed. She pointed at the couch and said, "Just throw some a that crap on the floor if you wanna park yourself somewhere."

Behan made a little room, and they sat within a foot of the bed.

"It's good to be careful, but nobody has to know you helped us. We can put you somewhere safe until this guy is caught if that's what you want," Josie said.

Judy studied Josie as if she were trying to figure her out then asked, "You the boss?"

"In Hollywood, yes," Josie said. "But I can arrange to get you anywhere you want to go."

"I ain't going nowhere. Prick needs to die."

"You know him?" Behan asked.

"I seen him with The Prince, here in the club."

"You knew Anthony Charles?"

"I knew him; I knew poor Uncle Howie and most of those boulevard kids that got themselves killed . . . I know Prince's brother, Eddie, too, that creepy piece a work." Her expression made it clear the mention of Ed Charles's name left a bad taste in her mouth.

"What do you mean 'creepy'?" Behan asked, giving Josie a quick look.

Judy wiggled closer toward the edge of the bed and said in almost a whisper, "What I mean is him hanging around this bar all the time watching his brother like some kinda gestapo or something. Anybody can tell he's more queer than Prince."

"Did you ever see Eddie try to pick up one of the boys or get friendly with any of them?" Behan asked.

"Nah, not Mr. High and Mighty fancy pants . . . too busy lookin' down his nose at all of us peasants . . . like his shit don't stink. I figured he did his hunting in the classier establishments. All he did here was spy on his brother."

"And Jessie Mata, you know him?" Josie asked. She was thinking they might've struck an information gold mine with this woman.

"Yeah, him too."

"Does he still come here?"

"Nah, not since Howie got his head blown off in the parking lot. Lotsa the regulars stopped comin' then."

"Has Ed Charles been back since his brother died?" Josie asked.

"Nope, so something good come outta it."

"Tell us what you know about Jesse Mata," Behan said.

"For starters, I know that ain't his real name. He told me it was his mother's name. Lotsa Mexican guys do that to fuck with immigration. Before you ask, I don't know his real name."

"What else? What does he look like? Where does he live? Who were his friends?" Behan asked. Josie could see he was becoming impatient for details.

"Whoa, big boy, I know you redheads got a short fuse but don't push me. I said I'd tell you everything and I will," Judy said, reaching over and patting his thigh in a very familiar manner.

"Sorry," Behan said.

That's a first, Josie thought, watching Behan's bright pink blush.

"He's Mexican, brags about it. Tall, dark skin, darker than most Mexicans I seen, good body and he knows it. That's why he wears that asinine bullfighter coat every chance he gets. Some of the boys say he's got black hair and dark eyes, but he always keeps his head and eyes covered in the bar."

"Is he a cop?"

"That's what Prince, what Anthony told me one time when he was high and talking too much as usual," she said with a half-smile that faded into an angry sneer when she added, "Mata is a vicious sonofabitch; I know that much."

"Why do you say that?" Josie asked.

"Those dead boys, three of them died right after they left here with Mata. I warned Anthony but he was so messed up . . . I don't think he cared. Sometimes I think that kid wanted to die."

"Where does Mata stay?"

"Rumor is he takes his boys to some dumpy rat-infested motel on La Brea. Koreans own it . . . looks and smells like a kimchi outhouse, but he for sure don't live there. Believe me, this dude's got money."

"How do you know?" Behan asked.

"I seen him wearing a Rolex and a gold chain this thick around his neck," she said, holding her thumb and forefinger about a half-inch wide, and bounced once on the bed before saying, "Oh, yeah, one time he had this ring on his right hand when he orders a beer, but when he gets another one, it's gone, so I'm thinkin' he forgot to take it off and puts it in his pocket maybe because he didn't want nobody to see it."

She went on to describe the large gold ring that looked like the head of a bull with small red stones for eyes and what appeared to be tiny diamonds around the edge. "And, he's also got this god-awful looking silver belt buckle . . . never can make out what it's supposed to be . . . just big and ugly like them rodeo cowboys wear."

"Shoes?"

"I guess, never looked," Judy said and seemed puzzled.

"Anything else?" Behan asked, letting the shoe question go.

"That's pretty much the whole enchilada except if this guy's a cop how do I know he ain't gonna find out I talked to you and come here to shut me up permanently to keep me from pointing him out?"

"Until we catch him, nobody but the two of us will know what you said," Behan promised and she seemed to relax. He reached into his briefcase and showed her a picture of Marvin Wright. "Could this be Mata?"

"Fuck no, nice-looking dude, but he's black, too fat, and not Mexican. I know the difference, Sweetie."

"Did you ever know Mata to carry a gun?" Josie asked.

"Not that I ever seen or heard about."

Behan asked a few more questions and gave Judy his contact information. She made it clear she trusted Red and was willing to deal with him, but only him. It wasn't a subtle message she delivered about intending to get to know him better. She wanted to keep living above the High-Top and said she would lie to Mookie, tell him she refused to talk to the police when he got out of jail or asked about it. If Jesse Mata came back into the club, Judy promised to let Behan know, but none of them really believed his return was likely.

THERE WAS little doubt in Josie's mind at this moment that Matador aka Jesse Mata and ex-officer Marvin Wright were two different individuals, but the question about which of them killed Howard Burke still had not been answered to her satisfaction. The gun carried by Marvin's bodyguard was the murder weapon but how and when did he get it, she wondered.

"What are you thinking about?" Behan asked, when they were pulling into the station parking lot. She hadn't said a word since they left the High-Top.

"Probably the same thing you are."

"Which is?"

"By all accounts we have a Latino or light-skinned black cop killing gay men on Santa Monica Boulevard. Howard Burke, who is gay, gets shot within yards of our other victims and yet I'm supposed to believe Marvin Wright, who is black and has no connection to Hollywood or the other victims, chose to murder him in the middle of our killing field, even though he could've shot him anywhere in the city."

"Nope, not what I was thinking."

"I know what you were thinking, Red, and if you do it, Miss Vicky will kill you," Josie said.

She'd seen that look on his face before when a pretty, young woman flattered him. It always resulted in an alcoholic binge, nights away from home, and banishment by his wife until she forgave him . . . again.

He was getting too old to do that, and more importantly, Josie needed him sober for the next couple of days. When the city yanked his ticket, he could cavort and drink all he wanted, but she could sense he was getting close to finding their killer, and they couldn't bring this complicated investigation to a successful conclusion with him working from the bottom of a whiskey bottle.

TWENTY

The Primrose Motel was on the West Hollywood side of La Brea Boulevard and came under the jurisdiction of the Sheriff's Department. Josie, Behan, and especially Marge Bailey and her vice officers knew it well since the criminal population used it as a base to infest their division.

During the last couple decades, civil injunctions to "cease and desist" required the name of the motel to be changed frequently, but its clientele remained constant. Josie also knew it was the last refuge on a road leading to life on the street. The oldest, worn-out prostitutes; drug users who'd spent their last dime and stolen from everyone; dealers at the bottom of the distribution ladder taking just enough off the top to stay high, and similar lost souls occupied the rundown rooms.

Judy's description of the motel had narrowed their search to the Primrose, and Josie knew this was the sort of place Matador could take his victims for sexual gratification before he strangled them. Josie was grateful the killer had carelessly let Anthony Charles and a few of the other boys live long enough to reveal some information and incriminating details. He'd been clever, but if he hadn't also been a little cavalier her investigation would be going nowhere.

Marge agreed to meet her and Behan at the motel after they finished interviewing the waitress. It was obvious as soon as they arrived at the Primrose the business had once again changed hands, and the Koreans no longer ran it. Two Hispanic women were behind the counter and the younger one who looked to be in her early teens was holding an infant.

"We need to see your register," Behan said, showing the older woman his ID.

"My mother doesn't understand English very well," the girl said, reaching under the counter and producing the hardbound register.

"How old are you?" Marge asked.

"Eighteen," she lied, quickly.

"Is the baby yours?" Josie asked, taking the edge of the infant's blanket to clean dried food and drool off its chin.

"No, she's my sister. What do you want?" the girl asked, turning the baby away from Josie.

"This scribble," Behan said, moving the register so the girl could see the illegible name. "Do you know who this is?" The girl shook her head and he continued, "He's stayed here a lot during the last four months. You must know something about him." He pointed to the same signature on several pages of the ledger, always the last person to register on each date.

The older woman took the baby and said a few whispered words to the girl. She seemed worried. Josie heard some of it and understood enough Spanish to know she was warning her daughter not to talk too much.

"Is your mother afraid because this man is a policeman?" Josie asked, pointing to the signature.

The two women looked confused and glanced at each other before staring at the floor.

"I'm going to close down your damn motel unless you talk to us. You fucking *comprende* that?" Marge asked, bending over to look directly in the older woman's face.

"He will take my children," the woman said, handing the baby back to her daughter.

"No, he won't, not if you tell me the truth. See this lady here," Marge said, indicating Josie. "She's the big boss. She won't let him hurt you if you talk to us."

The older woman stared at Josie and after a few seconds said, "Señor Mata, he brings *muchachos*, boys . . . one night, one . . . next time, another . . . *malo, muy malo*," she said slowly, shaking her head. "I tell him don't come. He say he's *la policia* if I don't do what he say, he takes my license . . . takes my children." She stopped and shrugged. "I do what he say."

"Did you see his face . . . without a hat or dark glasses?" Marge asked.

The mother shook her head but the daughter nodded and said, "One time . . . I went by his room and one of the boys he leaves the door open and I see Mata . . ." She stopped and blushed. With a slight smile and not looking at her mother, she added, "No clothes."

"Did he know you saw him?" Josie asked.

The girl wrinkled her nose as if she had just swallowed something distasteful, shook her head and said, "No."

"Does he have a room he usually stays in?" Behan asked.

"He says keep one room only for him. I take you," the woman said, reaching in a drawer for a master key. She walked around the counter and led them down the hall to a door with the number eleven over the peephole. It was the only room on that floor with a dead-bolt, and the key didn't work.

"Fucker changed the locks," Marge said. "Kick it, Red."

"Get a warrant," Josie said.

Behan was on his cell phone dictating a warrant in seconds. He talked to a judge in Hollywood who would sign it, and a team of his detectives would deliver the signed search warrant to the motel.

An hour later, the homicide team arrived with the warrant in hand and a locksmith who opened the door. While they were waiting, Behan had shown the woman and her daughter pictures of Marvin Wright and the bodyguards. They swore they'd never seen any of those men and the daughter described Mata exactly the way Judy had.

Expecting the worst, Josie was surprised to find an ordinary room, small but clean with an unmade bed. A pile of folded sheets and two blankets had been left on the bare, stained mattress. The women explained to her that Mata always brought his own linen and never allowed them inside. They seemed as curious and apprehensive as the police about what the room might contain. The door to the closet had another dead-bolt and was hidden by a heavy red curtain hanging from a wooden rod.

Josie opened the shades on the two windows facing the street. By La Brea motel standards, this was a decent room, she thought, as she watched Marge pull aside the closet curtain to make it easier for the locksmith to work.

When Marge was finally able to open the closet door, Josie moved closer to get a better look.

"Fucking jackpot," Marge said, gently punching Josie's arm.

Inside the narrow space on a row of wire hangers were the embroidered matador jacket in a clear plastic bag, a black cape, a couple pairs of Levi's, and a black hoodie.

They were wearing latex gloves but Behan stopped the search and called SID. He wanted to print every possible surface in the room before they touched another thing. The woman and her daughter were waiting in the hallway and he arranged for one of his detectives to take the daughter downtown to sit with a police sketch artist. She was the first witness he'd interviewed who'd seen Mata's face without a hat or glasses.

"This asshole is good," Marge said when she finished looking through the Levi's in Mata's closet. "There's nothing, not even lint, in his pockets. That's got to be Anthony's cape. Don't you think?" she asked, sitting beside Josie on the mattress.

"That would be my guess. Why do you suppose he picked this motel?" Josie asked, thinking out loud again.

"Because it's the perfect place to be invisible. Hard to find a piece of crap floating in a shithole full of human excrement," Marge said. "Are you hungry?"

Josie told Behan they were going to eat but he wanted to stay and wait for SID. He'd brought in another homicide team to start interviewing everyone who was staying or had recently stayed in the motel and workers in nearby businesses who might've seen or heard something. A Spanish-speaking uniformed officer was taking a formal statement from the woman who ran the motel. She seemed more at ease and willing to talk since the police had swarmed onto the premises and promised they weren't going to allow Mata to return.

"So what's it gonna be?" Marge asked when they were standing on the sidewalk in front of the Primrose. "Wanna walk over to that great pizza place, rub elbows with the whores and pimps, or pick up greasy chicken on Santa Monica among the lovely boulevard boys, or is it Nora's?"

"Nora's will do," Josie said, knowing several better restaurants had opened in Hollywood over the last few decades, but fast food or Nora's accomplished their mission of eating and getting back to work with as little interruption as possible.

They had just put in their order at Nora's when Josie's cell phone rang. It was Mac. He was in the station and wanted to know where she was. Within a few minutes, he'd come across the street and found their table in the dimly lit bar.

"Patrol's got Marvin Wright pinned down in an abandoned warehouse off Fairfax in Wilshire division, shots fired, SWAT's been called," he said, calmly reciting the information.

"Is Richards there?" Josie asked, standing and throwing twenty dollars on the table.

"Keep your money, Captain. I'll cancel the order," the bartender said, putting the cork back on a bottle of wine he had just opened.

"Kyle's the one that found Wright and called in the blue suits and . . ." he hesitated then added quickly, "Wright might've done some damage."

"Fuck," Marge said, grabbing a handful of peanuts off the bar. "Let's go." She stopped suddenly and asked, "Can he come? We might need the extra firepower."

Josie met Mac's hard stare and said, "No, sorry, not this time."

She nearly choked on those words and walked away from his look of disappointment mixed with anger. It was killing her not to let him come because she knew it was in his nature to be the cop leading the charge, the first one to face danger. But she also knew if she allowed him to go, Dempsey would make his life miserable before destroying his career. She didn't blame him for being angry and believed treating him this way was like forcing a thoroughbred to pull a hay wagon.

Marge got them to their destination on Fairfax in a few minutes. Uniformed officers in black-and-whites had established a perimeter several blocks out, surrounding the dilapidated building, and Josie located the makeshift command post in a tire shop at the end of that block.

"Where's Lieutenant Richards?" she asked the sergeant who seemed to be in charge.

He glanced down at the captain's badge on her belt and said with a condescending tone that suggested she was bothering him, "I'm guessing they got him at the hospital by now, ma'am."

"What the fuck happened?" Marge demanded, moving closer.

The sergeant had to have seen her lieutenant badge, looked her up and down, then took a step back before saying, "Look, ladies, I can't chat right now. I've got a command post to run. There's a nut job in that dump shooting at anything that moves."

Josie took a deep breath and before Marge could speak, she said, "This is your lucky day, Sergeant. Since you're obviously overwhelmed, I'm relieving you and taking charge of this command post." She tried to stay calm and not show her anger or her fear for Kyle's safety.

The man didn't move for several seconds. He almost smiled then looked at the faces of officers around him for a show of support that never came. Josie added, "Get out of my sight and find something useful you can do," before turning her back to him. He snatched his radio off the table and stomped away, pushing through a wall of officers in blue who were watching and seemed more than willing to follow a new leader.

"What's so funny?" she asked Marge who had a broad grin.

"Nothing, Boss, just admiring your technique in dealing with a patronizing asshole . . . my way probably would've got us in a whole lotta trouble."

"Right, catch me up," Josie said to another sergeant standing nearby who seemed to be enjoying the humiliation of his fellow supervisor. "Start with what happened to Lieutenant Richards."

The supervisor explained that Richards had been hit by one or two rounds when he approached the warehouse on a routine inspection. This was one of several places he'd gone to that day as part of Wilshire's task force trying to find Wright. He was ambushed as he walked away from his black-and-white but was able to broadcast a call for backup.

"How bad was he hit, Sarge?" Marge asked.

"Don't know, ma'am. Haven't had a chance to check with the hospital, but Sergeant Scott from West Bureau was here and went with him in the ambulance."

"That's a fucking comfort," Marge said sarcastically.

Josie had quickly studied the floor plan of the warehouse and repositioned officers on the scene before SWAT arrived. She spoke with the SWAT lieutenant and he wanted to try coaxing Marvin out with a negotiator before using force. Josie agreed but was struggling to keep her attention focused on what was happening around her and making the best decisions when all she wanted to do was drive to Cedars-Sinai emergency room as quickly as possible and be with Kyle.

Marvin had his cell phone and was willing to talk to them. The negotiator spoke to him as if the ex-cop's gibberish made sense, which it didn't. He complained LAPD had hitmen following him everywhere, and they had murdered his friend Jerome Handy. He wanted the department's fixed-wing aircraft to fly him to Costa Rica and leave him there with a million dollars in twenty-dollar bills. He threatened to kill himself and Tyler Jones, his remaining bodyguard, unless the negotiator allowed him to talk to his lawyer, his mother, a minister, an old girlfriend, and the handyman who worked on his mother's toilet last week and reminded him of his dead father.

It took three hours and two large Papa John pizzas before the negotiator made any progress. Marvin agreed to let Tyler come out.

The side door of the warehouse directly in front of a loading dock flung open. The big man Josie had seen with Marvin in the Wilshire captain's office stepped out into the headlights of several patrol cars pointed in his direction. His arms were stretched high above his head. He was shirtless, barefoot, and his big naked belly hung over the top of dirty grey underwear. The man was unshaven, with his hair matted and uncombed. He turned around in a complete circle several times to show the officers he didn't have a weapon.

A SWAT officer directed him to move out of Marvin's line of fire. He ordered the nervous man to kneel and then lie flat on his stomach with his arms out in front of him. He did everything he was told but seemed to have trouble comprehending and every command had to be repeated several times before he slowly complied and could be handcuffed.

Josie was watching officers talk to Tyler and place him in the back seat of a patrol car when Marge tapped her on the shoulder and said, "Boss, I could swear while everybody was concentrating on this douchebag, I saw something moving on the other side of that chain-link fence."

Josie told the SWAT lieutenant who said his officers had surrounded the building and assured her nothing was getting in or out without them seeing it.

"Could it have been one of the uniform guys changing position?" Josie asked Marge, following her as she made a wide circle behind the SWAT team and headed toward the back of the warehouse.

"Nope, they can't get in there."

"Then how . . ." Josie started to ask but decided to wait and see. SWAT's attention was focused on the negotiator and securing Tyler, so she had a few minutes to back up Marge.

What had been an asphalt parking lot to the rear of the warehouse was now cracked with potholes and covered in a thick blanket of weeds and dumped trash. It was surrounded by chain-linked fence with barbed wire on top to keep thieves from climbing over and stealing tools, wooden pallets, or strips of metal left behind when the business shut down.

There was a padlock on the gate, but Marge used the lock picks she kept in the glove compartment of her car and opened it quickly. Very little light from around the warehouse reached the parking lot but there was enough moonlight to see some of the bigger hazards surrounding them. Josie locked the gate again when they were inside.

After a few seconds, her eyes adjusted a little to the darkness and Josie could see as well as smell the garbage scattered around her, some still in plastic bags, a lot in piles where the neighbors, the elements, and time had deposited it. The weeds were difficult to navigate at night. Josie had seen a metal shed in a corner of the lot that she wanted to check, but waited and stayed with Marge until she finished searching behind stacks of junk and materials abandoned by whoever had last used the warehouse.

Josie's patience was wearing a little thin when she banged her knee against a sharp steel rod and tore her jeans.

"I've got to get back to the command post. What the hell are we looking for?" she asked, rubbing her knee and making no effort to hide her irritation. "Marvin couldn't get in here and if he did how the hell would he get out?"

"I'm looking for a fucking hole," Marge said, turning off her flashlight. "There were factory warehouses in this area that got shut down for using illegals. They got raided all the time and never got caught until the feds found tunnels. Illegals ducked into the tunnels, got outside the buildings, and disappeared."

"You think Marvin found a tunnel," Josie said.

"I fucking saw somebody in here. The gate's locked. There's no other way in. If I'm right, Marvin's still here because there's no way he gets his fat ass over that fence. If I'm wrong, we can go back and wait for Captain America to figure out he's trying to negotiate with a guy who's got a brain like a peanut butter and jelly sandwich."

"Maybe he went back into the hole," Josie said.

"Maybe, but let's check the shed. Your radio turned down?"

Josie pointed to her earpiece. She looked back toward the warehouse and saw lights still directed at the building, officers stationed around the perimeter. Nothing had changed, telling her the SWAT commander had every reason to believe Marvin was still inside. She trusted Marge but was beginning to feel a little silly about trudging around in the dark in the middle of a garbage dump looking for someone who might've used a tunnel that might or might not exist to get into a fenced lot from which he could never escape.

That feeling was gone as soon as they reached the shed and she saw two large empty oil drums had been dragged a few feet and placed directly in front of the door. There was enough space between the drums and the door for someone Marvin's size to get inside. The drag marks had clearly been made recently with clean deep tracks leading to their new location.

Marge placed her finger over her lips as she tiptoed closer to the shed and put her ear against the wall. Her smile grew bigger as she listened. After several minutes, she backed away and motioned for Josie to follow her to a location about twenty yards from the shed where dozens of wooden pallets had been stacked up to six-feet high. They had cover there but could still see the shed.

"Shithead's in there," Marge whispered. "He was talking to the negotiator but his phone died. I think I heard a police radio too."

"For a crazy guy, he's damn clever," Josie said.

She told Marge to unlock the gate again, go to the command post, and tell the SWAT commander to have his officers quietly set up around the shed, have the other uniformed officers move the perimeter in to surround the parking lot but keep everything off the radio. If Marvin had stolen a police radio, he was most likely monitoring what was said. She would stay and make certain he didn't try to leave but was confident he wasn't going anywhere. His plan was finally starting to make sense. She figured he intended to return to the warehouse and leave by the front door as soon as the police gave up. He knew everybody would go away if they thought he had found a way to escape.

Josie grabbed Marge's arm as she turned to leave and said, "Make Tyler show you where he went into the tunnel so SWAT can set up on it. Find out exactly where Marvin expected to come out in this parking lot."

"I saw him moving in the open so I don't think the exit's inside the shed," Marge said.

"Doesn't matter. He's not getting out this way. SWAT needs to make sure if he somehow goes back into the tunnel, they're waiting for him at the other end."

"Keep your head down, Boss," Marge said and jogged toward the gate.

Josie was relieved that Marvin Wright might be trapped and could no longer threaten Jorge, her, or anybody else, but she couldn't suppress the fear that his vendetta against Kyle had been successful. This standoff needs to end soon, she thought. Not knowing if someone she loved was alive or badly injured was making her crazy.

The SWAT lieutenant was smart. Less than ten minutes after Marge left, he was on the radio broadcasting that the suspect was no longer communicating on his cell phone and everyone should stay put while a bullhorn was brought in, which might take a couple of minutes. It was a stalling tactic to allow his officers time to get in position.

Shadowy figures were moving around now on the roof of the warehouse and a squad of heavily armed officers had entered the parking lot taking cover behind anything that offered protection. Josie recognized one of their armored vehicles and knew it could demolish the shed leaving Marvin in the open surrounded by enough deadly force to win a small war.

The only remaining question was, by afternoon would Marvin Wright be locked up in a jail downtown or lying on a cold metal slab in the LA County morgue? With Kyle in mind, Josie had a preference she'd keep to herself.

TWENTY-ONE

The greyish blue light of dawn slowly revealed those previously unidentifiable shapes and source of odors around Josie, and she could clearly recognize her surroundings as a filthy garbage dump. She knew any stealth approach to the shed was problematic now.

Josie met with the SWAT lieutenant and told him to do whatever was necessary to safely contain the situation. They both knew that was code for "kill the bastard if you have to but don't jeopardize our cops."

She tried to talk to Marvin on the police radio but he wouldn't respond. The lieutenant used a bullhorn to order him out of the shed with the same result. The weather forecast for that day was in the high nineties meaning in a few hours the metal windowless box would be an oven, probably well over one hundred degrees. There hadn't been any shots fired by Marvin since he crawled out of the warehouse. Josie guessed either he had run out of ammo or he was waiting to make his Butch Cassidy and the Sundance Kid exit in a flurry of senseless gunfire.

Marge had successfully convinced the bodyguard Tyler to show her the entrance to the tunnel in the warehouse.

It was on the factory floor under one of the work benches, and a dozen officers were left to guard it. The tunnel exit, he said, was close to the front gate inside the parking lot. In the dark, it looked like a cement pad where small containers were stored, but near the outside corner of the pad was a metal lid, three feet in diameter, sunk a few inches into the concrete. When the sun came up, Marge opened the lid and showed Josie steps leading to the dirt tunnel.

"How could Marvin have known about these tunnels?" Josie asked, helping Marge lower the lid again.

"He grew up in Wilshire, so his grandparents or neighbors probably told him. It was common knowledge if you lived or worked here at that time. I heard about it from a 211 victim who got robbed by a pimp. He'd just bought one of these warehouses, thought it was cool when one of the inspectors told him about the tunnel."

"I need to get to Cedars, but I can't leave."

"Why don't you send Mac. At least he can tell you what's going on."

Josie didn't answer. She could've called the hospital too but didn't. Not knowing was somehow more tolerable than learning bad news secondhand.

There wasn't much time to dwell on Kyle's condition. The SWAT lieutenant's calm voice came over the police radio.

"Shed door's opening, stand by," he said.

She was to the rear of the armored vehicle with Marge, and they crouched down, unholstering their handguns just as the metal door flung open and Marvin stepped out with a semiauto in his right hand. His arm was down by his side with the weapon pointed at the ground.

The lieutenant shouted at him to drop the gun. "Don't be stupid; drop the fucking gun!" he repeated.

Josie was close enough that she could see Marvin's empty, faraway stare, hear his incoherent mumbling—an irrational, fearful man who had lost touch with reality. He was sweating profusely; his hair and beard had grown out and were matted like Tyler's. His shirt was wrinkled, dirty and torn, with sweat stains covering the front. He'd lost a lot of weight, looked sick, and his dirty jeans hung low and loose on his hips. Everything about him told Josie he'd been living on the streets.

"You try, Captain," the lieutenant said, moving from the other side of the vehicle and giving her the bullhorn. "I'm not getting through . . . maybe a familiar voice."

Josie took it from him, not knowing what she could say that Marvin would want to hear or understand. She never had an opportunity to try; he began walking slowly toward them, raised the semiauto and fired two rounds, but before Josie or anyone close to her could shoot back she heard another louder retort and a spray of blood burst from Marvin's back. The bullet had done its damage exiting his body. He fell backward, hit the ground with his legs and arms outspread, and was still.

A team of officers moved from behind cover; one had an assault rifle pointed at the lifeless body. Another got close enough to kick the gun away, handcuffed Marvin, and quickly searched him for other weapons.

An ambulance had been on standby and within minutes the paramedics pronounced him dead. The police shooter had been on the warehouse roof, and he was quickly isolated to wait for the arrival of the Force Investigation team.

Chief Dempsey was on the scene within minutes and could be heard loudly congratulating the SWAT lieutenant and his officers. Josie watched as her boss stood over Marvin's body as if the ex-cop were a trophy kill. She didn't have much sympathy for the dead man but had so little respect for the deputy chief that just about anything he did seemed inappropriate and his reaction certainly was.

He finally got around to talking with Josie and Marge shortly after they finished giving their preliminary statements to the investigators.

"Good work, Lieutenant Bailey," he said, slapping Marge on the shoulder. "I understand you're the one who actually cornered our man."

"Captain Corsino and me," Marge said, edging away from him.

"You always manage to get yourself in the middle of everything, don't you, Captain," he said with a smirk.

"Following up on a possible murder suspect," Josie said, adding as an afterthought, "sir."

"There's no possible about it," Dempsey said, his face turning pink. "We've got the gun to prove it. By the way, where's Behan? Burke is still his investigation, isn't it?"

"He's working up a new lead on our serial killer," Josie said. She explained what they had found at the Primrose Motel and some of what the new witnesses had told them.

"That's fine, but Burke's murder is a priority. His suspect is lying dead over there. Your lead detective should be here."

"I'm here," Josie said. "And we still have nothing that ties Marvin Wright directly to Burke's killing. Behan's job is to find the killer and he will . . . whoever that might be. Getting a serial killer is just as important and he can do both."

Dempsey didn't argue. It was obvious he wasn't pleased and was more than eager to have the Burke investigation closed. His expression was a combination of disgust and annoyance, but he hurried away, summoning the SWAT lieutenant as if he had something important to say.

"Why the fuck are you still here?" Marge asked Josie as soon as the deputy chief was out of hearing range.

"It's all wrong, Marge," she said, shaking her head. "Look at him. I'm not buying that that mindless, homeless, tunnel rat was the mastermind of everything that's happened."

"I agree with you. So go to the hospital. I'll call Red and we'll tie up the loose ends while you check on Kyle."

She didn't argue and asked one of the uniformed officers to drive her to Cedars. He offered to wait and take her back to Hollywood, but Josie wasn't certain what she'd find at the hospital or if she'd be making that trip back to the office anytime soon.

Police officers were permitted to park near the back entrance of the emergency room where Josie got out, thanked the young patrolman, and moved quickly through the automatic glass doors and into the restricted area for trauma victims. She was peeking into each of the curtained-off stations until one of the nurses stopped her.

"Quit bothering my patients. I'll find your officer," the nurse said after Josie explained the reason for her search. The older woman sat in front of a computer and after several attempts located Kyle. "He's out of surgery and . . . in a private room in the north tower," she said, handing Josie a piece of paper with the room number.

"How bad . . ." Josie started to ask, but the woman interrupted her.

"Don't know, Hon. We do triage and stabilize; the surgeon fixes them," the woman said, wearily shaking her head. "If he's not in ICU that's a good sign. Now get out of here so I can do my job." She gently patted Josie's arm before hurrying toward a flashing light and a persistent high-pitched alarm.

Josie had spent many nights in this hospital's emergency room waiting and worrying with the families of injured officers, but had never felt the panic attack she experienced during those few moments it took the nurse to find Kyle's name. She wanted to think positively but after so many years in police work, she understood the cop curse, i.e., an officer could fire a dozen rounds hitting the suspect every time and the criminal would survive, but if a cop got shot once, he had a good chance of dying. There was no explanation; that's the way it was.

The afternoon visiting hours were just about over and the hallway on the third floor was almost empty. She found his room across from the nurses' station, but the door was shut. No one was around so she knocked softly, opened it, and saw him lying there in a hospital gown, eyes open with his head slightly elevated watching the television across the room.

He smiled at her and barely lifted his bandaged left arm, "Just saw you on the news. Don't worry. Marvin's a lousy shot."

"Was a lousy shot," she said, sitting on the edge of the bed and gently touching his face. "He's dead."

Kyle groaned as he moved to get comfortable. "Too bad, I was hoping we'd get a chance to talk to him."

She could see his eyes were glassy and his skin nearly as pale as the sheets. They had him medicated and drowsy.

"Why were you in surgery?" she asked.

Kyle pulled back the sheet, lifted his gown a little, and Josie saw the bandage and drainage tube on his side. "Not bad, little damage to the kidney, but I got another good one." Almost midsentence his eyes closed and as soon as he stopped talking, he was asleep. Josie straightened his gown and the sheet. She was exhausted and the space on his narrow bed was inviting, but she didn't want to wake or further injure him.

She located Kyle's doctor sitting outside the room at the nurses' desk studying a chart on the hospital computer. He explained that a bullet had penetrated the fleshy part of Kyle's upper left arm missing the bone and tendons and that wound would heal quickly with no permanent damage. Another round had entered his side and come out his lower back, nicking one of his kidneys. The doctor told her the prognosis for that kidney functioning again was uncertain but, "he's got another one and that's all he needs to live a good long life."

"You're saying he's going to be all right?" Josie asked. She was tired and a little punchy. The words weren't making any sense.

"That's precisely what I'm saying," he said, getting up with a groan. "But the man's been shot and needs plenty of time to mend, physically and mentally. He won't be going back to work anytime soon."

"Not a problem," Josie said. "As long as he's okay."

She explained her relationship with Kyle and asked if she could come and visit at odd hours because of her job. He didn't seem to care as long as his patient got enough rest. Josie called David, Beth, and Kyle's mother, told them about his injuries and where he would be for the next few days. They had heard a Wilshire officer had been shot and had been trying to reach Kyle and then her, but she'd turned off her phone when she and Marge were outside the shed. David promised he would come to the hospital as soon as the restaurant closed.

It wasn't until she spoke to her son that Josie realized how late it was. He was preparing for his dinner crowd. Her head was pounding, a reminder she hadn't slept, eaten, or had any coffee for hours. Caffeine deprivation was painful for an Italian-dark-roast addict. The hospital cafeteria was always open so she took the elevator down to the bottom floor and got their biggest cup of coffee and a stale chocolate cream-filled donut.

The sugar jolt revived her and the coffee gave her the energy to go back up to Kyle's room and check on him again. She had hoped Dempsey's adjutant, Sergeant Scott, might still be somewhere in the hospital and could arrange a lift back to the station so she could get her car. He'd made a big deal out of riding in the ambulance after Kyle's shooting, but the paramedics told her he'd flagged down a patrol car and left a few minutes after the ambulance arrived at Cedars. The little weasel did it all for show; no surprise there, Josie thought.

As she was about to phone the watch commander at Hollywood for a black-and-white "police taxi," two orderlies wheeled a small fold-up bed into the room, fitted it with clean sheets, and threw a pillow and light blanket on top.

"Doc said you looked like you could use this," one of them said. "Dinner's over but if you're hungry I can dig up a sandwich or something."

Josie wasn't hungry but was grateful. She thanked them and waited until they left before pushing the bed as close as she could to Kyle's. The mattress was too soft and lumpy, too short for her long legs, and smelled of bleach, but she didn't care. Kicking off her boots, she curled up on top of it. There was so much to do right now but here is where she wanted to be. She needed to sleep and wake up knowing he was alive and getting better. Everything else could wait.

TWENTY-TWO

When she got a full night's sleep, it was always a chore for Josie to get out of bed in the morning. She slept soundly and dreamed a lot. Kyle claimed it was entertaining during those nights to watch her talking and living through her imagination's wild adventures. His only real proof was the disastrous condition of her side of the bed when she woke up.

This morning as the warm sunlight hit her eyes, confusion about where she was, apprehension about where she should have been and if she was late getting there, were her first thoughts. She sat up and remembered, looked over her shoulder at Kyle in the hospital bed. He was awake smiling back at her.

"Slept good, didn't you?" he said, sounding like himself again.

She saw her blanket on the floor, the sheets pulled away from the mattress, and the cot on a slightly different angle from where it had been last night.

"Appears so," she said and asked, "How are you feeling?"

"Good enough to want out of here."

"Not gonna happen, lover," she said, getting up and giving him a long kiss. He held onto her for a few more seconds and she knew if he weren't so badly injured, they'd be in that tiny bed making love now. Instead she gently pulled away and said, "Doctor says you need to rest, but you'll be up and walking around a little today."

"Already did a turn around the floor. Besides sex helps me relax."

"Great. I'm going to use your shower," she said, glancing up at the wall clock. It was five A.M. and she wanted to get to Hollywood early. She felt recharged and knew the sleep helped but seeing Kyle awake and horny was the real reason for her energy surge.

The room was crowded when Josie came out of the bathroom. She was wearing yesterday's clothes but taking a shower and washing her hair was refreshing and she was ready to jump into whatever was waiting at the station. However she hadn't anticipated what was hovering around Kyle's bed—Mrs. Richards, Beth, and David.

They had been at the hospital all night while she slept and had just returned from breakfast in the cafeteria. Josie hugged David and Beth, but Kyle's mother made it clear with her body language she had no intention of having any physical contact.

"Hope you slept well," Mrs. Richards said to Josie in her best reprimanding tone while looking with disdain at the messy cot. "I couldn't sleep a wink all night . . . sick with worry."

"Sorry," Josie said, too cheerfully. "Doesn't he look so much better this morning?" she asked no one in particular.

"We walked the entire third-floor perimeter earlier," David said.

"Dad's tough," Beth said, smiling at David. "I mean, it's not the first time you've been shot," she added matter-of-factly while holding her father's hand. Josie guessed the remark was intended for her grandmother who gave the girl a look of exasperation.

"If it's all the same, I'd rather not make a habit of it," Kyle said, using the hand control to lower the top of the bed.

"Who sent the lovely flowers?" Mrs. Richards asked, pointing at the expensive-looking arrangement of white roses in a glass vase on the window ledge.

"West Bureau," Kyle said, and smiling at Josie, asked, "Dempsey does know I survived, right?"

"If you're lucky, he thinks you're dead, and won't visit, then you won't have to listen to him pretend he gives a shit," Josie said and heard a low gasp from Kyle's mother.

"Okay, everybody go away now, so I can get some sleep," he said quickly.

Josie waited until Mrs. Richards and Beth were done hugging him, and then she gave Kyle a hug and whispered in his ear, "For the next couple of days, hold onto that thought that sex is relaxing and we'll see if it's true."

THERE WASN'T much conversation on the elevator ride down to the hospital's parking level, but as they stood waiting for the attendant to retrieve their cars, Josie filled the others in on what she knew about the shooting. She urged David to be vigilant about using his security system until the Burke investigation was officially closed.

It was obvious to her that David and Beth had become friends. Her son was almost ten years older than Kyle's daughter, and Josie believed he should be a big brother not her love interest. Over the years, Josie had developed that critical cop skill of reading body language, but in this instance, it wasn't necessary. They clearly liked each other . . . a lot, and Mrs. Richards didn't seem any happier than Josie about the prospect of their growing friendship.

Her son offered to take Josie to Hollywood after Mrs. Richards and Beth finally drove away. When they were alone, she wanted to broach the subject of his relationship with Beth but didn't. A lifetime of dealing with David's sensitive nature warned her any advice she gave would result in frustration and overreaction on his part. She decided the perfect solution was avoidance—make Kyle deal with them.

THE RUMORS were flying around Hollywood station that morning about the gun battle in Wilshire and the death of Marvin Wright. Most cops take pride in the integrity of their profession and welcomed the news. The reputation of Lieutenant Kyle Richards was soaring with glowing reports of how he had tracked down the rogue ex-cop and nearly lost his life. A bit exaggerated, Josie thought, but Kyle deserved the attention and was certainly a hero.

Few people knew the role she and Marge had played in Marvin's demise and that was fine with Josie. She needed to stay off Dempsey's radar and one of the things that really bothered him was the fact that her officers admired her addiction to police work. He saw their loyalty to her as a sign of Josie's weakness. "They shouldn't like you. You're too lenient," he once told her. "They need to fear their boss if you want to get the most out of them." Her response was to compare her crime stats to the other four divisions in his bureau and show him Hollywood was far superior. Her relationship with her boss took a giant step backward after that day.

She located Behan and Marge in her office planning their interrogation of Tyler Jones, Marvin's surviving bodyguard.

"He was filthy and starving when we dragged him in here," Marge said, using her foot to push out a chair for Josie at the worktable.

"He was happy to get arrested . . . begging for a shower and a hot meal," Behan said, handing her a copy of the arrest report. "Claimed he was terrified of Marvin, 'crazy pit-a-ful fool' is what he called him."

"Where's Mac?" Josie asked. Her adjutant hadn't been at his desk when she arrived.

Marge shook her head and shrugged. "Haven't seen him since day before yesterday," she said.

"It's probably too early," Josie said. Although Marge was attempting to look unconcerned, Josie could tell something was wrong but wasn't going to pursue it now.

They discussed their questions and approach to Tyler's interrogation anticipating he might have information about the gun recovered from his buddy Jerome and possibly know something about Burke's murder. If Tyler had been with Marvin since his disappearance, Behan was intent to find a way to pry every detail from the man about their movements and activities.

A soft knock on the office door made Josie look up as Mac came in. He was wearing civilian clothes, still unshaven, and looked as if he just woke up.

"Didn't expect you here this early, Captain," he said, putting a copy of her schedule for the day on the table in front of her.

"Wanted to get some things done while it was quiet," she said. "You okay?"

"Shower, shave, and I'll be ready to go. Need anything now?"

"I'm good," she said and waited until he was out the door again before tilting her head and staring at Marge.

"Don't fucking look at me," Marge whispered. "Not my fault if he sleeps in the cot room. I'm not his damn mother. He can stay anywhere he wants . . . just not with me."

"We've been friends a long time, but I'm warning both of you you're playing with fire. That man has serious problems and nothing you're doing is helping," Behan said, getting up and gathering his reports.

"What I do in my personal life is none of your fucking business, Behan," Marge said.

"We'll talk about this later," Josie said. "Concentrate on Tyler. In two days, you're officially retired, Red. I need you to find whoever shot Burke and track down this serial killer. Let me worry about Dan McSweeney. He's my problem."

Josie watched them leave her office and had a bad feeling her problem might be more complex than she'd anticipated. Mac was complicated, a strong man with an armadillo shell and a glass center. She thought she was doing the right thing by paving the way for him to get back into police work but she worried now, after Dempsey's interference, instead of rebuilding his confidence she might be destroying the man.

The interrogation of Tyler wasn't going to start for another hour, so Josie got a lot of her paperwork out of the way. When Mac returned, he was wearing his uniform and was clean shaven. The dark lines under his eyes were still there but he seemed a little less tense, even smiled at one of her jokes.

"Have you been able to help Behan with the computer work?" she asked as they sat at the table assigning projects to her lieutenant watch commanders.

"The men's pants you found in that La Brea motel and the hoodie were expensive brands all purchased from a store on Rodeo Drive in Beverly Hills. The saleslady told Behan she remembered the customer because he was, and I'm quoting her, 'sooo gorgeous.'"

"Will she sit with the police artist?" she asked and he nodded. "Can I ask you something personal?"

"Why not," he said, sounding and looking as if he'd rather be eaten alive by a pack of rabid Chihuahuas.

"I have a gut feeling the stress of being here is getting to be too much for you. Am I wrong?"

"Not being able to do real police work is the only stress I have."

"When we catch the killer, Dempsey has no reason to keep you off the street."

"He'll find a reason."

"I'll fight him."

"You'll lose."

"What's he got against you?"

"Dempsey was my captain when that female sergeant brought her bogus personnel complaint against me. The court threw out the complaint, but they were especially nasty toward him for allowing the process to go forward. He took it personally."

Now it all made sense to Josie. Mac made Dempsey look like the fool he was, an unforgivable sin given the deputy chief's inflated ego. Josie knew the chief of police was a cop's cop and if he was told what Dempsey was doing he'd be furious. She'd make certain he found out. She'd been gathering everything she could find on Mac's complaint and lawsuit and had kept notes on Dempsey's arbitrary orders concerning her adjutant.

"Just keep doing your job and be patient. I've still got a few favors out there I can call in when the time comes. I'll get you back on the street," she said and was determined this time to keep that promise.

THE DOOR to the interview room was closed by the time Josie got to the detective squad room. Two homicide detectives were in the adjoining room watching through the two-way mirror so she dragged in a chair from the robbery table and sat beside them.

"You didn't miss much, Captain. They're just getting started," one of them whispered.

Tyler was sitting across the table from Behan and Marge. He had a protruding tummy and looked flabby like he had lost a lot of his muscle tone since the day Josie last saw him in Wilshire station. The jail jumper was a little baggy, but his hair had been trimmed and he had shaved and showered. Unlike Marvin he was somewhat articulate and spoke coherently about where he and Marvin had been and what they'd done.

"We had friends let us use their garage, but the neighbors complained so we mostly been on the street. Tell you the truth, I'm glad it's over. That whole business was so damn unnecessary."

"What are you talking about?" Behan asked.

"The dude was paranoid . . . he thought everybody was out to get him, even his mama . . . swore he saw you policemen spying on him behind every tree . . . kept running, hiding for no sensible reason I could see. We did stay one night at that dive in Wilshire, the Oaks, where cops almost caught us."

"You mean the Royal Oaks Motel on Venice?" Behan asked.

"Yeah, that's the one. Old Marv, he's popping off bullets like it's the damn OK Corral or Fourth of July or something. Scared the fuckin' shit outta me. I'm yelling, 'you're gonna kill somebody, fucker.' He's so scared he don't know what he's doing."

"Is that the same gun he had yesterday?"

"That's all he's got and it's not even his . . . kinda borrowed it from his mama's house. You already took the nice one outta his ride at the police station."

"What happened to his car?"

"Got repossessed soon as he stopped paying."

"What about the gun your buddy Jerome Handy was packing?" Behan asked.

"Here we go," one of the detectives whispered to Josie. "Truth or consequences."

"Jerome?" Tyler coughed and laughed. "Big, dumb ox, he'd shoot hisself if he got a gun . . . mean sonofabitch never needed one anyhow . . . jus' beat you to death. He robbed people with a butcher knife."

"He had a gun the day he was shot," Marge said.

Tyler shook his head and said, "Then you know more than me, Miss. Last I saw him was the day we left your police station. He got hisself arrested for hot prowl in some old lady's house around Westwood."

"How'd you find out?"

"How'd you think? He calls Marvin on his cell phone about a hundred times wanting us to bring bail to the Purdue police station."

"LAPD's West LA station?" Marge asked.

"If that's the one on Purdue. Old peanut brain thinks we got cash to get him outta jail when we can't hustle enough change for two Mickey D's burgers."

"Do you know how he got out of jail?"

"Didn't know he did, never saw him or talked to him again. Marvin saw something in the newspaper when Jerome got hisself killed."

"You're not lying to me, are you Tyler, about Marvin giving Jerome that gun?" Behan asked.

"What's to lie about? If Jerome got hisself a gun, he done it on his own . . . and seeing that fool never had a pot to piss in, he for sure had to steal it."

"Did Marvin kill the attorney Howard Burke in Hollywood or did he have Jerome do it?" Behan asked.

"Hold on there, officer, I don't know nothing about no killing."

"You never saw or heard anything from Marvin or Jerome about planning to kill a lawyer in a parking lot behind the High-Top Bar?"

"Hell no . . . wait is that the fag club in Hollywood? None of us ever been near that place. Don't want nothing to do with those people."

"What about shooting at Captain Sanchez in front of West LA station. Which one of them did that?"

"None of us did. The lawyers already told you that. We were with them at the police union office. They told you that."

"Marvin's rep admitted he didn't know for sure you and Jerome were there all morning," Behan said. "I'm thinking one or both of you slipped out."

"No, sir. I didn't go nowhere," Tyler said, looking at the floor.

"Did Jerome leave?"

"Couldn't say."

"WHICH ONE of you threw the Molotov cocktails at Captain Corsino's house in the middle of the night?"

"For sure that wasn't me and couldn't be Marvin neither because we was always together and I would of seen.
I can't know what Jerome's been up to lately, but how's he
even gonna find this Captain Core . . . whatever his name
is. How's he gonna know for sure it's his house?"

"You're not really telling me much, Tyler. I want to help
you but I need you to be truthful. Give me something for
the DA so he doesn't have to charge you with killing that
lawyer or being an accomplice on all those other things
Marvin and Jerome did," Behan said, slouching in his chair,
folding his arms, and glaring at the nervous man.

"Nothing to tell, man. Look at me," Tyler said, his voice
getting louder and strained as he started to fidget. "I been
living like some fucking bum, trying to keep my man alive
and stop him from hurting hisself. He couldn't hardly
remember where his mama lives or who the hell he is.
How's he gonna kill somebody or do all those other things
you said?"

"He's not," Josie said softly to herself, and got up. She'd
heard enough.

TWENTY-THREE

Thirty minutes later, it wasn't a surprise when Behan came into Josie's office and told her he was going to West LA station to get copies of the arrest report and booking information on Jerome Handy. If Tyler was telling the truth, she knew her suspicions that Marvin Wright and his cohorts had nothing to do with Burke's killing were starting to sound more plausible.

They had to retrace Jerome's movements to determine how and when the murder weapon got into his hands. He had it when he broke into Jorge Sanchez's house, so if he didn't have it when he was arrested, who did or where was it? Those were critical questions in Josie's mind.

She decided to go with Behan to West LA because it would give her an opportunity to check in on Jorge. They hadn't spoken since his shooting and she knew his use of force review board was coming up. Also, she wanted to ask him if the district attorney's office had forwarded its finding. Having been through the review process several times, Josie knew it was routine but waiting for everyone's stamp of approval could be stressful. She'd heard from Marion, Dempsey's secretary, who'd eavesdropped on one or two conversations, that her young protégé might be experiencing difficulties in coming to terms with having killed someone.

While Behan was in the West LA records unit, she went to the patrol captain's office toward the rear of the station. The door was closed but unlocked. She knocked, opened it, and walked in. He wasn't there and the top of the desk was clean. His adjutant, a female police officer, came in a few seconds later and looked startled to find anyone in the office.

"Captain Corsino, I'm sorry Captain Sanchez isn't in today," she said.

"Is he sick?"

"I don't think so, ma'am . . . just taking a few days off," the young woman said and added with some uncertainty, "I think maybe he needed to get away from all this . . . from us for a while."

Josie thanked her and didn't need to ask what 'all this' meant. She went to the other side of the building where the area CO's office was located. Captain Stuart Ames was at his desk talking and laughing with his secretary. He seemed a little annoyed when he saw Josie.

"What brings you to the Westside's sleepy hollow, Josie?" he asked sarcastically while slowly getting up to shake hands.

She waited for the secretary to leave and said, "I came to see Jorge . . . understand he's taken some time off. How's he doing?"

"Understandably still a little shaken by the incident . . . he needed a few days to move, said he couldn't live in that house anymore."

"Where did he move?"

"I think he's in your neck of the woods, Hollywood Hills, rented a bungalow somewhere off Laurel Canyon. My secretary has the address and his new phone number."

"Have you ordered him to the department shrink yet?" she asked. "Sounds like he might need help getting over this."

"Of course, he went right after the shooting, but I can't get him to go back. I've asked. He wants to work it out himself and I'm respecting his wishes," Ames said.

"Bad idea. It's better if he talks with a professional."

"I've never been in a shooting myself, but we're all cops. He has to learn how to handle the pressure. It's part of our job."

"That's bullshit and you know it, Stu. Lots of guys have trouble, nightmares, after a shooting especially if they kill somebody. You need to order him to keep seeing a shrink."

"I know how to run my division and take care of my people, Josie. From what Chief Dempsey tells me, you've got enough problems of your own without sticking your nose into West LA's business."

"Fine," she said, turning to leave, but came back and controlled her temper enough to say, "Jorge's my friend, not just one of your people. I'm going to talk to him and try to convince him to get help. If that bothers you, Stu, go do what you always do and whine about it to Dempsey." That's if you can get your nose out of his butt long enough to say anything, she thought as she left his office.

The secretary copied Jorge's new address and phone number and gave it to Josie. She put the slip of paper in her pocket and figured she'd try to stop by his new place sometime that evening before she went to the hospital. His new location was only a few minutes from Hollywood station, but she'd call first. Jorge was ambitious but he was a worrier too. She knew him well enough to guess he was hiding out until he was certain killing Jerome hadn't somehow damaged him or his career. Hopefully she could ease his fears and get him back to work.

When Josie went to the records section, one of the senior clerks told her Behan had been there and gone. She located him in the station's jail talking to one of the custody officers. He finished his conversation and motioned for her to follow him down the hallway.

"Jerome had been booked in this station a couple of times. Looks like Westwood is his hunting ground, breaking into condos just outside the UCLA village where there's lots of rich old ladies."

"Was he here when my place got firebombed?" she asked.

"I think so but I have to check the dates. He was arrested by West LA patrol right after he'd been with Marvin and Tyler at Wilshire station, the same day I confiscated Marvin's department semiauto."

"Did Jerome get filed on for his last arrest?"

"That's the strange part. I talked to the senior patrol officer. He says it was a righteous burglary, caught Jerome climbing out a window with stuff in his pockets. He should've been busted on his parole, but there was no record of his arrest. No one contacted his parole officer . . . I can't find any reports the officers wrote, nothing."

"How'd he get out of jail?"

"Walked out the front door. No charges filed or pending. Somebody signed the detectives' names on the release form, left it in the jail, and Jerome Handy was a free man. Detectives swear they never saw any reports and didn't release him; their signatures were forged. The arresting officers assumed his parole had been revoked and that was the reason they never got a subpoena to testify in court."

"You think Marvin was able to find a way to get Jerome released?" Josie asked, but she remembered the wasted confused man she'd seen at the warehouse and quickly dismissed that possibility.

Behan took a deep breath and showed her a copy of the form.

"Anybody could've forged this, but the names and serial numbers for the detectives are accurate. I'm thinking it has to be a cop who works here and knows them," he said. "The jailer's an old fart with bad arthritis in his hands and very distinctive handwriting. It wasn't him."

"Why would any cop want Jerome out of custody?" Josie asked.

"Damned if I know, but it's not long after he leaves here that he's breaking into Jorge Sanchez's house with the same gun in his hand that killed Howard Burke."

"You said he's been arrested several times in West LA. ID any cop who's had prior contact with him. Pull every crime report you can find connected to Jerome Handy and check with narcotics and vice for an informant package. I've got to get back to Hollywood," she said, returning the release form. "Need to get some work done so I can go to the hospital."

"Just go. Me and my guys can do this. I'll get a couple of them out here. Mac's arranged for the salesgirl from Rodeo Drive to work with our artist. We're about to take her composite and the one from the girl at the Primrose Motel and show them to everybody on Santa Monica Boulevard, every bun boy, runaway, every business. Somebody knows this Jesse Mata."

"But you're staying here to work on Burke's killer, right?"

Behan hesitated as if his answer was something he was reluctant to admit.

"It had to be a cop that got Jerome out of here, probably gave him the murder weapon and Jorge Sanchez's home address. We've been told more than once Jesse Mata or Matador is a cop. Burke got killed right in the middle of Mata's hunting ground. It would be fucking incredible to have two dirty cops working in the same neighborhood. My gut tells me we're looking at one guy for all these killings including Burke's."

"Maybe Burke had to die because he discovered Matador's real identity and then found out he was a cop. Matador makes it look like Marvin Wright killed Burke so nobody's looking at him," Josie said.

"And Marvin makes it completely believable by running and hiding . . . not because he's guilty but because he's a full-blown bipolar paranoid maniac."

"Good theory, now prove it. Find our dirty cop. We're running out of time, and Dempsey is salivating to dump this case on Marvin just to close it."

"Thought I'd talk to Captain Ames and see if he's got a candidate for someone in his division who might be clever or screwed up enough to pull off Jerome's escape."

"No, don't do that," Josie said quickly. "Stuart Ames is completely out of touch and he blabs everything to Dempsey. I'm going to see Jorge tonight. I'd rather ask him."

As she was leaving West LA station, Josie noticed a couple of her patrol officers coming out of the city attorney's office across the courtyard, and she hitched a ride back to Hollywood station. They were assigned several radio calls as soon as they were back in the division and Josie stayed with them until they finished. They were willing to drop her off sooner but she wasn't going to miss the opportunity to help them make arrests. A half-hour ride turned into two hours and if she didn't have so much work to do, it would've been longer.

Mac was waiting in her office when she arrived. He had received the results of preliminary blood tests on Marvin, Jerome, and Tyler. None of them matched the blood on the window ledge of the costume shop where Mata had cut himself stealing the Matador jacket.

"How's Kyle, Lieutenant Richards doing?" Mac asked, when she finished reading the report.

"I think he'll be coming home in a day or two."

"Great, good man."

"You should stop by Cedars. I'm sure he'd be really happy to see you."

Mac almost smiled and had started to leave when he stopped and said, "Commissioner Charles called about twenty minutes ago and said he would come by sometime later this afternoon. Didn't give me a time."

"Thanks, Mac, did he say what it was about?"

"No, but didn't sound urgent," he said, going back out to the admin office.

Josie had a Chamber of Commerce meeting in an hour and was planning to leave for Jorge's house right after that. The commissioner might have to wait until tomorrow. She was about to call him when he knocked on her door and stepped into the office.

"I apologize for coming on such short notice, Captain," he said, smiling and shaking her hand.

"No problem," she said, sitting at the worktable. Josie thought he was a very attractive man and figured Judy at the High-Top Bar was probably right about his sexual preference. He was very unlike his outrageous brother, Anthony, or his prickly sister and father. He was a prominent successful lawyer with a pleasant personality. Not someone

Josie would've expected to be unattached or without a significant other, man or woman, but then again there was that family gene thing.

"I just wanted to touch bases with you, see if there was any progress on finding who killed my brother or Howie Burke."

"We do have some significant leads," she said, and he straightened up a bit.

"Really," he said. "My father will be pleased to hear that."

"I'd say in the next day or so, we expect to solve the serial killings and identify Howard Burke's killer," Josie said and tried to sound more confident than she felt about that preferred outcome.

"Is Chief Dempsey aware of that?" he asked, seeming confused. "The reason I ask is he told the police commissioners at our meeting this week he was afraid the serial killings would remain unsolved and your dead ex-police officer had probably killed Howie but you were unable to close the case as solved."

"He was wrong," Josie said, and under her breath added, "As usual."

Charles was quiet for a few seconds, staring at her as if to satisfy himself she wasn't joking.

"Wonderful news," he said finally, getting up. "My family will be looking forward to the end of this week and some closure."

When he was gone, Josie cleaned off her desk, told Mac to go home, and drove to the Chamber office for her meeting. There wasn't much business to discuss there. She participated in early discussions about the Hollywood Christmas parade that took place after Thanksgiving every year. Her primary concern was safety and deployment of officers. She'd done it so many times her input was brief and practically the same as the prior year.

She left before the meeting was over, giving them the excuse that she had to get to the hospital before visiting hours were over. The real reason was boredom and her desire to visit Jorge with plenty of time remaining to spend with Kyle before he passed out in a medicated fog for the rest of the night.

Jorge's address off Laurel Canyon was one she knew. She had served a search warrant on that same street for a well-known rapper when she was a narcotics detective, and had recovered several kilos of cocaine. Most of the streets in the Hollywood Hills didn't have streetlights and were difficult to navigate at night but there was just enough time before sunset to see where she was going.

She turned the corner onto his street but immediately pulled to the curb behind a parked car half a block from the house. She was surprised but certain she recognized the four-door, black Mercedes-Benz parked in front of Jorge's home. As far as she knew, it had no reason to be there.

Any doubts she might've had disappeared when Ed Charles, carrying his suit jacket and tie, came out the front door and for several seconds hugged Jorge who was wearing shorts, no shirt, or shoes. It was far more intimate than a friendly good-bye. Charles got into the driver's seat of the Mercedes and drove away. Jorge waited in the doorway until the car was out of sight before going back inside.

"Now, ain't that some strange shit," Josie said out loud.

TWENTY-FOUR

Josie had forgotten to call and tell Jorge she was coming, but as she sat in the car watching Ed Charles drive away, she was grateful for that mental blip. There wasn't any good reason she could imagine that the police commissioner would be visiting the West LA captain at his home. Given what she saw, they were friends, very good friends. Shit, she thought, my protégé is gay, but why hadn't he or Charles mentioned their relationship? Jorge had to know it wouldn't matter. He never even told her he was friendly with the commissioner. That seemed odd to her.

She sat in the car a few minutes attempting to come up with some explanation why they would want to keep their friendship quiet. Jorge might've been conducting some side investigation for the police commission, but the hug she'd seen wasn't between business associates.

The best way to find the truth might be to ask Jorge. But instinctively, something told her not to do that. She waited a few more minutes then drove to the front of his house and parked. Before getting out of the car, she saw the curtain in the front window move a little. He was familiar with her city car, and she thought he'd have a few seconds to contemplate just what she might've seen on her arrival.

He opened the door as soon as she rang the bell. Now he was wearing a T-shirt, shorts, and shoes with white socks.

"Josie, what are you doing here?" he asked, moving aside for her to enter.

"I was at West LA today and they said you were taking a little time off. Thought I'd drop by, make sure you were okay," she said, giving him a quick hug. "I meant to call first but got busy and forgot; hope I'm not interrupting anything."

"No problem, come in, excuse the mess. I haven't quite organized my stuff yet. Got everything out of the other house in sort of a hurry."

"How are you doing?"

"Much better, just need some time," he said and laughed softly. "You probably think I'm a wuss after all the shootings you've had. My first one and I fall apart."

"It's a big deal taking a life even if he was a dipshit. I do think you need to talk to the department shrink again. It can't hurt and might help you cope a little better . . . unless there's someone else you trust and can open up to without feeling inhibited," she said and studied his expression looking for some indication he might mention Charles.

He started moving boxes off the couch to make a place for her to sit and offered to make them coffee. She accepted and waited while he went into the kitchen.

"This is a nice house," she shouted, getting up and walking around the living room.

"Thanks," he called back. "The rent's a little high but worth it for my peace of mind."

She looked down the hallway and peeked into the bathroom and the master bedroom. The king-sized bed was messy, and two whiskey glasses with a half-empty bottle were on the nightstand. She returned to the living room just as Jorge was coming back carrying two cups of coffee and a bag of chocolate cookies. He'd known her long enough to be familiar with her addiction to anything chocolate.

"I was looking for your bathroom," she said.

"Last door on the right," he said calmly.

She went into the bathroom, searched the medicine cabinet to see if he was taking anything for his nerves or if there was a supply of sleeping pills. There was nothing except a couple of toothbrushes and normal toiletries for men. She waited a few seconds, flushed the toilet, and came out.

"So do you think seeing someone might be a good idea?" she asked, taking the coffee and a cookie, sitting beside him on the couch.

"I'll think about it. Stu told me I could take some time off work and frankly, I think that's best right now."

"Maybe," Josie said. "But it's important to talk about it too. Is there anybody you can confide in, someone you're close to?" she asked, repeating herself, thinking the question had to be obvious as an attempt to draw a name from him.

"You," he answered, giving her that million-dollar smile.

"Thanks, but if you listen to Dempsey I'm the last person to give anybody advice . . . nobody else?"

He didn't respond but changed the subject and asked about Kyle. She gave him an update and noticed a blue Dodgers cap on the fireplace mantel.

"You a Dodgers fan?" she asked. She loved baseball, but didn't know he had any interest. She was hoping it belonged to Ed Charles and that would give him another opening to talk about their relationship.

"Not really, someone left that here; I keep forgetting to return it."

"I love the Dodgers. Does it belong to anyone I know?"

"No."

"Do you need any help putting your stuff away?" she asked, glancing around the room at the stacks of boxes. She really wanted to ask about Charles but a sixth sense warned her not to do it now. Years of police work had taught her not to ignore those subtle caution signs.

"Thanks, but no. It's kind of therapeutic doing it myself," he said, getting up. "How's the investigation on Burke going. Are we able to say Jerome or Marvin did it now that we've recovered the gun?"

"Behan's making some progress. At least you don't have to worry about Marvin coming after you anymore."

"Or you," Jorge said quickly.

"I've never lost much sleep over that one," Josie said.

She thanked him for the coffee, gave him another quick hug, reminded him to give some serious thought to seeing the department shrink, and left. There was still time to get to Cedars before Kyle went down for the night, but she had an urge to drive around the corner, park down the street again, and see if Charles came back. This was such an odd pairing—Jorge, the seemingly outgoing ladies' man, and the moody, genetically impaired gay police commissioner. She wondered if somebody at West LA station had found out about them and had blackmailed Jorge to get Jerome out of jail.

It bothered her that Jorge hadn't mentioned that he and Ed Charles were lovers or even friends. She'd given him plenty of opportunities to provide that information. He should've known after all these years she wouldn't judge him, but because he didn't tell her, Josie wondered what other secrets he and Charles were keeping from her.

Shortly after she had parked down the block, Josie saw Jorge's garage door open and his city car come out and drive away. She was tempted to follow him but didn't. Surveillance was tricky business. Tomorrow she'd confer with Behan and they'd have to take a more direct approach in asking both men about the relationship. It would be Red's last full day as an active cop. There wouldn't be any time left for delicacy or whatever it was that kept her from confronting Jorge.

The third floor of the hospital looked deserted when Josie got off the elevator. There wasn't a nurse or orderly in sight until she reached the nurses' station where they were gathered in a circle talking. Kyle's regular nurse waved at her and jumped up before Josie reached his room.

"He's already taken his meds. Sorry, he wanted to wait for you, but the doctor wanted him to sleep before we had to wake him again for his next round," she said.

"That's fine," Josie said. "I'll just look in now and head home."

She pulled back the curtain and saw Kyle was already in a deep sleep. He looked peaceful and his color seemed normal again. It wouldn't be a surprise if he were allowed to go home the next day. The doctor had told her he was eager to discharge patients. "Hospital isn't a good place to get well," he'd said.

Josie leaned over the bed to kiss him when her phone beeped. It was Behan. He asked if she could come back to West LA station. There was something he had to show her. She told him what she'd seen at Jorge's house.

"You need to get here," Behan said. He sounded concerned.

"What is it?"

"Not on the phone. I'll wait for you out front."

It only took a few minutes for her to drive from Cedars in Beverly Hills to the West LA station.

Behan was pacing outside the building's cramped lobby, smoking a cigarette, something she hadn't seen him do for a long time.

"I thought Miss Vicky made you give up that nasty habit," Josie said when she got to the bottom of the stairs.

"She did. Come inside, I've got to show you something," he said, dropping the cigarette butt on the ground and grinding it with his heel.

He led the way back into the nearly empty station, and she followed him through the records section to Captain Stuart Ames's office. When Behan opened the door, she saw Marge sitting at the CO's desk.

"What are you doing here in the middle of the night?"

"Going through a shit pot full of West LA personnel files," Marge said. "Disciplinary stuff, notices to correct, 1.28s, informant packages. You name it, everything."

"Captain Ames was a bit tight-ass about giving me access to his files. So I waited until he went home, called Mac and Marge, and we started looking."

"Mac is here too?"

"I sent him home about an hour ago when we got to lieutenants and captains. Didn't think he needed to know too much about guys that outranked him."

"Tell me you found something that justifies a burglary," Josie said.

"Pretty sure I have," Behan said.

He explained how he discovered the middle name Mata on an application to attend one of the department's out-of-state training classes. Marge had pulled every arrest report involving Jerome Handy and found that the same cop had arrested Jerome several years ago.

"At that time, there was an informant package made up for Jerome that's mysteriously disappeared from the narcotics office. There are ledgers kept in the OIC's safe with an informant number linked to every case Jerome got paid for and which cop paid him," Behan said.

"Just tell me who we're talking about," Josie demanded. She was getting impatient with his reluctance to give her a name.

"Your fucking boy wonder," Marge said. "Jorge Mata Sanchez. And in case you got doubts, his dad's name was Jesse. Personnel had it on his original application to come on the department." She handed Josie a copy of the application. It had Jorge's full name and listed his nearest relative as Jesse Sanchez, whose occupation was professional rodeo rider.

Josie sat on the edge of the desk. Confusion and disbelief were only a few of the emotions that had temporarily left her speechless. He was the one person on the LAPD she would never have suspected. Her mind was struggling to think clearly again, but she knew trusting and liking Jorge had probably blinded her to things she should have seen and questioned.

In almost thirty years, she had never allowed her feelings or prejudices to interfere with doing the job. The fact that he betrayed her trust and violated their friendship made her sad but mostly it made her livid. She knew her face had to be a bright shade of red by now.

"You okay, Boss?" Marge asked, keeping her distance. She was one of the few people who'd ever seen Josie lose her temper. It didn't happen often but they both knew it wasn't a pretty sight.

"I'm fine," Josie said, sliding off the desk and telling herself to calm down. "You did great work. We need to pick up Jorge. Do a blood match from the window ledge at Ozzie's Costumes and have our witnesses who made the composites ID him and check to see if his prints are anywhere in the motel room. Also see if that arson investigator in Pasadena got any prints from the broken Molotov cocktail bottles thrown at my house."

Her voice was steady but it felt as if she had a volcano in her chest about to blow. She had to be certain everything they did from this point forward made the court case against Jorge stronger when what she really wanted to do was grab the nearest wooden baseball bat and beat the living crap out of him.

"I'm guessing if we do a search warrant we're going to find that belt buckle. Remember Judy the bartender at the High Top said Mata wore one that looked like a rodeo buckle," Behan said.

"What about Ed Charles? Do we pick him up too?" Marge asked.

It was as if a curtain was lifting in Josie's brain. Now that she'd allowed herself to consider Jorge a suspect, the pieces were beginning to fall into place and her thinking felt on track again.

"We don't know if Charles is an accomplice or Jorge's next victim," Behan said.

"We made it difficult for him to get new boy toys off Santa Monica when we plastered his composites all over the boulevard and shut down his lair at the La Brea motel. So I'm guessing he had to get creative and Charles might be his next victim," Josie said.

"His MO is sex with his victims then kill them," Marge said. "If you saw what you thought you saw earlier, Boss,

WARNING SHOTS

they had sex, and I'm thinking there's about to be a vacancy on the police commission."

"He's not stupid so he's probably learned his lesson with Anthony about leaving them alive and letting them blab too much," Josie said.

"We need to find Ed Charles," Behan said and picked up the telephone. "I'll check Baldwin Hills."

Josie and Marge were quiet, watching him until he finished his conversation and hung up.

"That was his sister, Sandra. She said Ed was home until about twenty minutes ago. Didn't say where he was going but he was dressed in casual clothes, took the Porsche, and told her not to wait up," Behan said.

"Jorge doesn't know we're looking for him. Let's just stake out his house and arrest his ass when he comes home," Marge said.

"By then, Ed Charles might already be dead," Behan said.

"Where would Jorge bring him . . . back to Santa Monica Boulevard where he took the rest of his victims?" Josie asked. "It's got to be somewhere near the High-Top. That's where he's comfortable killing," she said, answering her own question.

She told Behan to give patrol a description of the Porsche and its license plate number and have officers look for the car in the area where the other young men had been killed, but make it clear all they should do is locate the car and not attempt to approach or arrest its occupants. She knew there was nothing more dangerous than an armed cop who knew he was going to prison and had nothing to lose.

Josie knew she should feel some guilt about Ed Charles being in danger. If she had asked Jorge about their relationship, he probably would've backed away from the police

commissioner. On the other hand, she figured having identified his next victim made catching him a lot easier. If
Charles got lucky, he'd live through the experience and be
able to testify. Either way she got her killer.

Behan sent a team of detectives to the Hollywood Hills
home off Laurel Canyon with orders to detain Jorge if he
returned. Marge had made copies of everything in Jorge's
personnel package kept in Captain Ames's office and the
one at personnel division. She carefully returned all the
West LA packages to the file cabinet and tried to leave the
office exactly the way they'd found it. Josie didn't want
to know how they managed to get in there, but guessed
Marge's expertise with lock picks had once again prevailed.

The original job application from Jorge had an address
for Jesse Sanchez in East LA. It was completed more than
fourteen years ago but Josie figured they might as well go
there and see if the old man was still alive and at that location. If they had any contact, the father might have some
idea where his son would be. She thought it strange that
Jorge would use his father's name and maybe an article of
his clothing to do his killing. In her mind, the possibility
of finding Jorge at that house was remote, but something
told her if the father was still alive, the trip wouldn't be a
waste of time either.

Marge had vice officers working a prostitution detail
on Hollywood Boulevard. She went back to the station to
move them down to Santa Monica Boulevard to help in the
search for the Porsche while Josie and Behan drove to the
father's house.

The time of night made it easier for Behan to drive
quickly across the city to the east side. They were silent
for most of the trip. Josie tried to recall all the clues that
should have been red flags pointing at her protégé. His

ambush couldn't have been Marvin's doing and the shots
were nowhere near the driver's side of the windshield.
Marvin didn't know her address, but Jorge did. How would
Jerome know Jorge's home address unless someone gave it
to him? Jorge had used Jerome as an informant in the past
and most likely signed him out of jail only to lure him to
his West LA home where he executed the man to silence
him and probably put the murder weapon in Jerome's hand
to take attention off himself. His expert shooting that night
should have been her best clue. Jorge was never that good
with firearms and had trouble qualifying.

She still wondered why he killed Burke. It had to
be because the lawyer somehow figured out that he was
Jesse Mata. Burke never gave any indication during the
board of rights that he believed Jorge was anything but an
LAPD captain. Except . . . that last day when Burke looked
upset and hurried out of the board room. She thought
it was because he was afraid of Marvin, but maybe that
was the day he realized Jorge and the "matador" were the
same man.

She felt a sharp pain over her eyes and rubbed both
temples trying to ease the tension. Stop thinking, she
thought. Let it play out.

"You okay?" Behan asked, as he was getting off the
freeway.

"Headache."

"No surprise there."

"I should've seen it sooner."

"Nah, I don't think so. The guy's a psychopath. He had
everybody fooled."

"For almost fourteen years he played the part of a cop,
a good cop, and all the while . . ." she didn't finish. What
was the point. It was like discovering you've got a mad dog.

You stop wishing it was Old Yeller and just put the damn thing down. She knew her damaged mutt definitely had to go.

THE ADDRESS Jorge had given for his father was in LAPD's Northeast division off Broadway in a heavily Hispanic part of the city. Josie recognized the area because a lot of Italians had lived in the neighborhood when she was younger, and she had visited several relatives who had homes there. She knew the crime rate had fallen in the last few years because most of the residents were either senior citizens or younger families with small children who had moved into the inexpensive housing. The gangs were less of a problem because of attrition. Those who weren't in jail were generally too old to embrace the lifestyle any longer.

The lights were on both inside the house and on the front porch when they arrived. Josie looked around for Jorge's city car or the Porsche. There was no sign of them. A detached one-car garage was to the rear of the house. She had Behan drop her off a few houses away so she could walk up the driveway and peek through a crack in the closed garage door. It was empty.

Behan parked, then met her on the front porch. Even in the dark, she could tell the house was old with peeling paint and dry-rot around the windows. The boards on the porch floor creaked, gave a little under their weight, and were in dire need of repair. There was one usable lawn chair by the door and a couple pieces of broken furniture and an old stove were stacked neatly out of the way.

She pressed the doorbell but didn't hear anything, so Behan knocked. The television inside got louder. He knocked harder. The curtain in the window to the left of the door was pulled back and a woman looked out and shook her head.

"Go away, too late!" she shouted.

Josie pressed her badge against the window and smiled at the woman. She wasn't very old, seemed to be about her age. The woman glared at her for a few seconds until Behan showed his badge then she let go of the curtain and moved toward the door.

"We'd like to speak to Jesse Sanchez," Behan said when she opened the door. The woman was short and thin with a hawkish nose but still had an attractive face. Her dark hair was pulled back in a bun and she wore a grey dowdy dress and clunky black shoes. She looked nothing like Jorge and had that constricted, unfulfilled aura of a spinster, Josie thought.

"He ain't here no more," the woman said. She looked worried, and the furrows in her forehead grew deeper as she spoke.

"Did he move or is he just away?" Josie asked.

"No, he ain't here cus' he's dead and buried," she said and stepped back a little. "You want to come in. I'm Sara, his stepdaughter."

The house was clean and neat inside. The furniture looked old but had intricate crocheted doilies on the arms and backs of the chairs and couch. Josie could see the table lamps had handmade silk cloth shades with wire frames. She'd had an aunt who made those shades years ago. She knew it was a lost art, very difficult and expensive to get anyone to do it now.

"These are wonderful," Josie said, touching the bottom of one of the more intricate shades.

"My mom's work from years ago. She sold them to put food on our table. She's gone now too."

"When did Jesse die?" Behan asked.

"About ten years ago."

"Is Jorge Sanchez your brother?"

"Stepbrother. Sit down," she said, pointing at the couch. "I just made iced tea. I'll get us some."

Before Josie could say, "don't bother," Sara was gone, disappearing into what she guessed was the kitchen. A few seconds later, she came back carrying two glasses full of ice and what looked like weak tea and put them on the table in front of the couch. She went back and returned with another glass on a small tray with a bowl full of packets of artificial sugar, left the tray on the table, took her glass, and sat across from them.

"Drink up and tell me what you want," she said.

"Do you stay in touch with Jorge?" Behan asked.

"Not since his daddy, Jesse, died. He don't come here anymore and I don't ask him to come."

"So you haven't seen him for ten years? Have you talked to him?"

"Haven't seen or talked to him since Jesse's funeral, and a long time before that."

"Jesse wasn't your father," Josie said.

"God, no," she said, almost choking on a sip of tea and when she could speak again added, "My mom married him and then him and his little boy moved in here with us."

"You don't sound as if you approved."

"Jesse was gone most of the time working the circuit, the rodeo, and sometimes he won enough or scraped together a few dollars to help with the bills but that was no marriage. Me and my mom was babysitters and when he was around, he was a bad father to Jorge."

"Why a bad father?" Josie asked.

"He beat that boy . . . strip him naked, use a belt 'til his skin was raw and that wasn't the worst of it," she said and hesitated as if the rest was too awful to talk about. "My mom, she tried to stop him but it didn't help. He never dare laid a hand on her or me . . . but that poor little boy."

"What was the worst of it?" Josie asked, thinking what she'd heard sounded bad enough.

Sara sighed and shook her head. Josie could see there were tears welling up in her eyes as she remembered and struggled to get the words out.

"I know he did . . . unnatural nasty things with that boy. I wasn't much older than my stepbrother, but I remember seeing that monster take Jorge into his bedroom and . . . have his way," she said, with an expression of disgust, looking at Josie as if she had said as much as she could tolerate.

"Did your mother ever call the police on him?"

"No, I told her what I saw but she didn't believe me, said Jesse would never do such a sinful filthy thing. Really messed up that boy."

"Messed him up how?" Behan asked. Josie thought she could probably answer that question.

"When Jorge gets bigger and stronger he's mean, sneaky mean, picking on things smaller than him . . . animals . . . other boys, but he always had the face of an angel and a way of talking so he gets away with it. In high school, he hit Jesse hard once, broke some teeth so my mom she kicked Jorge out. Never saw him again until Jesse's funeral and never after that."

"Did Jorge ever have a fascination with bullfighting?" Josie asked.

Sara's eyes opened wide and she asked, "Yes, how'd you know that?"

"Lucky guess."

"Jesse's professional name in the rodeo was the bull, El Toro. Every time Jesse hurt that boy, I know it sounds stupid, but I would cry, and Jorge would comfort me, promise that someday he'd be a matador and punish the bull."

"How did Jesse die?" Behan asked.

"Drunk, as usual. Police said it might've been robbers outside the bar, strangled him, left him in the gutter like the garbage he was. Nobody cared he was dead . . . especially me."

"What's your mother's family name?" Josie asked.

"Mata, like mine. I never married," Sara said. She took a deep breath and asked, "Can you tell me why you're asking all these questions. Is Jorge in trouble? Has something happened to him?"

Behan got up, and as she stood, Josie said, "I promise I'll come back and explain everything to you as soon as I can, Sara. But for now, if you want to help your brother, call us if he contacts you or comes here. He's in trouble and we need to find him before something bad happens to him or anyone else."

"Got to be a special place in hell for a man like Jesse, for what he done," Sara said, and then looked at the ceiling for a few seconds without speaking. Then she took their business cards and agreed to call them if her stepbrother contacted her. She stood in the doorway while they climbed down the porch stairs to the sidewalk but called out before they reached the car.

"It's not my brother's fault. Jesse was evil."

TWENTY-FIVE

The radio transmission began as soon as Josie got into Behan's car. A patrol officer broadcast the location of Ed Charles's silver Porsche. He'd spotted it pulling into the parking lot behind the High-Top Bar on Santa Monica Boulevard.

"Fuck!" Behan shouted as he started the car. "They were told to stay off the radio," he said, pounding his fist on the steering wheel.

"If we're lucky, Jorge's out of his car and didn't hear it," she said, knowing he probably heard it because they were never that lucky.

Marge contacted her on her cell phone and said she was waiting outside the club with a team of vice officers. They couldn't locate Jorge's city car, but the Porsche was parked in almost the same spot where Howard Burke's Tesla had been the night he was killed. Josie told her to keep the existing perimeter several blocks from the club with uniformed officers remaining out of sight and to wait until she and Behan arrived before entering the club.

Twenty minutes later, Behan's vehicle was pulling into the parking lot. Josie didn't see a single black-and-white or uniformed officer but she knew they were somewhere nearby in the shadows. She and Behan met Marge and her officers outside the back door of the club.

"It's your call, Red. How do you want to play this?" Josie asked.

"The three of us and the two vice officers go inside. You and me will confront Charles, Boss, while Marge and her guys search the club."

"My UCs have already been in there," Marge said. "Charles is alone at the bar drinking. He's talking to the bartender but nobody else. Looks like he's waiting for somebody."

"Let's just hope that asinine broadcast didn't fuck this up," Behan said.

He led them around to the front door of the High-Top. Several young men were gathered outside talking, drinking, and performing the usual pre-mating rituals that occur when it's almost closing time at any pick-up bar. No one seemed to be paying much attention as they went inside and were met with the stifling heat and odor of too many sweaty bodies in too small a space. The vice officers quickly blended into the crowd and Josie saw Marge climbing the stairs that led to the bartender's apartment.

The stools around Charles were empty. Josie and Behan sat on either side of him as he talked to Judy, who was standing on the other side of the bar refilling his whiskey glass. A few seconds after Behan got there, Judy turned her attention to him, smiled, and said, "Hello, my favorite redhead, what can I get for you, Sweetie," causing Charles to finally realize he wasn't alone. He looked from left to right and then behind him.

"What are you doing here?" he asked Josie.

"I was about to ask you the same question, Commissioner."

"What I do on my own time is none of your business."

"In this case, it is, sir," Behan said, and as concisely as possible, he explained everything they had discovered about Captain Jorge Sanchez.

Ed Charles slowly shook his head. It was obvious he didn't want to believe what he was hearing. By the end of Behan's story, his shoulders had slumped forward and Josie could see a slight nervous quiver in his lower lip as if he were about to cry. She didn't know if it was fear, remorse, or anger, maybe all three.

"Did he kill my brother?" Charles asked, attempting to control his emotion.

"We think so," Behan answered. "We're pretty sure he bought the cape Anthony always wore then took it after he killed him, so we couldn't trace it back to him."

"Tell me where Jorge is now, Ed," Josie said.

"He was supposed to meet me here," Charles said and rubbed his face with open hands for a few seconds. "I'm so stupid. We got together for the first time this afternoon. I believed him, trusted him."

"How did you meet?"

"Stuart Ames introduced us at your retirement party. He was funny and seemed interested in me. We were compatible," Charles said, swallowing a laugh. "He called last night out of the blue and I met him today at his house in Hollywood. Everything happened so fast. He made me feel . . . what's the difference. I'm such a fool."

"Don't feel bad. He's a genius at manipulating people," Behan said.

"Our affair, will it have to come out . . . in public?" Charles asked, wincing at the thought.

"We'll see," Josie said. "Important thing is you're safe, but we have to find him. Do you know where he might've gone?"

"No, sorry, he told me to meet him here before closing. There was something he wanted to show me. I had to stop by the office so I was later than I thought I'd be."

Marge came downstairs and joined them at the bar.

"He's not up there," she said.

"You've been in my apartment?" Judy asked. She was standing nearby, hands on hips, scowling. Josie had almost forgotten she was still there. "You've got no right . . ."

"You got the fucking right to remain silent or I'll book your ass for interfering," Marge said, getting within inches of the bartender's face before she could finish her protest. Charles started to object too but looked at Marge and remained quiet. He and Judy exchanged a glance that seemed to say, "Go ahead if you want to, but I'm not provoking that woman."

Behan left the two vice officers in the High-Top to watch Charles until closing. If Jorge didn't show, they would escort him home to Baldwin Hills and stay with him until Jorge was found. Like his brother, Anthony, the police commissioner had become bait, but Josie had a feeling this was the last place her protégé would show up tonight.

There was nothing to substantiate it, but Josie had a hunch Jorge was still somewhere within their perimeter. The broadcast about the Porsche came after the area had been secured. If his car was already there, he shouldn't have been able to get out. His picture and description had been distributed to every officer.

"We need to check again for Jorge's car," Josie said when she, Marge, and Behan were standing in the parking lot.

"I think he's long gone, Boss," Marge said.

"Tell me once more what he's driving," Behan said.

"It's a black Dodge Charger. His regular car is still out for a new windshield. There's a radio antenna in back but no emergency lights. I saw it when he left his house," Josie said. "He's still here, Red. He's addicted to killing, a junkie who needs his fix. If not Ed Charles then somebody. This boulevard is his hunting ground, familiar territory. He's going to do it here. He's got to."

"Okay, you don't have to convince me. I agree with you. Let's split up and start checking all the north and south streets off Santa Monica," Behan said. "If he's here we'll find him." He wanted to start on the west side and told Marge to begin at the eastern border of the perimeter. Josie got in Marge's car and they drove up and down each side street, north and south of the boulevard but couldn't find the Dodge Charger.

They were about to give up and return to the club when Josie saw what she thought was a sliver of light from the side window of the building where Anthony had been killed. She told Marge to park a half block away, and they would walk to the abandoned brick structure.

"A dozen fucking homeless kids must have used this place as a crash pad. It was probably them you saw," Marge said, taking a flashlight from under her driver's seat.

"Hurry up," Josie said, jogging toward the building. All the windows were dark now. She stopped at the alley where the building's escape ladder led to the roof, the route Mata had most likely taken to get away after killing Anthony Charles. Josie could make out the lines of what could've been a dark car parked behind the dumpster in the pitch-black alley. "Is it the Charger?" she whispered to Marge.

Marge moved carefully along the walls of the alley toward the car and got close enough to see around the dumpster. She disappeared in the darkness for a few seconds then hurried back to where Josie was waiting. "It's his, but he's not in there, must be in the building. I'll call for backup."

Before Josie could say anything, she heard what sounded like a high-pitched, woman's muffled scream from inside the building. She ran through the alley, past the car and ladder, around the corner of the building to the back door and found it unlocked. The interior was completely dark and Marge grabbed her arm before she could enter.

"Bad idea, wait for help," Marge said.

Josie pulled away and slipped into the reception area. She remembered the layout of the lobby, the huge space where dozens of cubicles had once been, covered now with dirty blankets scattered on the concrete floor for bedding, layers of garbage, broken furniture, and coffee cans turned over and strategically placed to hold candles.

"Jorge!" she shouted, getting behind what used to be the front counter. "It's me, Josie." Marge had followed her inside and was kneeling beside her. Josie whispered, "Go back to the alley and deploy officers where they can watch the ladder that comes down from the roof. It's the only other way out of here. The front door is chained on the outside. Keep everybody outside until I figure out who's in here with him."

"I'm not leaving you alone."

"I'm not going to do anything stupid. I just wanna calm him down and try to talk him out of killing whoever he's got with him."

"You're the boss," Marge said and crawled toward the back door. Josie could hear her giving orders on the police radio.

"It's over, Jorge. You're not getting out of here, buddy," Josie said, trying to sound calm.

"Help me, please," someone begged from the other side of the room. Now she knew it was a man with a high voice.

"Who are you?" Josie asked. She'd heard that voice before but couldn't remember where or when.

"Mookie," he whined. "Please don't let him hurt me."

She heard a thump, sobbing, and a moan.

"Don't kill him, Jorge," she said.

"Why not?" It was Jorge's voice, cold, indifferent.

"Because he's not the one you want," she said, trying to gauge where he might be hiding in the room.

"Maybe he won't die if nobody else comes in here."

"Nobody's coming in, yet, but you're not getting out either. The roof and that escape ladder are covered, and there's an army of coppers at the back door. By the way, Ed Charles knows you killed his brother," she said, just wanting to keep the conversation going until she could convince him giving up was his best option. She didn't want her officers dying in a shootout with him.

"Anthony was special. Ed . . . not so much."

"If Anthony was special, why'd you murder him?" She could hear him moving, feet shuffling, and it sounded as if he were dragging something on the floor. She laid on her stomach, trying to ignore the dried urine spots stuck to the concrete in front of her, and peeked around the counter. Her eyes had adjusted to the darkness, and she saw a couple of steel drums that she knew squatters used in the winter to build small fires, but she couldn't make out anything that looked like Jorge or Mookie.

She took her gun out of the holster, got to her knees, and crawled around the counter, got up and moved quickly to the wall outside the first individual office where the hallway began.

"I warned him never to talk about us, but he wasn't afraid of me even after I tried to kill him. That was Anthony . . . my impulsive, unpredictable prince, but then again he did taunt me by talking to you . . . almost dared me to kill him . . . so I did."

"Leave Mookie and come outside with me, Jorge. If you don't, you're going to die."

"Don't believe I can do that, Josie. Anyway, odds are my life's pretty much over," he said and laughed. "Good riddance, right?"

"Gotta ask," she said. "Who did you get to shoot at you in West LA?"

"Jerome, what a fucking disaster. Scared the shit out of me. He was supposed to hit the car, not the windshield. Asshole almost killed me."

"And Burke?" Just keep him talking, she thought.

"That was a bit of a miscalculation on my part. He pissed me off, tried to blackmail me, but I knew afterward it was a mistake to kill him. Unlike my dim boulevard beauties, his departure brought attention, demands from important people to find the culprit. Once you and Red got involved, I knew my fate was sealed. You are one tenacious bitch, Corsino."

"Prison's gotta be better than dying."

"You don't really believe that, do you?"

"You'd be pampered and die of old age on death row. This is California. Nobody gets executed. I know you. You don't want to die, Jorge, not like this," Josie said.

"You're a control freak, Captain C, but this one's kinda out of your hands."

"I talked to your sister, Sara. She told me everything," Josie said, leaning into the dark hallway trying to figure out which office in the long row of doors his voice was coming from. She wanted him to get pissed enough to step out in the hallway and give her one clean shot. It might be Mookie's only chance.

"Fuck my big-mouthed sister," he shouted and fired a round, sending a flash of bright light from what sounded like his .45 semiauto through the hallway, hitting one of the empty steel drums behind her. She had to jump back behind the wall; the explosive noise inside the closed space was deafening.

Before her ears stopped ringing she pulled the police radio out of her back jeans pocket and told Behan that she was okay. She didn't know if Mookie was still alive. He hadn't said a word since she'd heard the dragging sound, but she wasn't ready to give up on him and told Behan she needed more time.

"Negative, we're coming in, Boss," Behan said.

"Jorge," Josie called out but there was no answer. "Jorge!" she shouted again and heard a loud thud. She knew immediately it had come from the utility room and moved cautiously in that direction. The stairs in the middle of the room were empty and the trap door leading to the roof had been thrown open.

She heard a barrage of gunshots from outside the building as she ducked into the room, and then silence. Moonlight penetrated the gap where the trap door had been opened, giving the interior an eerie otherworld feel. She backed up, still holding her gun, while trying to see what was happening on the roof and nearly tripped over Mookie's small body. He looked like a child curled in a fetal position in a corner of the room. "Damn it," she said and checked for a pulse but knew it was pointless. The leather belt was still cinched tightly around his neck, cutting deep into the skin; his long stringy blond hair covered his face like a cheap veil.

"You okay, Boss?" Behan asked, his head and torso poking through the opening in the ceiling.

She didn't answer.

TWENTY-SIX

The roof of the abandoned building was crowded with uniformed police officers and homicide detectives milling around Jorge's body by the time Josie climbed up the utility room stairs and got assistance from Behan and Marge to pull herself out the trap door.

She had to believe Jesse's abuse had messed up the wiring in Jorge's brain, otherwise none of this made any sense. A talented man with so much potential and natural charm shouldn't need to take pleasure in preying on the weak. She had to admit after spending so many years navigating the underbelly of Hollywood, that although most people do learn to control or at least tame their baser impulses, for some it wasn't possible or even desirable. Jorge seemed to be one of those guys who wouldn't or couldn't.

THIS WAS Behan's last day as a homicide supervisor and he could have stepped aside and let one of his senior detectives take on the burdensome task of unraveling the complex crime scene. Cop-on-cop shootings were never simple and the fact that the suspect was a high-ranking officer made it even worse. Instead of leaving, he immediately took charge ordering portable lights for the roof and yellow crime scene tape for inside and outside of the building. He told one of the young police officers to start a list of names and serial numbers of everyone present, designated his best detectives to make phone calls to media relations, Scientific Investigations Division, and the coroner among others, and to start interviewing witnesses. Like the most talented orchestra conductor, he took charge and directed the players until they had given their best performances. Josie was certain, regardless of what the LAPD believed, his retirement wasn't going to be effective until he was satisfied with the preliminary crime scene preparations.

He ordered all nonessential personnel to get off the roof and in a few minutes Josie was standing alone staring at Jorge's battered body propped up and wedged between an air-conditioning unit and the wall. His white shirt and Levi's were smeared with dirt and blood, the handsome face barely recognizable. He'd been shot numerous times. He had moved only a few feet from the trap door before the volley stopped him. She guessed he'd started shooting as soon as he crawled onto the roof and had achieved the available-on-demand "suicide by cop" scenario. He'd been her friend and she should've felt worse, but Josie kept picturing Mookie's body.

Dempsey arrived at the same time as the coroner and was saying something to Josie but she wasn't listening. She and Behan had probably cleared all their homicides and none of her officers had been harmed, but celebrating or bragging about it wasn't what she felt like doing. When she did start listening, Dempsey was complaining about how he'd been denied access to the crime scene by a young police officer who didn't recognize him in civilian clothes. With his usual arrogance, he couldn't understand why anyone wouldn't know him and how important he was.

"Here's an idea. Wear your ID," Josie mumbled when she got tired of his bellyaching, and walked away.

"My guys took the police commissioner home about half an hour ago," Marge said, moving close to Josie and gently nudging her toward a corner of the roof where they could talk privately. "I haven't told the chief that Ed Charles was at the bar. I won't out the man unless you tell me to."

"No, don't," Josie said. "I need PC Charles to owe me a favor."

"I don't get it, Boss. What the fuck happened to Jorge?"

"You're asking the wrong person. I'm a cop, not a shrink. All I do is clean up the garbage . . . not my concern how it got that way," she said, knowing that was only partly true.

Marge shrugged and said, "Yeah, but when it's our garbage the stink sticks to all of us."

IT WAS late afternoon before the crime scene on the roof could be considered closed. The coroner had removed Jorge's body, sketches were done, pictures taken, evidence collected, and most of the witnesses interviewed. The police shooters had been isolated and taken back to Hollywood station to be interviewed by Force Investigation. A second crime scene had been worked simultaneously in the utility room where Andrew "Mookie" Romano had been strangled. The belt around Mookie's neck had a buckle engraved with a bull's head that seemed to leave marks that were a perfect match to those found on Jorge's other victims.

The evidence against Jorge should be overwhelming, Josie thought, once Behan's detectives got the blood match from Ozzie's costume store and the witnesses who made the composites had ID'd him. As his last official act, Behan planned to serve a search warrant on Jorge's new residence in Hollywood with a mission to find the ring Judy had seen in the bar.

Josie got a ride back to the station with the homicide supervisor, and they were in her office discussing details of what still needed to be done when Marge arrived with a fifth of rye whiskey in a brown paper bag and a box of donuts.

"I picked up breakfast," Marge said, putting three paper cups from the water cooler on Josie's desk.

"Perfect," Josie said. She opened the donut box and took the biggest most disgusting one she could find.

Marge filled the three cups halfway and gave one to each of them.

"I'm gonna make a fucking toast," she said, holding up her cup. "To Red, best damn detective in the best damn police station in the most fucked-up city in the world. We'll miss you, partner. If Miss Vicky doesn't throw your fat old-fart ass in the street after a week, I think you'll like retirement."

They emptied their cups and Marge poured a little more in each one.

"My turn," Josie said. She took a sip and held up her drink. "You're a warrior, Red. You fought to the end, earned our respect and love. You're gonna miss us." She drank a little more and added, "And here's to Miss Vicky, a very brave woman."

Behan topped off the cups again, cleared his throat and said, "I can't wait to get the fuck out of this hell hole and away from the two of you . . . too many damn women telling me what to do," he said grinning and emptied the cup.

"Now you can stay home and have one damn woman tell you what to do for the rest of your sorry life," Marge said.

They all turned when Mac came into the office. He was dressed in civilian clothes, clean-shaven, and looked more relaxed than he had in weeks.

"Morning," he said. "Congratulations on the investigation . . . but sorry about Captain Sanchez. Don't want to interrupt but I came to say good-bye."

Josie crumpled the cup and tossed it in the trash. "What are you talking about?" she asked.

"I'm heading over to personnel and resigning this morning."

"Why the hell are you doing that?" Marge asked. "We got the killer. You're off Dempsey's shit list."

"We all know he's a vindictive sonofabitch. He won't stop until I'm gone so I'm saving myself some misery and leaving with my pride intact," he said, and offered to shake hands with Josie. "I wanted to thank you for everything. I'd work for you anytime."

"How about Monday morning as a field sergeant?" Josie asked, still shaking his hand.

"Dempsey's not going to let you do that," Mac said.

"Take the weekend off and be here for any shift you want on Monday. Just let the watch commander know you're coming."

Mac stared at her, turned to Behan and Marge who both had serious expressions but didn't speak.

"Yes, ma'am," he said. "Thank you, you won't be sorry," he mumbled, backing out of the room and still not sounding as if he believed what he was hearing.

Marge waited a few seconds and checked the admin office before coming back and asking, "Really? When did Dempsey tell you he'd let Mac go back to patrol?"

"He didn't. But he will," Josie said.

Behan groaned and got up. "Hope you know what you're doing, Corsino," he said, shaking his head. "If you don't, I hope you can live with what you're doing to that man."

"Gotta go out for a while. You two need anything before I leave?" Josie asked, taking another chocolate donut. She pulled her keys out of her pocket and unlocked the oak wardrobe near the couch, removed a folder from the top shelf, and said, "Nothing? Okay, call on my cell phone if you want me."

"What's the point? You never turn it on," Marge said.

She left them in her office and finished the donut before getting into her car, threw the folder on the front seat, and drove slowly out of the lot. She was counting on the extra dose of sugar to keep her awake another hour or so.

Politics in the City of Los Angeles and in the bureaucracy of the police department wasn't something she enjoyed or ever wanted to participate in, but she'd make an exception this time. She called Ed Charles. He was still at the Baldwin Hills residence and she told him to wait and she'd be there in twenty minutes.

"I THOUGHT you'd be asleep by now," Charles said, when he answered the door. "That was a great job you and your people did last night." He sounded sincere but wouldn't make eye contact with her. Josie figured he was probably still embarrassed about his rendezvous with Jorge. She hoped that was the reason.

He led the way into his father's study and offered her coffee which she accepted. One of the servants brought in a tray and poured the coffee; she waited until he had gone and closed the door.

"I have a proposition to make," she said. He started to say something but she interrupted and continued. "Do you know David Jacobson?" she asked.

"Of course, he's the supervising jurist at the criminal courts building. He's a friend of my father's."

"David is my personal and family friend, my son's god-father and his namesake. He listens to me and takes my advice. David is retiring soon and I can give you my word that he will recommend and support your father as his replacement if you do something for me."

"Look, Josie . . ."

"Let me finish," she said and handed him the folder. "I want you to read this. It concerns one of my sergeants, Dan McSweeney, and Deputy Chief Dempsey. Dan won a court case that reflected badly on Dempsey and the chief has retaliated and harassed him since then, taking him out of the field and ruining his career. I've compiled every piece of information on Dan's case and detailed every vindictive action Dempsey has taken."

"What is it you expect me to do?" Charles asked, shift-ing uncomfortably.

"I want you to use the information in that file to per-suade the chief of police to allow McSweeney back in the field, and transfer Dempsey and his minion Tim Scott any-where but West Bureau with a warning to keep his hands off my sergeant."

Charles was quiet for a few seconds. He opened the folder and thumbed through the pages before saying, "I have to admit something, Captain. I owe you a huge debt not only for keeping my name and reputation out of the Sanchez case but for not revealing what you know about my family's . . . mental difficulties. It would be wonderful if my father could take David's place but it's not a prerequisite or even necessary for you to get my help. I promise I will do whatever I can do to assist Sergeant McSweeney. Just tell me when you need this done."

"Monday morning, sir. Not negotiable."

TWENTY-SEVEN

It was difficult for Josie to keep her eyes open during the drive to Long Beach. She wanted to sleep a few hours before going to the hospital to visit with Kyle that evening. The serial killer investigation was over. Burke's killer was dead, and she vowed to sleep for two days before returning to work and beginning whatever the next case was that certainly would eat away at those few precious hours she could manage for her personal life.

She made a promise to herself to take time off and live like a normal person for a day or two before starting the cycle again. Behan, her sounding board, would be gone when she got back to work. Her new homicide supervisor was a good man and a solid detective. He was the person Behan had recommended. The new guy had learned from the best detective in the city and convinced her during his interview that anyone who'd stayed with Red for ten years and hadn't killed him deserved to be promoted.

When Josie pulled into the driveway of Kyle's house, she noticed the side gate was open and wondered if Beth had come back. School hadn't started yet and a steady diet of

Mrs. Richards's company might've proven to be too much even for a devoted granddaughter.

The patio was empty but the kitchen door was unlocked too.

"Hello," Josie called out, standing in the kitchen and hoping anyone but Kyle's mother would answer.

Not getting a response, she went through the dining area into the bedroom and found Kyle asleep on their bed. He was lying on top of the comforter dressed only in his shorts and she could see he had a small bandage on his arm and another on his side with some bruising around the edges.

A lot of questions filled her head. What was he doing here? How did he arrive, how long had he been home, and so many more, but none of them seemed all that important. He was here. She was exhausted and wanted nothing more than to be on the bed next to him. She lay down fully clothed and closed her eyes, not intending to fall asleep but just wanting to rest a few minutes.

When she woke again it was dark. She reached over and Kyle was gone, but she heard noises in the kitchen and knew it hadn't been a dream. He was home.

She got up, took a quick shower, and put on a clean pair of sweatpants and a tank top and went into the kitchen. He was barefoot, still shirtless in his shorts standing near the stove. A bottle of chardonnay was open on the island. He reached over and poured her a glass.

"Should you be out of bed?" she asked, taking the glass.

"I'm hungry. Didn't think you'd feel like cooking."

"Cooking? Take-out from the barbeque place was my plan."

"Heard about Jorge on the news. There was always something not quite right about that guy," Kyle said.

"In the future remind me to listen to you. I'll tell you the whole story tomorrow. Don't really want to waste time on him tonight."

"Mac gave me a ride home from the hospital. He told me he was going back to patrol on Monday. How'd you pull that one off? I thought Dempsey was dead set against him being in the field."

"Called in some markers. What's for dinner?"

"Tell me later?" he asked.

"Sure, why not," she said, thinking he was probably better off not knowing how she had manipulated the system to get her way. "I need a break. What do you think about us flying to Vegas this weekend . . . maybe we could even get married?" she asked, half kidding.

Kyle sat on the chair beside her and said, "Terrible idea."

"Are you getting cold feet?" she asked, smiling.

"No, but marriage is important. I want my daughter and your son to be there. My mother unfortunately will show up whether we invite her or not. Besides, David's got a great reception planned, and I'm not missing his food for a cheap shrimp buffet at the MGM."

"You're right. Guess I just wanted something good to balance out the last couple of crappy days. You're home. That's good enough."

"Maybe we'll get lucky, and you won't get called out this weekend."

"Right, or maybe someday Marge will stop reminding me I mentored a crazed serial killer. We both know neither one of those things is likely to happen," she said, thinking she couldn't imagine her life any other way.